**The head of The National
Security Council spoke.**

"This involves a nationwide telecast scheduled to be released on prime time tomorrow. It takes in an interview with the Captain of the Alphard, *which is returning from Alcenar."*

The screen lit up with a picture of a man sitting in a plain, green-walled room. His voice came over with relative clarity: "The technology they have developed on Alcenar is fantastic. They have matter converters which can turn one element into another. I saw a whole road paved with sapphire—real sapphire. I broke some of it off, and I have it with me . . . ." The picture ended.

"I think he's mad!" someone said.

"But if he isn't?" Vanmore questioned.

WYNNE WHITEFORD
SAPPHIRE ROAD

ACE SCIENCE FICTION BOOKS
NEW YORK

To Gwayne Naug

This Ace Science Fiction Book
contains the complete text of
the original edition. It has been
completely reset in a typeface
designed for easy reading, and
was printed from new film.

SAPPHIRE ROAD

An Ace Science Fiction Book / published by arrangement with
the author

PRINTING HISTORY
Cory & Collins edition published 1982
Ace Science Fiction edition / April 1986

ISBN: 0-441-74962-3

Ace Science Fiction Books are published by
The Berkley Publishing Group,
200 Madison Avenue, New York, New York 10016.
PRINTED IN THE UNITED STATES OF AMERICA

1

THE PHONE CALL that changed Max Vanmore's life came at midday, just after he had climbed out of the roof-garden swimming pool of the Upolu. Still drying his heavy shoulders, he walked across the tiles to the phone in the shaded alcove, and pressed the button to open the channel.

"Vanmore."

The dark, aqua-haired Samoan receptionist appeared on the screen. "Call for you from the Postal Department, Mr. Vanmore."

"Could you put it through?"

Another face looked out at him, this time male. "Mr. Max Vanmore?"

"Right."

"I have a videogram for you from Australia. Could you identify, please?"

"One moment."

Vanmore walked along to the penthouse flat, glancing down over the railing. The Upolu was twenty storeys high, and he could see right along the sweep of coastline from Malua to Saluafata. Rain was falling over the sea, out beyond the reef. Below sprawled Apia, much as it had been in the twentieth century. He could see the large imitation-thatched roof of the old Tusitala Hotel, named long ago after the "Teller of Tales," Robert Louis Stevenson, who had died at Vailima in the hills just inland from here. Vanmore had never heard of

1

Stevenson until he came to Samoa, but since then he had read a recent local reprint of one of his books. Strangely, it had held him—even in a different age, people were people.

He returned to the alcove with his passport and air/surface driving licence, and held them in front of the camera lens adjoining the screen.

He watched the man's dark eyes take in the small portraits, comparing them with Vanmore's face. Evidently satisfied, he didn't ask for his thumbprint. He lifted a sheet of plastic material so that Vanmore was able to read it.

The first quick scan of the videogram stunned him, so that the letters seemed to blur out of focus for a moment. He pressed the RECORD key.

He took a deep breath, then re-read the message. Although he usually read at high speed, this time he plodded word by word, his lips moving like those of an actor in some farce.

"OK?" came the voice of the Postal Department man.

"Right. I've got it." Vanmore's voice grated like a rusting hinge.

When the picture flicked out, he ran back the tape to the beginning of the call, played it through until the videogram appeared on the screen, then held the picture and made a hard copy. He took the sheet from the slot and walked out into the hot sunshine again.

He went in to the penthouse, looked up a number, and punched it out. The screen blazed with multicoloured light, showing the bizarre interior of a women's beauty salon. A dark woman in a pink overall and pink hair looked at him with raised eyebrows.

"The Poinciana," she said.

"Could I speak to Rona Gale?"

"Well, she's just going under the dryer—"

"It's urgent, please."

The woman in pink hesitated, then moved away. A few seconds later Rona came on the screen, hair dishevelled, in something that looked like a pink cape.

"Excuse the hair, darling. I'm trying it lilac-silver. Do you—"

"Fine. Rona, I have to go back to Australia—straight away."

"You *what*? But we've hardly arrived here. Why, for God's sake—"

"Can't tell you on the phone, honey. I'll come down there. Five minutes."

He dressed quickly, then walked through the roof garden to where he had parked the rented airkar. The shriek of the oxyhydrogen motors climbed the scale. He took off, and swung down in a long curve over the harbour, which had been formed by a break blasted in the coral reef long ago, in the days of German and then British control.

Once, the harbour would have been alive with shipping, but there was not much sea traffic now. One inter-island hover-ship was beached on the wide inclined plane that had taken the place of wharves in so many seaports, and there were still some fishing vessels along the quay. A specialised freighter was loading timber, but that was all.

By the time Vanmore had landed in a downtown airkar park, the squall of rain he had seen earlier had swept in from the sea. When he reached the street, the rain was thundering down in a torrent, bouncing off the pavement in a silvery haze. People were sheltering under verandas, but he strode on, the rain plastering his hair to his forehead. Rain. It was here, in Apia, that Somerset Maugham had begun his play of that name. He was another of the old-time writers that Vanmore had discovered only since coming to Samoa. The place was like a museum of the nineteenth and twentieth centuries.

He found the Poinciana Salon and walked along the line of women sitting with their heads in dryers until he found Rona. She put her magazine down as he approached. Something in his face changed her expression. The bored poise suddenly slipped away from her.

"Max! What is it?"

"This." He handed her the copy of the videogram, and stood looking at her while she read it.

"Oh, Max! Your father—and your uncle. . . ."

"Dad, Uncle Rod, and my cousin, Jon—all three of them wiped out in the one explosion."

"But—what explosion? What happened?"

He pointed to the videogram copy. "I know only as much as that."

"But, darling—what are you going to do? Have you contacted the firm?"

"Not yet. I wanted time to think."

Rona beckoned to the woman with the pink hair. "Can you speed this up, please?"

Vanmore put his hand on her arm. "I'll slip over to the Upolu and pack our things, check out, then pick you up back here."

"No, don't do that. You go ahead. I'll be along in a few minutes in a taxi."

She came into the penthouse just as he had finished packing, a towel around her hair. She went to him without speaking, and for a minute they stood with their arms around each other.

"Sorry to wreck your holiday, honey," he said.

"Never mind. There'll be other times." She locked her arms around the back of his neck, rose on tiptoe, and kissed him. He held her very tightly for a few seconds. Then he stood back, holding her by the shoulders at arm's length.

"Let's have a look at that hair."

"I didn't give it time to dry properly." She began removing the towel. "There."

"Looks fine." He kissed her again, quickly, then turned her towards the outside view. "Take a last look at it, for now. We'll come back some day."

They stood looking down over Apia and its harbour for a moment, his arms around her shoulders.

They didn't talk much in the airkar on the thirty-odd kilometres out to Faleolo airport. He checked the machine in at the terminal, and they took an old-fashioned jet across to Pango Pango, where they had a delay of an hour before one of the big oceanic SSTs could take them to Australia.

"Wait here, Rona," he said, piloting her in to the coffee lounge. "I'm going to put through a call to the company."

The call took only a few minutes to get through, although he had made it a personal call to the company secretary, Quade Gannon. He looked at his watch. Two o'clock. That would be ten in the morning in the cities of eastern Australia, and nine-thirty in the centre of the continent, where the head office of Vanmore Titanium was located. In view of the tragedy, which must have disrupted the organisation, Gannon might not be in his office, but they should know where to locate him quickly.

"Your call to Australia," said an imageless voice, and then the screen lit up with a clear picture of Gannon sitting at his desk. He was dressed formally in a dark suit and fluorescent white shirt, and his large heavy face looked tired, as if he hadn't slept. He seemed fatter than when Vanmore had known him, and his fair hair was streaked with grey.

"Hi, Quade," said Vanmore. "I just heard. . . ."

"Terrible thing, Max. Deliberate, I'm sure of that." Gannon made a vague gesture. "Left us all in chaos, here. The two brothers had all the contacts—they believed in keeping control in their own hands. They were grooming young Jon to follow on some day, but he was like them. Kept everything to himself. Still, I won't go into too much detail on the phone."

"No. Listen, Quade, I'm on my way. SST leaving here in under an hour. Should hit Tullamarine in another two hours—say 12:30 your time."

"Have you booked from Tulla to Amadeus?"

"No."

"I'll meet you at Tulla with one of the company jets. I can fill you in on the way back to Amadeus."

"Right, Quade. I have Rona with me."

"How is she? Haven't seen her for four or five years."

"Different hair, otherwise the same. How's Joyce?"

"Joyce and I split about three years back." The large face broadened in a tired smile. "Like you to meet Bianca. Maybe tonight. Dinner?"

"Be fine. But I'll see you at 12:30."

"Right." Gannon glanced at his watch. "I'll organise it. Buon giorno."

As he switched off, Vanmore sat looking at the blank screen for a few seconds. "Buon giorno," he repeated to himself, and shook his head slightly.

When he got back to the coffee lounge, he didn't pick out Rona straight away, perhaps because of her upswept lilac-silver hair, and perhaps because she was turned away from him where she sat at a small table near the window. She was deep in animated conversation with a young Polynesian sitting alone at an adjoining table. He had a lively, flashing smile and a flower over his right ear. She switched her attention back to Vanmore as soon as she saw him, dismissing the Polynesian with a quick smile and a little wave.

"I took a chance and got you an iced coffee," she said as he sat down. "Unless you feel like something stronger?"

He shook his head. "Not today. I want to stay as clear as

possible." He drank some of his coffee and looked out through the tinted glass across the airfield. In the distance, the sharp volcanic peaks of Pango Pango showed a deeper blue against the sky, like a cardboard cutout.

"Did you get on to Amadeus?" she asked.

"Yes. Spoke to Quade Gannon. He doesn't think the explosion was an accident."

"Gannon." She thought for a moment. "I remember. Big fellow with one leg."

"That's right. He's meeting us at Tulla with a company plane. Wants to put me in the picture on the way up to Amadeus. He's been company secretary for the past eight or nine years."

"Do you trust him?"

Vanmore slowly shook his head. "In this game, it's safer to trust nobody—until you're really sure of them."

She looked out through the window, catching her reflection in the glass and making a small adjustment to her banana-silk dress where it clung to her firm, high little breasts, just showing the outline of prominent nipples. The light flashed on one of her star-sapphire earrings as she turned back to him.

"Do you think he's right about the explosion being deliberately set off?"

He nodded. "I'd say he's right in that, even without knowing any details. Dad and Uncle Rod knew too much about their technology to be blown up in an *accidental* explosion. Especially with young Jon with them. God, how often would the three of them be in the one place?" His teeth showed white in a grimace of sudden savagery. "No. Someone planned that."

"Who?"

He shrugged.

"Gannon?"

"Don't think so. He got on well with Dad and Uncle Rod—he'd want the status as quo as possible."

"Something like this happened to their father, didn't it? To your grandfather?"

"Yes. Shot with a laser from the roof of a building while he was officially opening a new port facility."

"Did they get the fellow who did it?"

"He fell from the roof trying to get away. Killed. Trouble was, they never found whether there was anyone behind him."

"This time—were they having much industrial trouble?"

Vanmore's voice took on a sharp edge of irritation. "Of course they were. Everyone has—more and more. If we're not careful, we'll have a complete national breakdown, the way the country did a long time ago. Then you get the army, or some such force, coming in to restore order, as they'd put it. And once that happens, you *might* get order restored—but the quality of life slips back hundreds of years."

He drained the rest of his coffee, then looked in the direction of the bar. For a moment he appeared about to rise, then he seemed to change his mind.

Rona said nothing. She understood him well enough to know when to back off.

While they were waiting in the lounge half an hour before takeoff, a newscast appeared on the large TV screen. There were several stories of social unrest in different parts of the world. Vanmore listened glumly. Change the names of the people and places and industries, and they could have been the same stories that had been telecast six months ago, a year ago.

"And now we have something different," said the newscaster. "The return of the *Alphard*. Some of my younger viewers might not remember it, but the *Alphard* is a spaceship which is within ten days of completing its third voyage between Alcenar and Earth.

"Alcenar, you will remember, is the third planet of Alpha Centauri A, one of the Solar system's nearest neighbours in space, and the site of man's oldest interstellar colony. . . ."

Rona looked suddenly excited. "Isn't that the ship young Ferris went away on? You know. Frank Ferris."

Vanmore nodded. "Listen," he said.

"The two systems of planets," the announcer was saying, "are separated by more than four light years. However, an improved type of drive evolved about a quarter of a century ago on Alcenar enables the *Alphard* to average more than half the speed of light over the journey. It makes the one-way trip in eight years.

"It first set out from Alcenar twenty-four years ago, reached Earth sixteen years back, then returned. Now, it's on the way here again, and will arrive in just ten days."

"I wonder if Frank Ferris is on it," mused Rona.

"You knew him pretty well, didn't you?"

"Yes. He intended to return." She smiled. "Frank. He'll be some sort of hero. Probably one of the first people to go to Alpha Centauri and back in time to meet some of the people they used to know."

Vanmore nodded, as if part of his mind was still elsewhere. "You realise he made both trips in hibernation," he said.

"So?"

"So he'll hardly have aged. Matter of weeks. When he left, he was twenty, I was twenty, and you were eighteen. Now, I'm thirty-six, you're thirty-four, and he's still twenty."

She thrust out her lower lip. "I'm almost old enough to be his mother. I wonder if he remembers me?"

"Of course he will. To him, he knew you only a matter of weeks ago." He made a sudden gesture as if flinging an idea away. "Anyway, we don't even know if he's on this voyage."

The supersonic transport had the blue and white markings of an American line. Its thousand seats were two thirds empty on the stretch of the flight between Pango Pango and Melbourne. By force of habit, Vanmore had fed in to the computer a request for seats adjoining a window, clear of the wing. He waved Rona to the window seat and sat next to her, saying nothing until the thin, muffled scream of the oxyhydrogen jets rose to herald their takeoff.

"I'm really sorry to cut your holiday short, Rona," he said, resting his hand on her knee. She placed her hand over it and squeezed it.

"You have to go to the funeral. I understand that, darling."

"Also, I'll have to spend some time at head office."

"I thought you weren't much interested in Vanmore Titanium. I mean, you have a perfectly sound business making synthetic star sapphires and rubies. What connection have those with titanium?"

He gave a short laugh. "Actually, quite a lot. Sapphire —and ruby—are both varieties of corundum. That's a transparent form of AL_2O_3—aluminium oxide, the hardest natural stone after diamond. It's their impurities that make the difference—chromium reddens the corundum to make what we call ruby. Titanium, as an impurity, makes it blue. Sapphire."

"But what about the stars in them?"

"Well, under some conditions, when the corundum crystallises, it arranges the little needles of titanium dioxide—what we call rutile—in three planes, sixty degrees apart, so you see them as a six-rayed star."

She was silent for a few seconds. "You take the magic out of them."

"No," he said decisively. "I put the magic into them. But how the hell did we get on to this? It's beside the point at the moment. I'm going back because I feel a sort of family responsibility. There's my aunt—Uncle Rod's wife—and Jon's wife and two kids. They're all dependent on income from the firm."

"Where does the ownership go?"

He looked at her profile for a long time until she turned to face him.

"The controlling interest goes to me. Fifty-one per cent. Didn't you know that?"

"I hadn't stopped to think about it."

His eyes looked from one to the other of hers, as if he were trying to see inside her skull. "Sure," he said in a neutral voice.

She looked out of the window for a while, then glanced back at him.

"This has changed you, Max. Already. And I've the feeling it's going to change you a lot more."

"Maybe," he said, but his thoughts already seemed elsewhere.

2

THE SUPERSONIC TRANSPORT seemed to be flying over the outskirts of Melbourne for a couple of hundred kilometres before it touched down at the old central airport at Tullamarine. Melbourne, with its countless satellite centres, had spread unchecked around both its bays and far across the plains to the west, and down the great valley to the south-east—a megalopolis almost too vast for ordered civic control. Although Vanmore and generations of his ancestors had come from this city, he was usually glad to get out of it.

He let most of the other passengers go ahead when the aircraft linked with the airbridge. Then he picked up their hand luggage—two small flying bags—and held them in one hand as he escorted Rona down the long slope of the bridge. The immense size of the SST lifted the outer end of the bridge high above the level of the upper concourse. The windows along the bridge were flecked with raindrops, and beyond was a grey, overcast sky.

The customs formalities were handled with electronic smoothness, and he soon collected their larger baggage from the carousel and dumped it on a motorised trolley.

"I'm cold," said Rona, hugging her arms around her body.

"Use yogi breathing," said Vanmore, steering the trolley towards the exit. "Two seconds in, four seconds hold, eight seconds out."

"Oh, that? I never remember it. All right."

As they went out on to the concourse, he saw Quade Gannon standing with two other men opposite the exit. Simultaneously, Gannon saw Vanmore, and they waved to each other. Gannon spoke briefly to his companions, then moved quickly forward.

He looked fatter than Vanmore remembered him, in a glossy grey leatheroid coat that fitted closely about the thick barrel of his body. His left leg had been taken off through the hip, and he held a single metal crutch under his left arm, swinging along with fierce energy.

"First of all, my condolences, Max." They shook hands, and Gannon acknowledged Rona's presence with a stiff little bow, then turned back to Vanmore. "We can leave any time you wish. I've got our own jet down below."

"Good," said Vanmore. Then, as if it were an afterthought, he glanced at Rona. "All right?"

"Of course," she said in an even tone.

They took one of the elevators down to ground level, and Gannon led the way along an almost deserted passageway towards a distant doorway where grey daylight streamed in. About halfway along, he said, "Just a minute," and pivoted round to look back the way they had come.

Turning, Vanmore saw two men coming along behind them. They were the men who had been with Gannon when they had waved to each other on the concourse.

"Two of our security boys," said Gannon. "I'll introduce you while there's no one around. Then you can just 'not see them' the rest of the way."

They were tough-looking, athletic, blank of expression. Gannon introduced them simply as Tom and Enzo. "This is Mr. Max Vanmore, son of K.J. And this is Ms. Rona Gale. I want you to take a good look at both of them, then watch over them as carefully as you watch over me. Right?"

"Right," snapped one of them, and the other merely nodded. Neither smiled. In fact, Vanmore found himself wondering if either of them were capable of a smile.

"Good." Gannon pointed along the passageway. "Let's go."

The company jet stood just outside, small and fast-looking, painted in the lime and flame-red colour scheme of Vanmore Titanium.

There was a pilot, co-pilot, and hostess aboard, although

the only passengers were Max, Rona, Gannon, and the two
security men, who sat at the back of the cabin. There were ten
seats, five on each side of the central aisle, and Vanmore and
Rona took the middle pair, while Gannon sat up front.

Soon after the machine was airborne, the orange-haired
hostess came back into the cabin and gave them a vivid, professional smile. She turned to Rona.

"Would you like to see the flight deck? We haven't the
stuffy rules of an airline. You could sit in the co-pilot's seat
for a while—you get a tremendous view from there."

Rona glanced at Vanmore, who nodded. She followed the
hostess up forward. A moment later, Gannon came down the
aisle, resting his hands on the backs of the seats. He eased his
weight down into the seat Rona had vacated.

"Max," he said, "how much do you know about the National Stability Council?"

"I know that Dad and Uncle Rod were members—although
they didn't give me any details about what decisions were
made there, or even how the Council operated."

"I see. I don't know much about it, either. But it looks as if
both of us are going to have to learn—fast."

"Could you develop that a bit?"

Gannon leaned forward across the narrow aisle, his folded
arms resting on his knee. "Yes. It seems each member of the
council has to own, direct, or have some substantial control in
a major component of one of the large, vital industries. You
know, energy, transport, food, aluminium, titanium, steel,
and so on. Also, each member has to be of high intelligence."

"How do they define that?"

"I don't know, but I think they're impressed by chemically
augmented intelligence techniques applied throughout child-
hood."

"I knew that much. Yes."

"So did I. But here's something I didn't know until this
morning. Each member of the council can nominate a successor. In the event of his death, the whole council interviews
the nominee. If he fulfils all their requirements—if he's accepted by the whole body of the council—he takes the place of
his predecessor."

"Who did our people choose?"

"Your father nominated you, conditional on your taking
over the directorship of the firm."

"And my uncle?"

"Your uncle nominated his son, Jon—but, as you know, Jon died with the others. His second choice was me."

Vanmore nodded. "Well, I think you deserve it. After all, you probably know more about the workings of the show than anyone alive, now." He suddenly extended his hand, and Gannon gripped it strongly. "It's a lot of responsibility, Quade. I learned that much from my father."

"I know. Rather frightening, in view of the way things are disintegrating all around us."

"Disintegrating?'

"Well, you know what I mean. The whole scene's getting more and more confused. Cost-push inflation. Another bloody strike looming up. Terrorist attacks aimed at straight blackmail. That's what the explosion was, you know."

"Was there a threat?"

"I think so. I think it was made to your father and uncle. Nobody's quite sure—they kept things under wraps."

"But who made the threat?"

Gannon shrugged. "Could have been any of several organisations. Their motives don't have to make sense. Look at that crowd that call themselves the Children of something. They believe we should live by the old sacred writings—and since neither Buddha nor the Bible nor the Koran mentions titanium, we're outside the pale, like the aluminium people. How do you reason with someone like that?"

"Security have any clues?"

"Following leads, they say." Gannon's tired eyes suddenly flamed with explosive anger. "They said that at Port Kalamurra."

"Yes, I remember that." Vanmore felt the pressure of his own rage mounting. "I remember the way Dad felt when the sniper shot his father. He said: 'It's not just a personal thing, Max. Everybody loses. A thing like this pulls down the average.' "

For a time, they looked down at the flat, yellow landscape rolling by below, with its occasional belts of irrigated green.

"Anyway," said Gannon. "The past is past. You can have K.J.'s office, if you like, on the twenty-fifth floor of the Tower. Or your uncle's, if you prefer. They're both vacant, now, and adjoining."

"I'll take Dad's."

"Right. Then I'll move in to the other one, if that's OK with you."

"Sure."

"Incidentally, there's a penthouse at the top of the tower. Both brothers used it when they had to spend the night back at the office—it happened a lot, because some of their overseas contacts were made in the middle of the night. Anyway, I've fixed it for you and Rona to stay there while you get your bearings."

"Thanks."

Rona and the hostess came through the door from the control cabin. Gannon stood up, hands on the backs of the seats.

"Perhaps we could meet at K.J.'s office this afternoon. There's a lot to discuss, and the sooner we get started the better."

Vanmore looked at his watch, which he had adjusted to Amadeus time. "How about three o'clock?"

"Fine, Max. Three." He vaulted up the aisle to the front seat, using the seat-backs on either side of him, and then Rona came down to the one he had vacated.

"Hi," she said. "The pilot's name is Martin. Quite nice—freckles and a sort of lop-sided grin. He said we'll be flying right over Lake Eyre."

"Good," said Vanmore.

"He said it used to be more than a hundred and fifty metres below sea level, before they cut the canal through from Port Augusta. Now, Martin says, it covers twenty-nine thousand square kilometres, and they bring sea-going freighters into it."

"Good," said Vanmore again.

"God, Max, is 'good' the only word you remember?"

"Sorry, honey. I've got a lot of fast thinking to do."

"Of course. Sorry." She said nothing for quite a while. When the broad, blue expanse of the now flooded Lake Eyre basin appeared ahead of them, slowly swinging below them, she touched Vanmore's arm.

He had flown over the lake before, and now he felt a sudden stab of guilt at leaving her out of his thoughts. He pointed out the various ports around the shores of the lake—all of them specialised—and the ore freighters, which their altitude made toylike.

"There's not much irrigated land around it, is there?" she said.

"The irrigation has to come by pipeline. That's sea water down there—straight up the canal."

"Of course." She gave a little laugh. "I don't think things through much, do I?"

He smiled. "Well, it's a cute image, honey. But how about starting to phase it out?"

She sat very straight for a few seconds before answering, then her head came round sharply. Spots of red flared on her cheeks. "I said all this was changing you. Now you want to change *me*."

He was uncertain how to answer, and ended by saying nothing. Rona sat silent, looking straight ahead. After about half a minute, she made an abortive little movement of her hand towards her face, then put both clenched fists in her lap. He caught the glisten of a tear on her cheek as she turned her head away to look out of the window.

"Hell!" he said, with sudden, inward-directed savagery, "don't take any notice of me, honey. I'm sorry."

A minute or two later, Gannon turned round in his seat. "Down to the right, Max. You can just see Port Kalamurra."

Vanmore had to lean across to look out of Rona's window. "Hard to see much from here," he called.

"What *is* Port Kalamurra?" asked Rona in a controlled voice.

"One of our port installations. Got a historical significance for us. My grandfather opened it eighteen years ago—that was where someone on the roof of a building shot him with a pulsating laser."

She turned her head. "You mean—that was where they assassinated him? While he was opening the port?"

Vanmore nodded. He jerked his head in the direction of Gannon. "Quade was there, at the back of the platform where my grandfather was standing at the microphones. Quade was one of his young assistants—only about twenty-four, I think. Anyway, the laser beam that killed my grandfather went through Quade's thigh."

Rona looked at the broad back of the man in the front seat. "God, no wonder he's paranoid about terrorists."

"I don't think it's all paranoia, Rona. I think there's some justification."

Over the red centre of the continent, the jet began to lose height. Vanmore touched Rona's arm and pointed over to the left.

"You can see Mount Conner, there—the big red outcrop with the vertical cliffs. Then Ayer's Rock—there, and you can just see the Olgas beyond it."

Still dropping, they began to pick up turbulence from the uptrends rising from the sun-baked ridges of bare rock. The pilot banked steeply to the right, bringing them into calmer air over the blue waters of Lake Amadeus.

"But it's enormous!" Rona's eyes were wide as she looked down at the lake. "It's like the sea."

"It used to be a dry lake-bed, most of the time," said Vanmore.

"Did they bring in sea water, the same as Lake Eyre?"

"No. This basin's a couple of hundred metres above sea level." He made an effort to restore communication between them. "It's fresh water. They pipe it all the way from north Queensland."

"But it seems to stretch further than you can see."

"It does. Over three hundred kilometres. They brought the level up, so the lake extended to take in Lake Neale, to the north-west, and on westward to Lake Hopkins, over the Western Australian border. In places, it's forty kilometres wide."

Along the north-east shore, behind a tree-lined esplanade, were the towers of forty-year-old Amadeus City. As the jet swung low over the water for its approach run, Vanmore pointed ahead.

"That's the Titanium Building. The one with the top painted in bands of lime and flame-red."

"It's one of the highest."

"Fifty storeys. No need for that height in this area, but when it was built it was supposed to add prestige."

The company airstrip slanted in from the edge of the lake close to the tower. The jet touched down smoothly and taxied towards a line of hangars at the tower's foot. More security men met them as the plane rolled to a halt. None of them seemed capable of smiling, either, but they looked efficient.

Out of the plane, the heat struck them like a blast from an iron foundry. Vanmore slung his jacket over his shoulder. Gannon had shed his leatheroid coat, and wore his white shirt open-necked and outside his belt. He led the way across to the side door of the tower.

"I thought it better for you not to have a formal meeting with the company personnel out here," he said. "Safer for all of us."

"Good idea. Plenty of time for that."

They passed in to the building through an airlock of doors that hissed open and shut automatically, and the fresh, cool air inside made them realise the full ferocity of the external heat.

As they entered, a man who had been sitting near a fountain stood up and rode quickly to meet them, his attention focused on Vanmore.

"Max Vanmore? I'm Ashton Marsh, National Stability Council."

Vanmore took his extended hand. Marsh was very tall and loose-jointed, as if his limbs had been strung together like those of a marionette. His long, tanned face was dominated by a pair of intense eyes that did not quite match each other.

"Sorry to pressure you at a time like this, Mr. Vanmore, but we'd like to arrange a meeting of the Council, with yourself and Mr. Gannon here, as soon as possible."

"I understand the funeral is at one o'clock tomorrow," said Vanmore.

"How about meeting tonight?" asked Marsh quickly. When Vanmore hesitated, he said, "I think the situation demands that much urgency." He looked at Gannon. "You'd agree with that, Quade?"

Gannon nodded.

"All right," said Vanmore. "Where? And when?"

"At the Council Roundhouse on the Esplanade—eight o'clock tonight."

Vanmore raised his eyebrows. "I thought the members of the Stability Council were scattered all over Australia."

"So are the Roundhouses. There'll be only three of us here, but the rest will be present as holograms—just as we'll be holograms in each of the other Roundhouses from one end of the country to the other."

"OK. I'll be there," said Vanmore.

"And I," added Gannon.

"Fine. Eight tonight, then." Marsh turned and went striding out through the double doors.

Vanmore turned to Gannon. "How many are there on the council?"

"I don't know. We'll find out tonight, I suppose. Meanwhile, I'll show you two the penthouse."

The elevator ran in a transparent tube up the outside of the tower, overlooking the lake. Gannon pressed the button for the fiftieth floor—the top one—and the lift accelerated smoothly upward. Rona gasped as the panorama of Lake Amadeus widened below her.

"Look Max. You can see right over to the Olgas. And the Rock."

"Uluru. Grandfather told me an aboriginal legend—remind me to tell you."

Their baggage had already been brought up to the top floor, and stood just outside the lift. Vanmore hadn't seen Gannon organise its movement, and decided he must have arranged it in advance.

The view from the large windows of the penthouse was arresting, across vast reddish plains broken by twisted, rocky ridges. Near the shores of the lake were forests of eucalypts and casuarinas and acacias, but out beyond the reach of the irrigation channels the landscape retained its thin, ancient cover of spinifex and clumps of stunted mulga.

"I live down on the Point," said Gannon. He lifted the tip of his crutch and indicated a number of houses on a small point of land jutting into the lake of the westward. "Green place right at the end. Be glad if you'd come down there for the evening meal. Make it early because we have to be at the Roundhouse by eight. Say six o'clock. Bianca can look after you for the evening, Rona, while Max and I are finding our way round the Stability Council."

"Thank you," said Rona.

"Anything you want, use the internal phone. My number's 9." Gannon swung across to the elevator, waved to them as the door slid shut, and was gone.

"What was he saying on the plane when the hostess took me away?" asked Rona.

"It seems both he and I have been proposed for the National Stability Council—in place of Uncle Rod and Dad."

"God, that carries a lot of clout, doesn't it?"

"Yes. Not many people know exactly how much." He walked across to the drink dispenser. "Coffee?"

"Uh-huh." She opened the sliding door that gave access to the roof garden, then immediately closed it again. "Whee! It's hot out there."

"Better keep the door shut," said Vanmore. When the coffees were ready, he carried them across to the titanium table near the window. "Pretty smooth on details, Gannon, isn't he? Like thinking of this place, getting our luggage sent up, and so on.''

"Yes." Rona stood sipping her coffee, looking down through the double-glazed windows. The buildings of the city sprawled in either direction along the lake shore—modern, uncluttered, bold in design. Suddenly she looked up. "He gets about very well on his leg, doesn't he?''

"I believe he had the muscles strengthened. The way some athletes used to do, fifteen or sixteen years ago, before they banned the technique from competition sport." He looked at his watch. "Hey, it's news time.''

He activated the television set, and when the fanfare introduced the news they both sat on the sofa facing the hologram alcove.

There was no mention of the deaths of the Vanmore Brothers. The main item concerned the return of the *Alphard* from the Alpha Centauri system. Much of the story was as they had heard it in Pango Pango, but this time more details were added.

"Two young Earthmen have made the double journey from Earth to Alcenar and back—an Australian, Frank Ferris, and an Indian, Ras Aiyar—"

"Frank Ferris!" Rona's eyes were alight. "He *is* on it.''

"Yes. Listen.''

The hologram showed a few old pictures of the *Alphard*, taken on its previous visit to Earth. The commentator's voice went on: "The ship is at present under deceleration of 1g. It will reach the Transfer Station in ten days. We promise you live interviews with some of the people aboard, including the two young Earthmen—Australian and Indian—who have made this immense voyage to man's oldest interstellar colony.''

"He's going to be quite a celebrity, young Frank," said Rona.

"How was he selected to make the trip? I forget, now.''

"Oh, the Centauri people announced there were three or four vacancies on their ship for the return journey. Some of their people had stayed here. Frank heard the offer early, because he was working with a news magazine. He volunteered straight away. I think the magazine might have helped him a lot—they saw a chance for easy publicity. Anyway, he was selected—

and this Indian fellow. May have been one or two more—I forget the details.''

''Well, the magazine people will probably get behind him when he comes back, so he'll be on top of the world.''

''I don't think so, Max. The magazine folded not long after he left. He'll be away out on his own.'' She turned down the sound as the news veered off onto other subjects. ''He'll be terribly on his own, Max, when you come to think of it. All the people he knew are suddenly a generation older than him.''

''Well, he knew that would happen before he volunteered.''

Rona walked into the kitchenette. ''What would you like to eat?'' she asked, punching the MENU key and consulting the display terminal. Vanmore went across and stood looking over her shoulder, his hand gently caressing her deltoid.

''Only something light, cherie. I'll try 17 and 44.''

She punched the numbers, following with a choice of her own.

''How do you feel about Quade Gannon?'' she asked as they waited.

''Why?''

''I don't like him, somehow. Most of the time he seems to ignore me.'' She turned to look over her shoulder into his face. ''So do *you*, sometimes, the last few hours. But with him, it's sort of built in.''

''Maybe. But he's been under a hell of a strain the last few hours, remember.''

''What's his woman like?''

''Bianca? No idea. Joyce, the last one, was a bit of a playgirl. I don't know whether he's kept to the same type, or gone for the opposite—I've seen different fellows react various ways.''

''Find out for me if you can, Max. Remember, I've got to spend this evening with her.''

''I'll try. I'll be meeting him at three o'clock.''

Their food emerged from the cubicle, and they took it over to the titanium table by the window and began to eat. For a time, at any rate, the tension that had built up between them seemed to have abated.

At 2:30, Vanmore looked up a list of internal extension numbers and punched ''7'', the number of his late father's office. He didn't expect any response, and was about to cancel when a woman's head and shoulders appeared in the hologram. She was a thin, hard-looking woman who must have been attractive twenty, even ten years ago. Her grey hair was cut short, and her eyes looked reddened behind rimless glasses.

"Mr. K.J.'s office," she said.

"I'm his son—Max. You'd be—"

"Elsa Perry. His private secretary."

"I'd like to see my father's office, Miss Perry."

She glanced down as if checking something. "Mr. Gannon will be coming here at three o'clock," she said.

"I know. I'd like to come down now. I'll see you in a minute or two."

He switched off, kissed Rona, then went to the elevator. He rode down to the twenty-fifth floor, then stepped out into the silent, deeply carpeted foyer. At the far end was a door marked BOARD ROOM, and on the right, near it, another marked K.J.V. On the other side of the foyer was a door with the initials R.G.V.

Miss Perry was waiting as he went in. She wore a close-fitting, dark grey suit that was like a caricature of a man's.

"I'd like to express my sympathy, Mr. Vanmore," she said in a precise, rehearsed little speech.

"Thank you, Miss Perry. I believe you were my father's secretary for the past ten years or so?"

"Twelve years. His confidential secretary, yes. I'm told you'll be taking over as Director?"

"Yes. But by degrees. I hadn't expected anything like this to happen, of course."

"Nor did any of us." Her voice shook slightly. "Your father was a marvellous man—in ways most people didn't know about." She sniffed. "I suppose you'll be bringing in your own secretary."

"No. My own business is on a more limited scale. I have no one with the experience to handle this."

"I'd be glad to help my successor pick up the threads."

"Miss Perry—or can I make that Elsa?—what's this about a successor? You've been doing the job for twelve years. Who else is more qualified?"

She looked away. "Well—if you don't mind the age difference—"

"What I'm looking for is expertise. I think I can trust my father's judgment. Now, suppose we get to work."

She showed him over the suite of offices his father had occupied. The outer office, where he had entered, was simply a reception space. It opened into a larger one with an oval table in the middle and a desk near the double-glazed windows that looked out over the lake. An unobtrusive door led from this main office to a smaller, inner room lined with files and reference books on shelves up to the ceiling. From this, another door led along a short passageway to the board room. Vanmore looked in. Its colour scheme jolted him slightly. The windowless walls were lime green, and the chairs and the large, oval table were flame-red.

He walked thoughtfully back into the small room with the array of files and small visual display terminals, and its single desk. This was where K.J. must have done most of his work.

He looked again into the main office. "Elsa," he said, "there's something I don't understand about the geography of this place."

"I don't follow, Mr.—"

"Max. There must be another large room in here, between the board room and the passage and these rooms. But there seems to be no way into it."

She looked at him with an air of increased respect. "I don't think anybody else ever noticed that—certainly not as quickly as you did."

"Could I see it?"

She hesitated. "Oh, well," she said, "you *are* the Director now." She went out to her own desk and returned with a flat magnetic key. She walked in to the inner office, moved some books on a shelf, and inserted the key in a barely noticeable slot in the shadowed back corner of the shelf.

A section of an adjoining bookcase pivoted silently until it stood at right angles to the wall, revealing a dark doorway. Vanmore stepped into it, and at once lights came on in the room beyond. It was circular, with a ring of TV alcoves broken only at the point of entry.

"What is it?" he asked.

"The hologram room," she said in a hushed voice.

He stepped inside. "Where do all these terminals link up at the other end?"

She was watching him intently, two bright spots of red on her pallid cheeks. "You understand, this is all extremely confidential. I'm not even sure I should be showing you this."

"Listen, Elsa, it's my office. I would have found what was

in here, anyway, even if I'd had to have someone break in with a jackhammer.''

"I suppose so," she said in a resigned voice.

"I think you'd better fill me in on the whole story. Huh?"

She made an attempt at a smile, which didn't reach her eyes. "Actually, these terminals are linked directly with others in the offices and homes of some members of the National Stability Council.''

He thought that over for a while. "But I understood they contacted each other through the Roundhouses like the one down on the Esplanade.''

"Officially, yes. But K.J. and a few of the others believed the council had become too large, too unwieldy. Too many members to be able to make quick decisions. You see?"

He nodded. "I'm beginning to see, I think."

"K.J. told me something like this—using different techniques, of course—has been going on in most large governments for centuries. Perhaps for thousands of years. You have an inner group within the main group that thrashes out the hard decisions beforehand. Then they can act with a clearcut goal when they meet in open council.''

"Who can you actually contact through these terminals?"

"No one knows that. K.J. didn't even tell *me*."

"But you had the key to this room."

"I got it from his desk. After he— died."

"I see." Vanmore held his hand out. "I'd better take it now, Elsa."

She hesitated. He looked at her eyes, switching his focus from one to the other. Her stiffened neck seemed to vibrate with inner tension. Suddenly she held the key out at arm's length.

"Of course," she said.

"Thanks, Elsa. It'll be safer with me. Do I just push this door shut?"

"It locks automatically."

He tried the key once, then put it in his pocket. "Elsa, Quade Gannon is meeting me here in a few minutes. Does he know about the hologram room?"

She shook her head.

"I see." He smiled. "Let's keep it that way for a while, eh?"

As they walked out to the main office, she turned to face him, and for the first time since they had met her lips curved in a genuine smile. "You know," she said, "you're very like your father."

"Me?" He was astounded. "But everyone has always said we're quite unlike."

"I don't understand that. To me, you're like the same man at a different age." Abruptly she looked away. "I suppose I shouldn't have said that."

"Not at all. It's interesting." He gave a wry smile. "Perhaps it's the environment."

A buzzer sounded at the outer door. Vanmore glanced at his watch.

"That'll be Quade Gannon. Would you let him in?"

3

ELSA PERRY WALKED to the reception desk and glanced at the closed circuit video screen, then pressed the release. "Come in, Mr. Gannon. Mr. Vanmore's just arrived."

Vanmore had moved quickly in to the small inner office, and now he sat behind the desk. "I'm here, Quade," he called.

Gannon came through the outer office with the oval table, and swung in to the inner room as if he were used to the place. At the door he stopped sharply, his jaw swinging momentarily open.

"Christ!" he said, "you gave me a shock for a moment."

"Why? You knew I was in here."

"The way you were sitting, I suppose. For a second, I thought—never mind." He leaned his crutch against the corner of a bookcase and sprang lightly to the chair opposite the desk. "I have all the arrangements for the funeral tied up, Max. Tomorrow, one o'clock, out at the Crematorium. There won't be many there. Once, it would have been almost a state occasion. Now, too large a crowd is simply inviting another 'hit.' "

"Any clue yet who planted the bomb?"

Gannon shook his head. "Nothing as yet. If it's a terrorist group, they may be waiting for a news announcement before they claim responsibility. If it was for extortion, well—" He spread his hands. "K.J. and R.G. were the only ones who knew where the demand came from."

"I notice you've managed to keep the story away from the media. How did you arrange it? When I looked at the news a while back the main story was about the ship coming back from Alcenar."

"Yes," said Gannon, and lapsed into brooding silence. As the silence prolonged, Vanmore looked across at him more closely, and saw that his attention seemed focused at an infinite distance.

"What's wrong?"

"Eh? Sorry." Gannon dragged his attention back to his immediate environment with an obvious effort. "Just a side current of thought." He gestured vaguely when Vanmore made no reply. "You know, Bianca came from the Centauran system."

"*Your* Bianca? From Alcenar? I didn't know that."

Gannon rested his broad hands on the desk and looked down at them. "Not from Alcenar, originally. From a settlement on one of their other planets. One they called Chiron. Heavy-gravity planet."

"How did she get here?"

"The *Alphard,* on its previous voyage—sixteen years ago. She was one of the Centaurans who stayed here until the next trip. I think the other two were a historian and a biologist."

"And Bianca?"

"Her people had developed a technique for chemically increasing muscle power. Originally, they'd evolved it to help them deal with their high gravity. She brought her expertise here." He smiled momentarily. "You remember when a few athletes put up some fantastic records? Thousand metres in less than two minutes, and some unbelievable high jumps?"

"I know. The Athletics Association banned them from competitive sport."

"That's right." Gannon slapped the hard muscles of his thigh. "I had this treated by her, and followed on with a course of physiotherapy—that was about fifteen years ago. Saw her professionally over the years, but I wasn't really close to her until a year or so after I split with Joyce."

"I see."

Gannon looked at Vanmore as if finding something hard to express. "They're a lot different from us, you know. In their thinking, I mean."

"In what way?"

"Something to do with their hard environment. Serious, cautious, conscientious. I suppose that comes of living in a world where one mistake can easily kill you. Tremendous emphasis on accuracy. Gets on your quince after a while. Anyway, you'll meet her tonight."

"Looking forward to that."

"Right," said Gannon. Suddenly, he looked at Vanmore with a curiously naked expression in his eyes. "She told me once she intended to return to her own system one day. I don't doubt she meant it."

Vanmore nodded. Evidently, Gannon thought she might leave on the next Alcenar-bound voyage of the *Alphard*, which was now very close. He switched the conversation on to a different track.

"Tell me, Quade, just how did you manage to keep the story of the assassination out of the media?"

"To tell the truth, I'm beginning to think that what I did really hadn't much to do with the final result. I think the Stability Council killed the story. They probably thought it would be unstabilising—that the idea of a terrorist assassination might spread."

Vanmore looked at him thoughtfully, rubbing his chin with his hand. "Be interesting to know just how they clamped the lid on it."

"We might find out some of it tonight."

"Some of it. Yes."

Gannon stood up, his fingers resting lightly on the edge of the desk. "I'll see you and Rona at my place at six, then. A bit earlier, if you like. Bianca and I like to watch the sunset over the lake as we eat. By the way, you right for transport?"

"Yes. Rented an airkar."

"Could have fixed you up with a Company vehicle."

"I know. But after what happened to my father and uncle I'd rather not be too easily recognisable when I'm moving about."

"You have a point there. See you at my place."

Gannon reached back for his crutch without looking at it, and slipped it under his arm and swung out. Vanmore heard him talk briefly with Elsa Perry, then after he had left she came in.

"Did you tell him about the hologram room?" she asked.

Vanmore looked up at her with bland innocence. "What hologram room, Elsa?"

In the relief of tension, they both laughed.

He rode the elevator down to the ground floor, then walked across to the westward-moving beltway that ran along the side of the Esplanade. A breeze off the lake tempered the fierce afternoon heat to a slight degree, but he could still feel sweat running down his back.

He stepped off the beltway as he reached the airkar yard. The machine he had arranged to rent looked as clean as it had done on the video, and it was an inconspicuous olive green. He took it for a trial flight along the shore of the lake and back to the yard, where he finalised the contract. It was just after five when he flew to the top of the tower and parked the airkar on the highest of the landing flanges, on the side of the tower away from the lake.

He locked it, then walked through the damp little roof garden to the penthouse. When he went in, Rona was wearing a new dinner dress. It was made of what looked like metallic foil that rippled with changing bands and waves of diffracted light, fitting her as closely as a second skin between breasts and hips. Black, high-heeled boots reached her knees.

"How do I look?"

"Marvellous, as always."

"What's Gannon's woman like?"

"Something you'd never guess in a hundred years."

"What, for godsake?"

"She's from the Centauran system—from the place they call the heavy planet."

"How long have people lived there?"

"I don't know. Anyway, you can ask Bianca." He glanced at his watch. "Ready?"

"Wait on. Bit of perfume, then I'm right."

He went ahead out to the airkar. As he emerged from the tunnel that led through to the steamy roof garden, with its dripping sprinkler bars, he noticed another airkar parked on the topmost flange of an adjoining building, slightly below his level and only a few hundred kilometres away. It was grey, with coppery, reflective windows that hid whoever was within.

He didn't think much about it just then. Rona came aboard, and he took off, hovering for a few seconds just above the flange and checking his instruments before plunging over the two-hundred-metre drop.

He swung down in a wide curve towards the Esplanade, with its attractively uneven lines of tamarisks and casuarinas. Then, suddenly, in his mirror, he saw the grey, copper-windowed airkar following.

Coincidence, he told himself. Then he thought of the explosion and sudden fear dried his mouth and throat. He dived to gain speed, travelling only a few metres above the laser-sawn stone retaining wall edging the lake.

Rona looked around through the back window, and when she spoke her voice was unexpectedly taut. "Is that thing following us?"

"I don't know. Let's find out."

An avenue ran inland between two of the high buildings on the Esplanade, and he swung the airkar sharply. Ahead was a large shopping centre.

"It's still coming," said Rona. "God! What do we do?"

By the time he had circled the shopping centre and headed back to the lake shore, it was obvious that the grey machine was tailing them. He glanced at Rona. Her face was pale and set. It came to him that he had never seen her in danger before—never seen her extended. She was standing the tension well.

He followed the sea wall around to the Point, with the grey machine about a hundred metres behind him and slightly higher. He picked out Gannon's house—the last one, two-storeyed, of green brick. At the last possible moment, he threw the airkar around and swung it down into Gannon's private parking area, partly under the wide, transparent, cantilevered wing jutting from the house. There were two other airkars there, and a wheeled vehicle like an enclosed van.

"They went straight over," said Rona.

"Right! Into the house, quick!"

But the grey airkar was back sooner than he had anticipated. He seized Rona's hand and pulled her under the shelter of some thick boobialla trees. The airkar went past about fifty metres up, slowly. Hands clasped together, they watched it go back around the curve of the shore until it was a speck in the distance. Then he led Rona towards the front door.

Gannon opened a sliding glass door as they approached. He

was wearing a wraparound happicoat of yellow towelling, and his bare leg looked very hard and muscular. "Heard you land. Get lost on the way in?"

"No. An airkar followed us down here from the flange on the building next to the tower. Grey. One-way glass windows. We kept under the trees until it had gone."

"Get its registration number?"

"No."

"You did the right thing in hiding. The way things are, you can't be too careful." He moved aside. "Anyway, come in."

The lounge, a large, semi-circular room on the lake side of the house, had double-glazed, polorised windows from floor to ceiling, right around its curved side. From the doorway into the other part of the house, an unbelievably broad, squat woman in a white, ground-length cloak waddled in.

"Bianca, this is Max Vanmore, and Rona Gale. Bianca Baru."

With surprising speed, the woman moved across to Vanmore, looking up at him with dark, hazel eyes beneath a wide forehead. She flung her cloak back from her right shoulder, and reached up to grasp his hand.

"Good to meet you, Max." Her voice was relaxed and unexpectedly deep, and her hand felt disturbingly strong. Vanmore glanced down involuntarily at her bare arm. Both his hands could not have encircled the massive biceps.

"Glad to know you, Bianca," he said, and she spun towards Rona.

"Like your dress, Rona." She took Rona's slim hand in hers, and pressed it against her cheek.

"Bianca's from the Centauran system," said Gannon to Rona.

"I know someone who's just coming back from there," said Rona. "Frank Ferris. He went there on the *Alphard*."

"He would have gone to Alcenar," said Bianca. "I'm from Chiron. I came here on the trade ship sixteen years ago."

"The same ship?"

"Yes. Eight-year journey each way, in hibernation. I'm making up my mind whether to go back this time."

"I thought we'd decided you were staying," said Gannon sharply.

Bianca's cloak whirled as she spun to face him. With her head set almost immovably between massive shoulders, she had to turn her whole body to look around, but her immense strength enabled her to move in a flash. "*You* decided, Quade, I'm still considering."

Gannon seemed about to reply, then changed his mind. A muscle throbbed in his cheek. He moved over to the console.

"Care for a drink, anyone?"

He pressed the LIST key, and an impressive range of drinks appeared on the display terminal. He punched out their requests, then slid out a magnagrav tray with four glasses and pushed it towards the others. One of the glasses was enclosed, with a flexible transparent tube coming from the top of it. Bianca took it, inserting the tube between her lips.

"Thanks, Quade," said Vanmore, raising his glass. "But not too much of this—I want to stay clear for tonight."

Gannon drained his glass quickly. "I get nervous, sometimes, if I see things too clearly."

"Most people have an illogical streak," said Bianca in her level voice. She moved over to the sofa, and with a quick thrust of her stubby legs sprang backwards on to it, sitting with her short, almost round boots sticking straight forward. She reached up her hand. "Sit here with me, Rona. We have too much of a height gap."

She pulled Rona down alongside her and put her massive arm around her shoulders. Rona looked at Vanmore with one eyebrow raised. Standing, Bianca had seemed little more than half her height, but on the sofa she gave the impression of being nearly three times her size.

"What's your home planet like?" asked Rona.

"Don't think you'd enjoy it, dear. Gravity of nearly 200 centigees. I weigh 160 kilograms here, but on Chiron I'm over 300."

"God, how do you move around?"

"Well, we're built for it. Our ancestors had to be carefully selected, and their children genetically and surgically modified. We have stronger bones, stronger hearts, tougher system right throughout. And we use our muscles more completely."

"Do you like it here?"

"Interesting, Rona. But I'll go back some day—not sure when."

Gannon snorted. "We'll see." He glanced at his watch, then said, "If we want to get to the Roundhouse without hurrying, it might be a good idea if we ate now. All right?"

Bianca took a small remote-control keyboard from under her cloak, and tapped some of the keys with her left hand. Rona, Vanmore, and Gannon made their selections from the numbered menu that appeared on the far wall, and a touch of a few more keys made a section of the wall revolve, bringing a gleaming autokitchen into view, with its microwave cookers and pressure vessels.

"Do you do your own programming?" asked Rona.

"Of course. No creativity in following the numbers." Bianca remained on the sofa as she cooked the meal. Under the cloak she wore a one-piece blue suit that left her right arm and shoulder bare. Vanmore noticed that it was only her right arm that was gigantically overdeveloped. The left arm was strong, but normal in proportions, with a swift-moving, supple hand that danced over the keys. Evidently this was an adaptation to Chiron's savage gravitation—the arms were differently specialised for heavy and light work.

Lids lifted from dishes to let the smell of food flood the room, and Vanmore suddenly found that he had a ferocious appetite. They took their food across to a circular table and sat around it. Bianca pulled over a low chair with some mechanism built under it. She sat on it and touched something that started the soft hum of a motor, and the chair lifted her until her eyes were on a level with those of the others.

For a time they all ate in silence.

"This is superb, Bianca," said Rona.

"Thank you. I've given myself more than the rest of you, but I have a big body. It needs a lot of fuel."

Sitting level with the others, her body seemed to dominate the group, the thickness of her trunk keeping her erect. She was on Vanmore's left, and she ate lefthanded, the enormous right hand resting passively on the table. Near her elbow he could see her slow, powerful pulse, and the huge barrel of her rib cage rose and fell steadily and deeply.

The rest of us, he thought, probably seem as alien to her as she does to us—unless she's got used to us in sixteen years. He remembered when he had spent some time in southern India. At first, the innumerable dark faces had seemed strange to him. Then, after a few weeks, when he unexpectedly came face to face with his own reflection in a mirror, the light-skinned face had looked like something from another world.

Gannon glanced several times at his watch.

"How are you travelling down to the Roundhouse?" asked Bianca suddenly.

"Airkar, I suppose. Why?"

Her eyes rolled sideways to look at Vanmore. "What about the people who followed you here? Do you think it'd be safe?"

"We'll have to chance it," said Gannon.

"Suppose I drive you down in my van?"

Vanmore broke in. "Wouldn't your vehicles be well known to people likely to be involved?" He looked from Gannon to Bianca. "My airkar's rented—that's least likely to attract attention."

Bianca seemed to weigh up both sides of the argument for several seconds before she replied. "I think you're right."

"Very careful girl, Bianca," said Gannon.

Her thick brows came down in a steep V. "On Chiron, we *have* to be careful, or we don't survive. Our gravity and atmosphere don't forgive many mistakes."

Gannon said to Vanmore, as he finished his meal, "Your airkar, then." He stood up. "Now, if you'll excuse me, I'm going to change."

He went off into the inner part of the house. Vanmore turned to Bianca.

"Is Chiron closer to your sun than Alcenar, or further out? In other words, is it your Venus or your Mars?"

"Neither. You see, in the Alpha Centauri system we have two main suns, a yellow one that's a twin to yours, and an orange-red, almost the same size but only a third as bright. With me?"

"Yes."

"Now, Alcenar's the third planet of the yellow sun, but Chiron's the second planet of the red one. We're only about half as far out from the red sun as you are from yours, so the disc of our sun looks about four times the size of yours."

"How far apart are the suns?" said Rona.

"Imagine a red sun circling yours about the orbit of Uranus, and you have the picture. Sometimes it comes in nearly to the distance of Saturn, and it makes its full circuit once in just over eighty years."

"So your sunlight is all red?" pondered Rona.

"Yes. The yellow sun often shows in the sky at night."

"Like our moon?"

"Smaller, and much brighter. As much as 600 times brighter. We get some beautiful effects, sometimes." Bianca had lowered her chair as Rona and Vanmore stood up, and once again Vanmore found her sleek brown-haired head level with his waist. At this moment, a phone bell sounded somewhere else in the house.

"Excuse me," said Bianca, and she began to waddle towards the door in the far corner of the lounge in the direction of the bell. Abruptly, she leaned forward, put her right hand on the floor, and vaulted forward in a series of long leaps like those of an ape moving on its hands. The movement was so swift and inhuman that it shocked Rona and Vanmore into looking at each other after she had disappeared.

"I wonder if those two ever make love to each other," whispered Rona.

"I've no intention of asking them," said Vanmore.

Rona moved towards him and put her arms around the back of his neck, pulling his head forward and down, and kissing him hard on the mouth, her tongue playing with his lips. Suddenly she drew back.

"Be careful, Max, when you go down to the council."

"I'll be all right, honey. I told you—I trust nobody until I'm sure of them."

"But the danger may be from people you don't see. Your father and uncle never saw the people who killed them. So—be careful."

He held her tightly until they heard Gannon coming back. He was wearing a dark suit and fluorescent silver shirt.

"Ready?" he asked Vanmore, and then he looked around. "Where's Bianca?"

"She went to the phone," said Rona.

A moment later Bianca came back into the room with her quick, waddling gait, very erect. It was hard to connect her with the explosively violent, anthropoid movements they had seen a short time ago.

"Someone calling to tip me off about a T.V. program I mustn't miss," she said.

"Good," said Gannon. "Well, Max, we'd better go."

As they walked to the airkar, Max looked back and waved to the two women, who were standing just inside the glass door. Bianca had her right arm around Rona's waist, holding her almost possessively against the round bulk of her shoulder. Simultaneously each lifted a hand to wave, and Bianca's lips signalled, "Ciao."

The Roundhouse looked a vaguely sinister building at night. A thick, circular wall of laser-sawn stone supported a shallow dome of a metal that appeared to be bronze, although it did not show the slightest sign of corrosion. There were no windows, and the single, heavy-looking door was of the same metal as the dome.

Ashton Marsh emerged from a ground-car as they approached, his lank height unfolding like a carpenter's rule. With long strides, he intercepted them near the door. He placed his right hand against a metal plate in a recess in the wall.

"You'll be 'printed' for this later assuming your selection goes through," he said. The door slid silently open, and, as it clicked to its full opening, lights came on in the building.

Marsh led the way in, and as he waved his hand over a plate on a column the door closed behind them. Opposite, about a third of the circular wall was taken up by hologram alcoves in three tiers. Vanmore did a quick estimate—about thirty in each row. Say ninety altogether.

Facing the alcove were six comfortable-looking chairs, fixed, with floodlighting throwing them into a bright glare. There were small consoles with microphones and banks of keys in front of them, and fixed T.V. cameras pointed at them from different directions.

"As you see," said Marsh, "we have six places. Generally we only use three—the others are for council members visiting the area. Let's sit down."

"It's only ten to eight," said Gannon.

"No matter." Marsh sat in one of the central seats, Vanmore on his right, Gannon on his left.

"Are all Roundhouses like this?" said Vanmore.

"Internally, yes. All over the continent."

Three sets of hologram cameras had begun functioning as soon as they were seated. Vanmore was aware of a feeling of rising tension.

"What happens now?" asked Gannon.

"We wait," said Marsh complacently. He gestured to the alcoves. "In a few minutes, all the rest of the council will appear as they enter the other buildings and switch on."

After a minute, four of the alcoves in different parts of the array lit up almost at the same instant, as if at a pre-arranged signal. The heads and shoulders of four people—two men and two women—appeared in the alcoves, three-dimensional and startlingly alive.

Vanmore had the immediate impression that the four had been watching him and his companions for some time before appearing themselves. They showed none of the curiosity that he would have expected in the first second or two of confrontation with a person strange to them.

One, near the middle of the central tier, drew his attention, perhaps because he had appeared just a fraction of a second before the other three. He was a man in athletic middle age, blond, freckled, with cool blue eyes that looked uncomfortably observant. A name board in front of him read: Capt. S. Kranzen, Dept. of Defence. Something about him made Vanmore feel a little uneasy.

He was reminded suddenly of an encyclopedia which dealt with *Intelligence* under several headings, one of which was *Intelligence, Military and Political.* Captain Kranzen looked a classic example of intelligence military and political—he seemed to radiate an aura of cold, rigid authority that assumed immediate mastery of any interpersonal relationship he encountered.

Vanmore looked at the other three faces. None of them looked young. One of the women wore a white overall like a surgeon's or an electronics technician's. She had black-rimmed glasses, and her head was completely bald. The other woman looked thin and birdlike, and the man might have been a retired engineer, with a jutting chin and grizzled, close-cropped hair.

"We're a little ahead of time, Marsh," said the first man to appear. "But we may as well use the time to get to know our newcomers. I'm Kranzen, as you see."

Marsh introduced his companions. "Max Vanmore, Captain Kranzen. Max is the son and nominee of Kelvin Vanmore, who met with such a shocking end less than twenty-four hours ago. And here, Quade Gannon, secretary of Vanmore Titanium and nominee by default of Roderick Vanmore, on the death of his primary nominee."

"Yes." Kranzen gave the ghost of a smile. "We can cut the formalities, Marsh—we've seen their dossiers. What we want to establish now is their basic attitude to the Council—their goals, if you will."

Vanmore was the first to speak. "I learned something of the Stability Council from my father. He drummed into me quite early the importance of stability to a nation, and the idea of responsibility."

Kranzen looked steadily down at him. "Did he have any suggestion for improving our methods?"

Vanmore's mind raced. He thought of the hologram room hidden behind his father's office, and the link-up of the secret inner group within the council. Was Kranzen one of them? Were the four people who had appeared in advance of the meeting time all members of the inner ring? He decided to take a plunge.

"He did have one criticism," he said, "although I suppose it's hardly my place to repeat it."

"What was it?" snapped Kranzen.

"He *did* think the Council rather unwieldy. He often suggested that some kind of internal steering committee might make for smoother decision-making."

Kranzen looked at him a long time. They were all looking at him.

"That seems a rather sensible suggestion." The speaker was the bald woman in black-rimmed glasses.

"It does indeed," said Kranzen, still looking at Vanmore. "I think we might discuss this further. We won't bring it up before the whole Council, yet—but it's worthy of thought."

Suddenly another alcove lit up, and immediately Kranzen's eyes flicked sideways to something just out of the field of his hologram cameras—possibly some light or other signal warning him that another channel had been opened. Neither he nor the other three early birds said any more, and within a few minutes nearly all the alcoves were filled with a sea of faces, some of them men, some women, most of them noticeably older than Vanmore or Gannon.

Right on eight o'clock, someone announced the election of chairman for the night. How the choice was made, Vanmore wasn't sure, but he noticed all of them looked down, and apparently pressed numbered keys. The chairman turned out to be the grey-haired man with the jutting chin, whom Vanmore had thought looked like a retired engineer. His name was Szabo.

"We have two major items on our agenda tonight," he said. "One is the examination of our two nominees, Max Vanmore and Quade Gannon." He went into a brief summary of the events that had brought them here, then called on one of the other members to produce dossiers on the two candidates.

The dossier on Vanmore was projected on a large screen at one side of the alcoves. Evidently all the Roundhouses had similar screens, all at the moment filled with data on Max Vanmore. He scanned it with a deepening sense of insecurity. He had no idea how anyone could have amassed so much data on him. His school record from the very beginning, interests, people he had known, people he had forgotten, everything of importance he had ever done, and many things of which the importance escaped him.

All over the country, his detailed history was being analysed. The growth of his own firm, VanStar, and various other operations. Fortunately, all his ventures so far seemed to have turned out well.

"And now," said Szabo, "we vote."

Each screen had a row of coloured lights in front of it. As soon as the voting opened, four green lights blazed simultaneously—Kranzen's and those of the other three who had come early. Others followed their lead, until more than half the alcoves showed green lights, with a few yellow, which evidently signified abstention from voting. Presumably red meant no, but no red lights came on.

"Carried," said Szabo. "Max Vanmore, you are elected to the National Stability Council on a provisional basis. You do not have voting rights straight away, but you are free to speak on any subject in which you have special interest or special knowledge."

"Thank you," said Vanmore. He looked along the tiers of alcoves. "And thank you all. I know my father felt his membership of this Council was an incalculable honour, and a heavy responsibility. I'll have to feel my way for a while, but I hope I can eventually fill his place as effectively as possible."

There was silence, where he had expected at least some murmur of applause. Had he overdone it?"

Szabo acknowledged his speech by simply bowing slightly and saying, "Thank you." Then they went on with their examination of Gannon. The same routine followed—the dossier projected with chilling clarity on the screen, then the vote. This time, there was not the immediate appearance of the four green lights. The lights came on in ones and twos, some green, some yellow. Three or four times, different members asked Gannon questions about some aspect of his career, and he answered. With each reply, a few more green lights appeared, and finally Szabo gave his verdict: "Carried."

Gannon, perhaps influenced by the lack of response to Vanmore's speech, confined his reply to a brief "Thank you." Vanmore reached across in front of Marsh, and shook Gannon's hand.

"And now," said Szabo, "we pass on to the second item on our agenda.

"This involves a nationwide telecast scheduled to be released on prime time tomorrow. It takes in a preliminary interview, at long range, with the Captain of the *Alphard*, the Alcenar ship on its way to Earth, and due here the week after next. Also, interviewed was a young Australian, Frank Ferris, who had made the journey to Alcenar and back.

"We've received an exclusive preview of the interviews by vortex beam from the transfer station. It's been suggested that the part involving Ferris may present a stability risk. Are we in agreement that we watch and evaluate?"

Green lights flared.

"Right," said Szabo. "Let's have the picture."

The screen lit up with a picture of a man sitting in a plain, green-walled room. "This is Rik Dane, of United," he was saying, as if the opening had been cut, "speaking from Earth Transfer Station Number 3, in synchronous orbit above meridian 135 degrees east. In ten days from now, we promise you live interviews with Captain Rance, of the *Alphard*, and Frank Ferris. You have heard a preliminary interview over long range with Captain Rance, and now, by the same technique, we bring you picture and sound from Frank Ferris. . . ."

At this point the tape had been edited, because it jumped immediately to a picture of very poor quality, showing a figure which Vanmore recognised as Ferris. Somehow, he looked even younger than when Vanmore had known him.

His voice came over with relative clarity: "The technology they have developed on Alcenar is fantastic. They have matter converters which can turn one element into another. I saw some examples of this. I saw a whole road paved with sapphire—real sapphire. I broke some of it off, and I have it with me. . . ."

The picture ended.

"That's the significant part," said Szabo. "What's the general feeling about that?"

"I think he's mad," said one member.

"But if he isn't?" queried another. "After all, we know these Centaurans have carried out very advanced research. They developed the drive that powers the *Alphard* when our so-called experts said it was not feasible."

"That's not the immediate question before us," said Szabo. "All we have to decide at the moment is whether or not we allow this part of the broadcast to proceed as we heard it."

"I'd say kill it!" came an emphatic voice.

The next comment came from the bald woman. "It may, or may not, be true that they have an economy so absurdly rich that they can afford roads paved with sapphire. But I'd say it was more likely that young Ferris was mistaken, or duped." Her voice remained cool and level. Vanmore read the little name board in front of her: Dr. G. Lester, Dept. Biological Research.

"True or not," came another man's voice. "It could be highly unstabilising."

"Let's vote, then," said Szabo, after a short interval of silence from the alcoves. "Green, we let the broadcast run as presented. Red, the Ferris segment is deleted."

A mixture of lights flamed along the tiers—red, green, and yellow. It was obvious without a count that about seventy or eighty percent were red.

"Then the segment will be killed," said Szabo. He looked across at one of the alcoves. "Will you handle that, Vic? Right. Any other business?"

Quite abruptly, the meeting closed. It had taken little more than half an hour. The lights went out in the alcoves, and the floodlights and the hologram cameras snapped off, leaving the Roundhouse in only moderate illumination. Somehow it looked very large and empty with the vigorous electronic life drained from it.

Ashton Marsh jackknifed to his feet. "Well, that's it. Congratulations, you two, on your election." He shook their hands, and they went out into the night.

On the way back to Gannon's place, Vanmore said, "Now I'm beginning to see how they operate. I never realised there was that type of safety valve on our news broadcasts—did you?"

"No idea. I've taken it for granted the news came through without any delay. In other words, I thought it was a 'free press,' to use the old term."

"What did you think about Ferris and his story?"

"I don't know. It's unbelievable—and yet, I'm sure *he* believed it. He looked young, though, and impressionable."

"I know. But remember what he said? 'I saw a road paved with real sapphire. I broke some of it off. *I have it with me.*' Now, whatever he's got, other people on the *Alphard* must have seen it."

"Then you think it might be true?"

"I don't know. Gives you a nasty taste, doesn't it? Leaves you feeling you're not quite sure of *anything*."

"No. They *are* very advanced. Look at their space drive."

As Vanmore was swinging the airkar down towards Gannon's carport, Gannon gave a gasp of mild surprise. "The van's gone."

Vanmore parked the machine, and Gannon sprang out as soon as it touched down, making for his front door. He broke into a curious, skipping run, with two leaps on his foot for each forward swing of his crutch. He palmed the lock-plate to open the sliding door, and Vanmore, following, heard him call Bianca's name as he went into the house.

"There, Rona?" called Vanmore as he stepped inside. The only sound he could hear in the house was the tap, thud of Gannon's step up to the bedrooms, then back again. Fear began to come to him, with the taste of metal in his mouth.

When Gannon returned to the lounge his face had a greyish pallor, and he looked somehow older. "They're gone," he said.

"Well, Bianca's probably taken Rona somewhere in her van."

"Not like her. She'd have left a note on the chalkboard in the passageway." Gannon's eyes looked dark and haunted.

"They'll be back," said Vanmore, but he knew he wasn't even convincing himself.

4

WHEN VANMORE AND GANNON had taken off in the airkar for the Roundhouse, Rona and Bianca had stood inside the glass door until the machine swept out of sight behind the casuarinas on the lake shore.

"Well," said Rona, "I wonder how long they'll be?"

"I don't know, kitten. Hours, I suppose. Their Stability Council's a big deal." She still had her arm around Rona's waist, holding her gently but immovably against her side. Rona could feel the deep, steady movement of the great rib cage, and it seemed the rate of Bianca's breathing suddenly grew faster.

She put her hands on the encircling arm to try to disengage it, but under the smooth, creamy skin the enormous muscles were like iron. As if absent-mindedly, the hand turned slightly and one of the long, strong fingers caressed Rona's breast.

"Well," Rona said, "they're out of sight, now. I suppose we may as well sit down."

"Of course. Come and I'll get us something to drink— Chironian style."

With an upward movement of her arm, Bianca lifted Rona effortlessly so that her feet were just clear of the floor. Turning, she padded quickly across the room and swung her down on to the sofa.

"God, you're strong," gasped Rona.

Bianca laughed, her eyes very bright. "Just a normal Chiro-

42

nian," she said, and moved over to a small cupboard, taking out a curiously shaped bottle of green liquid and two glasses. "Haven't much of this left, but I don't think I'll be needing it around here much longer."

"Are you really going back on the *Alphard*?"

"I'm going to try. I'm tired of this man's world." She crossed to Rona with the two glasses, which had transparent covers over their tops, with flexible tubes. Although Rona was sitting on the low sofa and Bianca was standing, their faces were on the same level.

"A man's world?" Rona accepted one of the glasses. "I thought we were supposed to have equality."

"Do you really believe equality of sexes works here?" Bianca put the flexible tube of her glass between her lips and drew off some of the liquid.

Rona smiled. "Not in practice. No. Does it work on your planet?"

"We have no men on Chiron."

For a few seconds Rona said nothing. "I don't think I heard that properly, Bianca. I thought you said you had no men on Chiron."

"That's right, kitten. All girls and women. If one of us wants to mate with a man, she has to go to Alcenar, or somewhere further. But most of us inseminate artificially when we want daughters—we can control the sex of our children, of course."

Rona tried her drink. It was too sweet for her taste, but she drank some without comment. She felt she needed it.

Bianca leaned forward, put her right hand on the sofa, and swung herself up alongside Rona. The sofa compressed noticeably under her weight, and she slipped her monstrous right arm around Rona's shoulders, holding her lightly against her.

"It's good to have an intelligent woman to talk to for a while," she said. "I'd love to be able to take a girl like you back to Chiron, but I can't. Our gravity would kill you."

"How did you come to have a planet with no men?" asked Rona. "I mean, I can see how you can keep it going, but how did it ever start that way?"

"It was men who started it—and they made a Frankenstein."

"What's a Frankenstein?"

"Oh—just an old expression." The fingers of her left hand ran lightly down Rona's thigh. "Alcenar is something like Earth. Now in the same system they had this other big planet, Chiron, rich in metals, petroleum, coal for making nylon and dyes, a real El Dorado. But out of reach—because of its surface gravity of 194 centigees. You with me?"

"Yes."

"So the genetic engineering boys created a new type of man—and woman—to live and work in that gravity. It meant they wouldn't necessarily fit in anywhere else, but they could live on Chiron. You see?"

"Uh huh."

"Well, quite early it was found that the males tended to be aggressive when they came in contact with so-called normal males from Alcenar. Also, under a gravity of 194 centigees the male is very liable to scrotal hernia and a few things like that. So they let the male Chironians die out, and built up a totally female population."

"And you've kept it going?"

"For generations. Eventually, some of us went back to Alcenar, and that's where the fun started. We had quite an impact on their civilisation. They weren't used to women like us. You can't easily push a Chironian woman around."

"But how—" Rona made a vague gesture. "How do you have any social life without men?"

Bianca laughed. "The same as anywhere else. We have family structures like any other society—sometimes one woman has a career while her mate raises the daughters, and in other cases two women share tasks. We do all the things mixed societies do. Art, music, athletics—although our sports have a different emphasis. The more important with us are discus, javelin, weight-lifting, wrestling, swimming."

"But what about affection? Love?"

"You mean sex?"

"Yes. But isn't the most natural form of sex between man and woman? They used to say that's what made the world go round."

"Maybe your world, kitten. Not mine." She still had her right arm around Rona, and when Rona tried to push it away she caught both her slim hands in her huge one, and held them firmly while her left forefinger stroked the front of Rona's neck from the chin downward. Rona stiffened, and Bianca released her with a little laugh.

"Sorry, kitten. I haven't given you time to get used to me." She eased slightly away from her. "Affection is very natural, with us—" She seemed about to say something else, but stopped.

"It's hard for me to imagine a world without men," said Rona. "Are all the women like you?"

Bianca extended her arm in front of her. "Each of us has her right arm hypertrophied—her main arm, as we call it. Our whole system is set up for that. Our vehicles are steered by the main hand. We use our minor hand for anything that needs delicate manipulation."

Rona felt a slowly rising anger within her. "But that was a monstrous thing for those men to have done. Forcing women to live on a world where they wouldn't live themselves."

Bianca gave a deep laugh, and Rona could see the vibration in her cavernous rib cage. "It's our world, kitten. And now nobody can take it away from us. They're welcome to come down to the surface and try to live there."

Abruptly, she looked at the slim wristwatch on what she would have called her minor arm, and flung her body into a standing position.

"Are you game to listen to an illegal telecast?"

"What d'you mean?"

"It'll have to be a secret—even from your man."

Rona shrugged. "He doesn't tell me everything, so I suppose there's no need for me to tell him everything." She hesitated. "But you *did* say illegal? I don't think it's ethical to do anything that might get Max into trouble."

"Don't see why. I'll tell you what it is, anyway. I have a friend who's an amateur radio freak. She can pick up vortex beam signals from satellites to the aerial that feeds the Stability Council Roundhouse. They get a preview of news stories that go on the air the next day."

"Why not simply wait for them?"

"Because sometimes they kill the story. Perhaps only one in a hundred, but they're usually the most interesting ones. Anyway, it's not far from here. Are you game?"

"Frankly, I don't think I'm interested enough."

"Pity. Still, it mightn't have been very interesting. They

were going to try a long-distance interview with people on the *Alphard*. Incidentally, I think one of the ones they're talking to is your young friend Ferris."

"Frank Ferris?" Rona sat straight up on the sofa. "How long will it take?"

"Well, they'll be listening to the same thing at the Round-house—and I suppose they'll discuss it for a while afterwards. If we come back as soon as it's finished, we'll be home before the boys, and they need never know."

Rona thought for a moment. "Why not?"

Bianca's plump cheek dimpled slightly. "That's my kitten! But we'll have to hurry." She turned, and bounded apelike into the passageway, using her main arm. She returned quickly in a hooded black coat with its huge right sleeve ending in a leatheroid glove with hard padding across the knuckles, so that she could use her fist as a third foot.

"Don't worry, kitten. We'll be back before the boys."

She led the way out to the blue electric van, and Rona climbed in beside her. It had Chironian-type controls, with a small steering wheel that Bianca turned with her right hand, its gloved fingers spanning the indented rim. Her left hand rested on a keyboard-type console, and her legs, too short to operate pedals, were simply braced against a board.

She drove through a series of twisting avenues and lanes that led away from the lake, although Rona's sense of direction was soon confused.

"The lass we're visiting used to be one of my physiotherapy patients. She doesn't get about much. Spends all her time as a radio and TV ham."

She stopped the van under a clump of tamarisks by an ir-rigation canal, on the other side of which lay a thin line of houses, with dark plains beyond.

"We'll have to cross the footbridge and walk a bit. Come on."

She locked the van and led the way over an arched foot-bridge. The night was so still that stars were reflected in the mirror-smooth water of the canal.

A path ran along the far side, and Bianca reached up her left hand to take Rona's. "Hurry," she said, "let's run."

Using her gloved fist against the ground, she bounded for-ward in the semi-darkness, towing Rona along as quickly as she could run. Ahead was an isolated house with a lighted green veranda, and Bianca released Rona's hand and leaped up on to the veranda, pressing an old-style bell-push.

By the time Rona had joined her, the door was opened by a gaunt, white-haired man in shorts, with rimless glasses perched near the end of a long, thin nose with a red, bulbous tip.

"Ah, Ms. Baru," he said. "Charl's just watching a telecast."

"She rang me about it. May we go through?"

He stood aside with a flourishing gesture, and Bianca waddled briskly down the passage, Rona following. A knock on a closed door brought the sound of a bolt sliding, and the door was opened by a thin girl in a striped green T-shirt and grubby white slacks.

"Rona, this is Charl. Rona."

"Hi," said Charl, tilting her head back to look at Rona through rimless glasses similar to the man's. She was obviously his daughter—her thin, bulbous-tipped nose was a smaller version of his. "Just starting," she said, and moved aside to let them in to a room cluttered with masses of electronic gear linked by tangles of wire. She bolted the door as soon as they were inside, and moved awkwardly to a jury-rigged control panel on a bench.

"How are the legs?" asked Bianca.

"They get me there." Charl glanced at Rona and indicated Bianca. "I wouldn't be able to walk if it wasn't for this monster."

"Like your choice of words," said Bianca.

"That's affection. You're my favourite monster. Ah, here's the picture."

They watched the screen, Rona sitting on a ricketty-looking chair while Bianca stood beside her. The picture was not three-dimensional, but it was in full colour and of a fair quality. The segment was the one which Vanmore, Gannon, and the whole National Stability Council were watching in what they believed to be secrecy. Rona wondered how many other leaks existed throughout the continent.

Suddenly, Frank Ferris was on the screen.

Rona's eyes widened. "God, he looks young!"

Charl glanced at her in surprise, and Bianca said, "She knew him."

"Yeah?"

Then they were all listening to what Ferris was saying, while Charl fiddled with a vernier-type dial in an effort to improve the sound.

". . . the technology they have developed on Alcenar is fantastic. They have matter converters which can turn one element into another. I saw some examples of this. I saw a whole road paved with sapphire. I broke some of it off, and I have it with me. . . ."

"What?" ejaculated Charl.

"Sapphire?" Rona looked from Charl to Bianca as if to verify what she had heard. "A whole road of it?"

"That's what he said," said Bianca in an awed voice.

"But you've been there. Is it true?"

Bianca didn't answer straight away. "I suppose it is," she said at length. "They *do* have some blue roads there—shiny, crystalline blue. I just took them for granted."

Charl stared at some private vision. "They must be ages ahead of us. . . ." Abruptly, she came back to the present. "Listen, you two, for crisake not a word to anyone about this! Nobody's supposed to know it except the Council, yet. It's all right for me—I don't see many people. But if you let it slip, someone's going to wonder where you got hold of it."

"Don't worry," Bianca said. "Have I ever spilt anything?"

"But Rona. Does she know? I mean—"

"She knows," Bianca assured her. She looked at her watch. "Say, we'd better head back. Might be some awkward questions to handle if our men get home before we do. Thanks, Charl."

Charl moved across to her. "Anything for my favourite monster."

Bianca turned to Rona. "Come on, before we're insulted."

Outside, as they walked along the path towards the bridge, Rona said, "Bianca, do you think that's true? About the sapphire road?"

"Could be, kitten. I simply don't know. And since it's sixteen years since I came here, that makes twenty-four years since I've seen Alcenar. This boy saw it only eight years ago. Anyway, as I said, they had some blue roads when I was there. I could have driven over sapphire without knowing it."

"Did you ever hear of a matter converter?"

"Seem to recall hearing the term, yes. But I don't know

much about it. Biology and human engineering were my specialties.''

"Of course."

They went along in silence for a while with their arms linked, Rona walking quickly, Bianca's feet pattering on the ground with a tempo like that of a fast run. But as they neared the footbridge, Rona suddenly stopped.

"Wait!"

"What's the matter?"

"That airkar over the other side—parked near your van."

"What about it?"

"It's like the one that followed Max and me when we came down from the penthouse. I can see the grey colour where the light from one of the houses strikes it. And the windows—you can't see through them from outside."

"Keep your voice down, kitten," whispered Bianca. She drew Rona across under a clump of trees and bushes growing along the margin of the canal, so that they could look across without being seen. Fortunately there was some loud music playing from one of the houses the other side.

"There's a man waiting near the van, I think," murmured Rona. "Yes! See? Under those trees!"

"Let's move along so we get his silhouette against the light on that veranda."

They worked their way silently along behind the bushes, until they had a good view of the waiting figure. He wore a close-fitting one-piece suit, in spite of the heat of the night, and his head was hidden by a helmet with a shining, one-way visor.

"What'll we do?" whispered Rona, kneeling down alongside Bianca and sitting back on her heels, so that their heads were on the same level.

"We wait for a while, and think."

"But Max and Quade will get home and find us missing."

"Can't be helped. We don't know who these people are. You couldn't trust a fellow who's masked." She pondered for a while.

"We can be sure of one thing, kitten. They didn't follow us here in that airkar. After I parked the van and we walked over the bridge, we would have seen it in the air. I think they must have bugged the van. Could have done it with all our vehicles

—they stand out under the big carport most of the time, and all these people would have to do is stick a small tracer somewhere under the body.''

"Why are you so sure they didn't just follow us?"

"Because they don't realise we're this side of the canal. See? He keeps looking up and down the road over that side, expecting us to come out of one of the houses over there. Or Quade, or Max—they wouldn't know who brought the van here."

Rona had a sudden idea. "Your friends had a ground-car beside their house. Could we get them to run us back?"

"No. It's not fair to involve them. I can deal with these fools in the helmets."

"Who are they?"

"Some kind of security setup, I'd say. Who's paying them, who's behind them, is anyone's guess." She touched Rona's arm. "Wait!"

A second helmeted man had emerged from the airkar. He sauntered down to the one near the van and they conversed for a short time. Then he went back, and in a few seconds the airkar took off, its lights coming on only when it was airborne. It swung off down the length of the canal towards the lake, and they watched it until its lights were hidden by the high buildings near the Esplanade.

The man in the helmet took something from his pocket, and they heard a metallic click. The light from beyond him gleamed on the barrel of a weapon as he checked it, and there was another sound like the snap of a steel spring as he put it away again.

"Fair enough," whispered Bianca as if to herself. She began searching for something among the detritus under the trees, and found a large section of broken branch. Rona would have needed both hands to lift it, but Bianca hefted it easily in her right hand, feeling the balance of it. "Listen!" she said softly to Rona. "When you see me go to the van, run like hell across the bridge. I'll be aboard by the time you get there."

"But what about *him*?"

"He won't worry you." She swung the branch easily back and forth with her giant arm, using her left hand to hold her coat about her to give her arm free movement. Rona was watching the man across the canal, perhaps thirty metres away. He turned slowly, his back to the canal, scanning the houses on the far side.

From the corner of her eye, she saw Bianca blur in an incredible explosion of movement. The branch spun like a boomerang across the canal on an almost flat trajectory, and there was a blood-chilling impact as it struck the helmeted man across the upper part of the back. It rebounded high in the air and clattered to the ground, while the man sprawled face-downward, unmoving.

A curtain was drawn aside from a lighted window in one of the houses, and someone looked out. However, as there was no further sound or movement outside, the person soon lost interest, and the lighted rectangle of the window darkened again.

With appalling speed, Bianca raced across the bridge, using her arm to hurl her body along. Within seconds, her squat, massive figure was beside the fallen man. Gripping his shoulder, she flipped him over on his back. Rona had the unreal feeling of looking at a faked film where the action had been speeded up to an impossible degree.

Bianca took off the man's helmet and looked at his face. His head moved. With a movement almost too swift to follow, she backhanded him across the jaw with her gloved hand, and he lay still. She took the weapon from him, put it in the helmet, then flung both into the canal with a splash.

Leaving the man where he lay, she rushed silently for the van, and Rona sprang to her feet and raced across the bridge. A moment later they were both aboard, and the powerful electric motors whined as Bianca swung the machine down the road.

"Did—" began Rona, but her voice grated, and she had to start again. "You didn't kill him, did you?"

"No. He'll need some bone manipulation, and his jaw might be cracked. But that's all in a day's work for a fellow who carries a gun."

"You got a look at him. Did you know him?"

"No. Wouldn't want to."

For a time they travelled in silence. Rona looked covertly at the woman beside her, as if she were a stranger she was seeing for the first time, almost as if she were a creature of a different species from the human. At least as different as one of the great anthropoid apes, yet with a woman's brain and senses and emotions.

"You were good in that rough spot, kitten," said Bianca

suddenly. "You didn't panic, or go to pieces."

"You were the one who got us out of it. You're a very dangerous lady." Rona glanced sidelong. "But nice."

Bianca grunted. She drove down on the Esplanade where they could look around the curve towards her house, and immediately pulled the van into the kerb, switching off the motors.

"They're home. That means we have to work out our story." She turned herself round in the seat so that she was facing Rona, her eyes steady and direct.

"What can we tell them?" said Rona.

"Some of it. Not all. We can't tell them about the broadcast—you realise that. But I *must* tell Quade about the bugging of the van and the men who waited for us." She gestured towards the house. "That could happen again. Any time. Perhaps to Max, too. They'll have to be warned."

"Are you going to tell them how you flattened that man with the gun?"

"Oh, that part of it's all right. Quade knows I'm capable of that, anyway." The corners of her eyes wrinkled in a half-smile. "He says I'm the most efficient bodyguard he could possibly have. No, all we have to hold back is the part about Charl and the telecast. If they knew we saw that, we'd be in terrible trouble."

"Well," said Rona, "we could say you took me to see a friend of yours—I didn't get her name—and on the way back we saw these horrible men with the grey airkar and the guns."

Bianca's eyes seemed to sparkle. "Perfect!" She turned to face forward again. "Let's go!"

5

VANMORE, STANDING NEAR the glass door, saw the blue van returning before Gannon did.

"Quade! They're coming! Around the Esplanade."

Gannon loped across the room and stood beside him, shading his eyes with his hand to look out into the night. "You're right," he said, as the van passed under another of the overhead lights, and he immediately opened the door.

They both stepped out onto the veranda. The outside air was cooler, now, with a light breeze coming in over the lake. As Bianca swung the van into the carport the men hurried to meet it.

Rona sprang out before it had quite stopped, and ran towards Vanmore with outstretched arms. He put his arms around her and held her tightly against him, his spread fingers caressing her shoulder-blades as they had not done for quite a time.

"You're trembling," he said. "What happened, honey?"

She kept her face buried against his neck, so that her reply was muffled.

"Come inside," he said.

"Yes," said Gannon, around the other side of the van. "We'd better all go in."

In the lounge, with the outer door closed, Gannon made hot drinks for the two women, while Rona steadied herself with an obvious effort. Bianca seemed completely poised.

"Now," said Gannon. "Where did you go?"

Bianca gave a short laugh. "It's not a question of where we went. It's what happened when we tried to come home." She glanced at Rona, who took up the story.

"It was that grey airkar with the one-way windows, Max. The one that followed us here—you know? We went to pay a short visit to a friend of Bianca's, and when we came out this thing was parked near her van."

"What?" shouted Vanmore.

"But *how?"* demanded Gannon.

"They must have a tracer somewhere on my van," said Bianca. "Probably got one on your airkar, too, Quade. Obviously someone wants to keep track of our movements."

"What did they do?" asked Vanmore.

Rona took over the story. "When their airkar flew off, one of them waited near the van—with a gun. We saw him checking it. Bianca was wonderful! I've never seen anyone move as quickly!"

"What did you do?" asked Gannon, looking at Bianca, who had thrown back the hood of her coat.

She smiled, her cheek dimpling. "I had to use a little Chiron-style force on him. There was a log handy, and I threw it from thirty or forty metres away. Hit him across the spine."

"Where is he now?"

"I suppose he's still on the ground, out along the bank of the irrigation canal that runs past the sub-station."

"How was he dressed?"

"One-piece suit. Grey. Looked like a uniform. And a helmet. I took his helmet and gun away."

"Where?"

"The canal." She slipped off the black coat and tossed it over a chair, then swung herself up on to the sofa. She looked up at Vanmore. "Your girl kept her head very well, Max," she said.

Vanmore was still standing with his arm around Rona's shoulders. Suddenly she looked up at him.

"What happened at the meeting, Max?"

Gannon cut in. "Never mind about that just now. We'd better find out who's involved in this." He stalked across to the passageway, and the others were silent as they heard him tap out a number on the visiphone.

"Enzo," he said after a short interval, "can you get over to my place right away? Bring Tom, if he's there—and whatever you need to look for a bug hidden on our van. Possibly another on the airkar. . . . Right. We'll see you.''

He appeared at the door of the passage, and stood for a moment as if undecided.

''I think I'll let Ashton Marsh know about this,'' he said.

''Why him?'' asked Vanmore.

''Well, he *is* on the Board.''

''You mean the Council?''

''Yes, the Council—but he's also on our Board of Directors. But I thought you knew that.''

''No. Listen, Quade, I just got here today, remember? There's a hell of a lot I don't know about our setup.''

''I'm sorry—I haven't told you the people on the Board, yet. But there's been so much—''

''Never mind now, anyway. You can fill me in tomorrow. Go ahead, if you think he has any ideas.''

Vanmore walked in behind Gannon, after excusing himself to the two women. He watched as Gannon tapped out Marsh's number, and waited. The small alcove lit up with the hologram of a plump woman with a parrot nose and prominent eyes.

''Ah, Mrs. Marsh. Is Ashton there?''

''One moment, Mr. Gannon.'' The woman hadn't seemed particularly surprised to see Gannon's face, as if he were in the habit of calling Marsh often.

Marsh appeared in a few seconds, stripped to the waist, with a towel across his shoulders. ''What is it, Quade?''

''Something I think you should know. When Max Vanmore came down to my place prior to tonight's meeting, someone followed him in a grey airkar. While we were at the meeting, the same machine followed Bianca when she went out with Max's lady in her van. Any idea who might be behind it? . . . No, she didn't imagine it. . . . No, I don't think it's a police matter—do you? . . . Quite so. Well, in any case, we'll meet at the funeral tomorrow.''

Vanmore had moved back into the lounge as Marsh began to talk, so that he heard only Gannon's side of the conversation.

''Well,'' he said, as Gannon returned. ''Did he have any suggestions?''

Gannon shook his head. ''We'll see what my security boys can dig out.''

Tom and Enzo arrived in a black airkar within a couple of

minutes. They both had the same look, as devoid of expression as an Easter Island statue. In fact, they looked very similar, except that Tom was blond and Enzo dark. They surprised Vanmore a little by greeting both him and Rona by name as soon as they came in.

Bianca seemed to know them quite well, and they listened attentively as she described what had happened by the canal. When she told them she had knocked the helmeted man down by throwing a log across the canal, they didn't appear surprised. Enzo looked up as Rona vouched for the truth of what Bianca had said.

"Don't doubt it, Ms. Gale," he said. "Ms. Baru's a very strong lady." He flexed his arms. "She treated me."

"And me," added Tom. "We're a couple of the fellows you've probably heard about. Broke world athletic records right and. left, and then the Athletics Association took them away from us." He turned to Gannon. "Anyway, I'll check the vehicles for tracers. Perhaps Ms. Baru could take a run out with Enzo to where she left this fellow with the helmet. Enzo might be able to get him to fill in a few details."

"Good idea." Bianca slipped on her coat, and went out to the black airkar, Enzo walking beside her. Tom lifted a metal toolbox he had brought with him. "I'll check over your vehicles, Mr. Gannon."

"Right," said Gannon, and Tom went out. "Good boys, those. Used to be professional athletes. Bianca's techniques of increasing muscle power made them world-beaters, but of course they were out of a job when the Association found out. She was treating me at the time, and she asked me to help them—I found them a security job, and they've been loyal to me ever since."

Vanmore nodded. "You're pretty well protected, with those two *and* Bianca."

"Unfortunately, that's no protection against high explosive, or a laser beam." Gannon sat heavily on the sofa, extending his leg along it. "What a day! Eh? Do you realise it's not twenty-four hours since the explosion that killed your father and uncle?

"It *is* rather incredible. Not much more than twelve hours ago, we were in Samoa." Vanmore looked at Rona, who nodded.

"Not a care in our lives. All I had to worry about was what

colour to have my hair tinted, and where we'd go during the afternoon.''

"What about your own business?'' asked Gannon, looking at Vanmore.

"It's fairly streamlined. Almost runs itself, now. Anyway, I was on a week's holiday, so no one's expecting to see me for a few days.''

"Good. I should have explained, having the funeral tomorrow probably seems indecently soon—but I wanted it carried out as quickly and unobtrusively as possible, to give people less chance of planning another 'hit.' You see?''

"Yes. But what people?''

Gannon spread his hands. At that moment, Tom reappeared at the outer door. He walked in, looking down at something in the palm of his hands.

"That should be the lot,'' he said. "Five of 'em.'' He held his hand out, showing five tiny metal specks, each with an almost invisible whisker of wire.

"Five,'' ejaculated Gannon.

"Two on the van, two on your airkar, and one on the airkar Mr. Vanmore's renting.''

"What?'' Vanmore looked at the tiny tracers. "How the hell did one get on *my* car?''

"Where's it been from the time you picked it up?'' asked Tom.

"Let's see. From the hire yard, I tested it a bit, then flew it to the landing flange on top of our building.'' He went through all the movements of the machine, while Tom listened without apparent interest.

"Probably happened on the landing flange. This other car on the adjoining building—*might* have come across and landed alongside yours for a minute while someone planted the bug. Don't think so, though. It'd be a conspicuous thing to do, wouldn't it? More likely someone in the building slipped out and planted it. It was stuck under one of the struts of the landing gear, by the way. Someone could have walked past and slapped it on almost without missing a step.''

"And how about the four on my vehicles?'' asked Gannon.

"Well, they're in the carport a lot of the time, aren't they? With bushes around, that'd make it a kid's game.''

Outside, the black airkar whirred down to a landing. A few seconds later, Bianca came in, followed by Enzo.

"Gone," she said laconically.

"Had he walked away, or did someone collect him?" asked Gannon.

Bianca gave a short laugh. "He didn't walk away—I can guarantee that. Wouldn't you agree, Rona? No, I think his friend came back in the airkar and found him. We found the log I threw, so there's no doubt about the place."

"How about checking the local hospitals?" suggested Vanmore.

"We could try," said Gannon, "but I think they'd fly him out to a hospital a long way away from here. Adelaide, Melbourne—you wouldn't know where to start looking."

"We can try, if you like," said Tom. "Don't expect too much, though." He put the tracers on the corner of a sideboard, then as if on an afterthought he took two of them and put them in his pocket. "I'll get these examined and see if we can find out where they were made."

"A thing like that's not going to have the maker's name," said Gannon. "However, you can try."

"Want us to shadow you out to the funeral tomorrow?" asked Tom.

"Yes. You'd better do that," said Gannon.

As the two security men were leaving, Enzo turned in the doorway with a sudden flash of white teeth. It was the first time Vanmore had seen either of the men smile. He indicated Bianca.

"Say, you know? This lady is really terrific! You should have seen the size of that log! Right across the canal! Pow!" He drove his fist into his palm, then was gone into the night.

Bianca took her coat off and folded it. "Glad I've impressed somebody," she said.

Rona yawned, and Vanmore put his arm around her. "I think we'd better head for home. It's been a day and a half. Thanks, Quade. And thank *you,* Bianca, for looking after Rona."

After he took off in the airkar, he swung it in a circle just above the rooftops, looking in every direction, before he switched on its lights. As they flew up towards the top of the Titanium Building, Rona glanced back several times to see if they were being followed. Reaching the building, he flew slowly right around the top of it, hovering a few times and flooding the roof garden with the brilliant glare of his landing lights. Satisfied there was no one on the roof, he landed, and they walked through the tunnel from the landing flange to the penthouse. He didn't feel really safe until they were inside.

Just before they went to bed, they stood together at the window. The moon, just entering its third quarter, was low over the eastern end of the lake, large and golden.

"Is this really happening to us?" asked Rona in a small voice.

"I was wondering the same thing," he said.

"That man had a gun, tonight," she said, and he felt a tremor run through her slim body. He tightened his grip on her shoulders.

"Sounds as if Gannon's woman handled him very effectively," he said.

"She's something else altogether," she said. "You know what she told me?"

"What?"

"On this planet she comes from, they don't have any men. The gravity is nearly twice ours, so they modified the women to live there."

"Why no men?"

"Hernias, and other reasons—they had men there at first, but when the gravity gets that high it's not feasible to use them. So you have this terrible world of monstrous women with stumpy legs and enormously strong right arms."

"Lucky for you, tonight."

"Yes. Oh, what happened at your meeting?"

"Oh, of course—I haven't had time to tell you. Quade and I were both accepted on the Council."

"Just like that? Straight away?"

"That's right. The meeting takes in people all over Australia. You see the others in hologram form, and they see you. There's a big team of them—about ninety, I'd say."

"Any women?"

"Some. Maybe twenty, twenty-five." He laughed. "Most of them are quite old—men *and* women."

"Are you the youngest one there?"

"Very possibly. But I'm sure of one thing. There's a small clique that seems to run the thing, as far as major decisions are concerned."

"That used to happen on our local shire council. Perhaps it always works like that."

"Maybe it does. Anyway, let's go to bed."

"Best suggestion yet, darling."

With the lights out, the room was not completely dark, because the moonlight slanted in through the windows. The golden colour had gone as it rose higher, and under its cold, pure light the lake was a sheet of steel.

"You know something?" he said, staring up at the dim ceiling.

"What?" she asked sleepily, snuggling closer to him, her arm across his chest.

"Something else just struck me as odd. This fellow Ashton Marsh. He's on the Stability Council, you know. He saw me about it when we first arrived, remember?"

"I remember. He didn't seem much interested in me—I know that."

"True. Well, it turns out he's on our Board of Directors."

"So?"

"Well, it's odd that he said nothing about it when we met. He must have known I'd meet him in the first Board meeting we attended. Unless he didn't expect me to live that long."

It took a few seconds for the implication to sink in, and then she suddenly squirmed violently into a half-sitting position in the bed.

"Do you think someone is trying to wipe out the whole management of the company?"

"It's a possibility you've got to look at. When I first heard of the explosion, I thought it was engineered by some individual crackpot, or maybe a small group of crackpots. Now, I don't think so. There's some sort of organisation behind all this. Technically sophisticated." He yawned. "God, I'm tired."

"So'm I. S'jet lag. Say we leave it all till the morning?"

"Good night, honey."

He kissed her, turned towards her with his uppermost arm around her. Quite soon her breathing became deep and regular, with a tiny rattling sound at a certain point in each breath. Carefully, he disengaged his arm from her, then rolled on his back and stared up at the dimly visible blankness of the ceiling.

He must have slept very deeply, because when he awoke it seemed his eyes had been closed for only a moment—yet the moon was now close to the zenith, and the eastern sky was lightened by the greenish pallor of the dawn. From the movement of the moon, he calculated that he must have slept for at least five hours, which was his normal ration.

Rona was still asleep—in the state of so-called rapid-eye-movement sleep—he could see the slight stirrings behind her closed lids, and the small movements of her mouth. He slid out of bed quietly, went into the bathroom, and splashed cold water in his eyes. The building was silent as a desert.

The hidden hologram room came into his mind. He dressed quickly and went to the elevator.

He did not ride down to the twenty-fifth floor, but to the twenty-seventh, where a cafeteria was located. He went into the deserted room and got a glass of orange and mango juice from a dispenser, listening carefully for any sounds on the nearby floors. Satisfied that there was no one about, he located the emergency stairway and walked down two floors to the twenty-fifth.

He went in to his suite of offices, using his keys, shutting the door behind him and moving without turning the lights on—there was sufficient light from the rapidly brightening sky, now, for him to find his way about. He went in to the inner office, then moved some books from the end of the eye-level bookshelf and inserted the magnetic key in the slot.

Again, a section of bookcase pivoted to give access to the dark room beyond. He moved in as it swung fully open, just as the lights automatically came on.

Now that he was able to look at the room alone, he examined it more critically. First, he checked that he could not accidentally lock himself in, then he closed the door. The wiring in the room looked as if none of it had been built in during the construction of the tower. It was neat, professional, yet somehow with a temporary look, like something an experienced electrician might knock up for an amateur stage production. Then he remembered—young Jon, his cousin, had been trained as an electrician and radio technologist, as part of the Vanmore Brothers' principle of keeping a wide spread of expertise within the family.

The hologram alcoves were numbered—one to nine. He looked at them again. Eight of them. He checked along the numbers painted above them—one, two, three, five. . . . That was it. Number four was missing from the series. Then he realised it—*this* was number four. He noticed a line of nine small green light globes on the side wall, each bearing a painted number—and number four was alight. Presumably, it was also burning in all nine of the hologram rooms—wherever the others were located.

He traced a wire from it back towards the door, then noticed the contact switch automatically operated by the door as it opened. There were two contact switches, actually, one controlling the indicator light, the other the main overhead lights in the room. He tested them by pushing the contacts with his finger. The one controlling the overhead lights could be bypassed by an ordinary wall switch, but the green light—together with the number four light in each of the other eight rooms like this one—would come on automatically as soon as someone entered the room.

He went back to the outer office and found an adhesive tape dispenser, then he took it back to the hologram room and taped the contacts of both switches. Now the lights in the room were under his control, through the wall switch. He could come and go in the hologram room without anyone knowing in the other terminals.

When someone officially told him about the hologram rooms, he would be able to co-operate—if he believed in what they were doing. But as long as they kept him in ignorance of their existence, he had no compunction about finding his own way into their inner circle.

He looked around at the hologram alcoves before he left. Screwdriver, pliers, a few switches, and some wire—that was all he needed. Smiling grimly, he closed the room and went out of the office, locking the outer door behind him. He walked up the stairway for two floors, then entered the elevator in which he had ridden down to the cafeteria level. It had not been used in his absence. He pressed "50" and rode back up to the penthouse.

When he went in to the bedroom Rona was still deeply asleep. He made two cups of coffee, then took them in to the bedroom and set them on the table alongside the bed. He sat on the bed and gently stroked her neck.

She grunted a little, and he held her coffee in front of her. She woke slowly, a few strands of the lilac-silver hair hanging across her forehead, and yawned with her eyes still shut.

"Impossible," she muttered, still half asleep. "There

couldn't be any such thing as a road made of sapphire. . . ."

Slowly, he put the cup of coffee down on the table. He leaned close to her.

"A road made of what?" he whispered.

"Sapphire," she murmured. "A sapphire ro—" She opened her eyes. They didn't focus at first, and then she saw Vanmore. Her eyes darkened as the pupils expanded enormously, and her mouth opened.

"What sapphire road, Rona?" He shook her by the shoulder. *"Where did you hear about a sapphire road?"*

"You're hurting me," she protested. "I don't know. Yes, I do. It was from you."

"Me?"

"You were muttering something in your sleep."

"I never talk in my sleep."

"You did last night. Something about Frank Ferris. Something about a sapphire road. Or did I dream the whole thing?"

He looked at her for a long time. He didn't speak.

"Could I have my coffee, please?"

He handed her the cup. She drank a few mouthfuls.

"It's possible," he said after a time. "I was very tired last night. Perhaps I did say something as I slept."

"Yes. I've never heard you talk in your sleep before. Anyway, it didn't make much sense, did it?"

"I don't suppose it ever does, if people talk in their sleep." He drank his own coffee, while she thoughtfully sipped hers, sitting up in the bed with her knees drawn up.

6

ABOUT SEVEN O'CLOCK Vanmore dialled breakfast, and after some protest Rona got up and joined him at the table near the window.

"I'll have to get something black to wear for the funeral," she said. "All I have in my luggage is holiday gear."

"All right. And while you're shopping, could you get a few items for me?"

"Such as?"

"Couple of screwdrivers, light and heavy, a pair of pliers, adjustable wrench about this big, a roll of insulation tape—"

"Hey, hey! Too early in the morning for me to remember all this. Can you write it down?"

"Sure." He took a small notebook and began writing.

"What's it all for, anyway?"

"Oh, I wanted to fix something in the office."

"Can't you get someone else to do things like that?"

"Not this time. I think the place may be bugged. The fewer people who know what I'm doing, the better." He tore the page from the notebook and handed it to her. "There."

"Right. Will comply. Listen, I'll get something like a black suit this morning. Can I call on you in the office and see what you think of it? At the same time—" She waved the piece of paper. "I can give you these."

"That's fine. Best if you could have them all wrapped up in a parcel so no one could see—"

At that moment, the bell sounded in the TV alcove.

He glanced at his watch. "Who's that, at this hour? I suppose it's Quade—not many people would know I'm here."

But it was a long-distance operator whose image appeared on the hologram. "Mr. Max Vanmore?"

"Yes."

"I have a call for you from Nu Karnatika."

"Go ahead."

"Putting you through."

The man who next appeared was about Vanmore's age, tall, lean, and dark, his black hair streaked lightly above the temples with grey. He held his head back with an air of relaxed, confident authority. His teeth and the whites of his eyes flashed in a brief smile of recognition.

"Ah, Max. Long time, eh? My sympathy in your loss."

"Rajendra! Thanks—but I hardly expected a call from you at this time. Must be the middle of the night, there."

"About 3 a.m. But that's not as altruistic as it sounds, you know. I often have overseas contacts that need to be handled in the middle of the night."

"How did you find me?"

"Through your company secretary. I've had a lot of dealings with Quade. We buy quite a lot of your titanium, you know. The highest-grade stuff."

"Is that so? I don't know much about where our output goes, as yet—I came into the scene only yesterday. Why do you need so much high-grade titanium?"

"Our space program. We're making a really big thrust in that area, you know." He gestured. "Prestige, you might say —but also it's paying off as far as our economy is concerned."

"I've read about some of Nu Karnatika's projects. Mining in the asteroid belt, for instance."

"Yes. Our first ship, the *Harappa,* has paid for itself several times over in the fourteen years it's been operating. But you remember our motto, don't you?"

"Something about growing, wasn't it?"

"To Live Equals To Grow. You recall? Our new ship is an extremely advanced piece of engineering. We've gone on from where America and Russia and Japan have stagnated. We're using the same drive principle as that used on the Alcenar ship."

"How did you get hold of that?"

"Simply by observing their ship on its last voyage here. Our boys were able to work out the drive, once the Alcenar people had demonstrated that it could be done."

"You mean you have a ship that could reach the Centauran system in eight years?"

"Even slightly less, if our calculations are correct."

"But that's something even the Northern Alliance hasn't tried to achieve."

"My dear chap, Northworld is suffering from political hardening of the arteries. They've had their so-called universal peace so long they've become afraid of making any effort towards change. Mark well, Max, any future steps forward are going to be made by we people on the fringe, as it were."

"You may be right, Raj."

"History tells me I'm right in this. Tells me with many examples."

"I don't doubt it. Look, I appreciate your calling. We'll have to meet some time."

"That could be quite soon. Today, in fact."

"Today?"

"I'm flying out to the funeral of your late father and uncle, as I'm one of the major consumers of your highest-grade product. I'm doing this partly out of respect for esteemed business associates, and partly to ensure smooth co-operation with the new management."

"But the funeral's at one o'clock today, local time. That's in less than six hours from now."

"No problem, Max. I have an extremely fast jet." He looked down, evidently at a watch. "I will see you, Max, no doubt, at the funeral."

"You know where it is?"

"Quade Gannon just showed me a marked local map, and I took a hard copy." Again, the sudden, flashing smile lit up his dark face. "I will see you."

Vanmore lifted his hand in a wave as the hologram faded.

"Who was that?" asked Rona as he returned to the table.

"Fellow called Rajendra Naryan. His father and grandfather built up one of the old Indian states into quite a dynamic country. Used to be the state of Mysore long ago, then they changed the name to Karnatika in the middle or late twentieth century. Since Rajendra's father's time they've called it

Nu Karnatika. It's independent, and scientifically quite advanced."

"Where'd you meet him?"

"Training institute in San Francisco, and on a special course in Kyoto."

"So you were both engaged in picking the brains of Northworld?"

"You could say that. Him more than me. He had unlimited money at his disposal—I didn't. America, Japan, Russia, United Europe—he studied all over the Northern Alliance. Probably paid off—he's a very bright guy."

"It paid off for you, too, darling—didn't it?"

Vanmore was silent for a time before he answered. "Yes, but I think we had different goals. I just wanted industrial success. He wanted to build an empire."

"I thought empires went out of fashion with steam trains."

"The name did. When you think of it as the expansion of power—that'll never go out of fashion as long as there are people."

About eight o'clock, Vanmore rode the elevator down to the twenty-fifth floor and let himself in to his office. He opened a large stack of Company mail. A few organisations had not heard of the change, on account of the news blackout.

He switched the phone through to the inner office, then went in and sat at his father's desk. Some of the papers on the desk had still to be dealt with, but most of them referred to matters of which he had, as yet, no detailed knowledge.

While seated at the desk, he noticed a small pedal projecting from the inner side of the righthand set of drawers, just near his right foot. Experimentally, he touched it with his foot, and a shallow drawer slid silently out, almost into his lap.

Clipped to the top of it was a compact laser pistol, placed so that the butt was free of the drawer. It was arranged so that a simultaneous tap of his foot and grab of his right hand could leave him holding the pistol in less than a second, below the level of the desk top. He checked the battery and found it showing full charge.

He weighed the weapon in his hand for a few seconds, then rested it across the back of his left wrist and sighted on a spot on the far wall. Thoughtfully, he put it back on its clips and pushed the drawer in until it clicked home.

It was something he hadn't expected. Still, his father had known more about the setup than he did. Not that it had helped him in the end.

He sat in the silent office, regretting that he had not seen more of his father during the past ten years. They had grown apart, and only now was he beginning to understand why. He'd have to be careful the same kind of distance didn't come about between him and Rona.

In the midst of his thoughts the phone rang. He opened the channel and found a square-faced, white-haired man looking out at him.

"Mr. Vanmore?" His voice was deep and clear.

"Yes."

"I'm sorry to take the liberty of intruding on you at this time, Mr. Vanmore, but my name is Evan Hart. Shop steward, Amalgamated Titanium Workers' Union."

"What can I do for you?"

"First, I'd like to express on behalf of my fellow workers our sympathy in regard to your loss." He sounded as if he were following a carefully rehearsed speech. "Secondly, I'd like to arrange a meeting with you as soon as possible—unofficially, if you prefer—to discuss your views on the future of the work situation in the Company."

"It's a bit early for that, Evan. I haven't had time yet to make any detailed assessment of the firm's potentialities. In fact, I haven't even attended a board meeting. Suppose you get in touch with me in a few days?"

Hart nodded. "Could I call you tomorrow?"

"Make it the day after. I should know more, then, and we could arrange a meeting."

"Good. The day after tomorrow, then."

About a quarter to nine, Elsa Perry came in. He heard her moving about in the reception office, and then she walked through and stood at his door.

"Oh, Mr. Vanmore. I didn't expect you to be here. Did someone ring through to you?"

"Fellow named Evan Hart."

"Oh, the shop steward? Bit of a cheek, wasn't it? At this time?"

"Well, I suppose his fellows are pushing him to find out

what's going to happen to them.''

"What'd you tell him?"

"Nothing—except a date for him to get in touch with me. Two days' time.''

"Sounds fair enough. How did he seem?"

"All right, as far as I could see. Businesslike."

"H'mm," said Elsa as she walked back to the outer office.

Vanmore spent the next hours studying flow charts showing the movement of ores and metal through the Company's widespread plants. Around ten o'clock Elsa rang through to him.

"Ms. Gale to see you, Mr. Vanmore."

"Send her through, Elsa."

Rona came in, wearing a close-fitting black suit, black hat, and shining black boots.

"Suitable?" she asked.

"Perfect."

She moved closer, and kissed him. "I like your secretary. No threat at all." She put a supermarket carry-bag on the end of his desk. "Those are the things you wanted."

"Good." He put the bag into the bottom drawer of his desk. "Thanks. D'you want to eat before we go out there?"

"No, I don't think so."

"Well, I'll pick you up about twelve fifteen."

The crematorium was located on the shore of the lake about twenty kilometres north-west of Amadeus City. It stood in a formal cypress grove between the flat empty vastnesses of lake and desert. It was an area that made it easy to maintain security, with just the one road running along the shore, and an airstrip nearby.

By prior arrangement, Vanmore and Gannon had flown out in their separate airkars, keeping within a few hundred metres of each other all the way. Rona occasionally looked apprehensively behind for signs of pursuit, but Gannon's machine was the only one in view.

The only airkars at the crematorium site apparently belonged to the chaplain and the funeral director and their associates, and the police were represented by a large, twin-rotor jet helicopter. Vanmore flew in a circle around the small group of buildings, dominated by a chapel with stained-glass windows and the strangely sinister crematorium itself, with its chimney. He could see no one lurking among the trees, but that meant little—an assassin would make certain he wasn't seen beforehand.

He landed, and Rona got out with him. Gannon landed nearby and came across to them, using two crutches instead of his usual one, so that his movements seemed somehow more measured and dignified. Bianca, alongside him, seemed even shorter and broader than usual in a hooded black, ground-length cape.

"We're well ahead of time," said Gannon.

"What's that?" asked Rona in a tense voice, pointing at the sky across the lake.

It was no ordinary airkar. As it drew rapidly closer Vanmore could see that it was a high-performance jet helicopter with double rotors. As it circled the area at low altitude, just as he had done, he saw that it was dull green and carried army markings. It landed, and out stepped Captain Kranzen in full military dress uniform.

He was taller than Vanmore had thought when he had seen him on the hologram. He strode across with a springing, animal energy that advertised immense muscular power, out of all proportion to the visible bulk of muscle he carried. He left at least two other uniformed men waiting in the helicopter. It was obvious from his greeting that he knew both Gannon and Bianca well, although he showed little warmth.

Vanmore introduced Rona to Kranzen, and he bowed formally, stiffly. She said later she had almost expected him to click his heels.

"It looks as though most of us are here," said Kranzen.

"Yes," said Gannon. "R.G.'s wife won't be here, nor will Jon's wife. My suggestion. I thought it safer if the relatives stayed away."

"Quite," said Kranzen. Suddenly he spun towards the north-west. He lifted a wrist radio to his lips and spoke in a quiet voice, and at once the twin rotors of the army helicopter began to revolve.

Now Vanmore saw what had caught Kranzen's attention—a fast-flying jet coming in at low-level, as if on a landing run. It passed over them, quite low, and they could see its gaudy crimson-and-saffron colour scheme.

"Rajendra Naryan," said Vanmore, as the machine swung

in a wide curve over the desert, its flaps and undercart coming down.

Gannon turned. "But he spoke to me only this morning—from Nu Karnatika."

"I know. He has a very fast plane."

The jet touched down on the strip. It was of Indian design, a model Vanmore didn't know. It parked a respectful distance from the army helicopter.

Rajendra emerged, spoke to someone still on board the jet, then walked across to the group. He seemed to know everyone there except Rona, whom Vanmore introduced.

The rotors of the army machine had stopped spinning.

Then the funeral director came out of the room adjoining the chapel and outlined the procedure of the ceremony to Vanmore, who was to lead the others in.

As they were walking slowly in the direction of the chapel, another airkar came in over the cypresses. It was grey. For a moment, Vanmore had the impulse to throw himself flat on the ground and pull Rona down alongside him. Then he saw this machine did not have one-way glass in its windows.

As it swept down on to the strip, he could see there was only one person aboard.

"Who's this?" asked Rajendra, who was a couple of paces behind him, and it was Kranzen who answered.

"Georgia Lester—she wasn't sure she could be here."

Vanmore remembered seeing the name Lester printed somewhere within the past twenty-four hours. Then it came to him. Dr. G. Lester, Department of Biological Research. The name board in front of the bald woman with the black-rimmed glasses on the Stability Council.

She came into the chapel after the others had entered, tall, slim, in a hooded steel-grey cape. All that he could see of her was her pale, long oval face and her glasses, framed by her hood.

Vanmore and Rona took their places in the front righthand pew, while the others grouped themselves in the seats somewhere in the middle of the chapel, as if none wished to be too prominent. The three coffins stood on trestles in a row, each surmounted by floral tributes.

The chaplain began his address, but somehow Vanmore did not concentrate on it after the first few sentences. It seemed to him that the man had not really known his father, nor his uncle and cousin, and was simply putting together suitable phrases that he had no doubt used many, many times.

While the voice droned on, he replayed in his mind memories of his father. When he had been a boy, and his father's hair had been dark and his body lean and taut, there had been an intense friendship between them that had transcended any generation gulf.

Then, by slow degrees, Vanmore Titanium had come between them, a small operation that had grown into a colossus beyond the most optimistic dreams of its creators.

It had grown in many directions they had never anticipated, absorbing more and more of Kelvin Vanmore's life. It was only now that Max was beginning to understand the complexity and the tensions that had shaped his father's lifestyle.

At last the talking ceased, and the funeral director, who had been standing near one wall, unobtrusively pressed a button. The coffin of Kelvin Johannes Vanmore sank slowly out of sight with a terrible finality that shook Max with a violent tremor until Rona's hand squeezed his, bringing him back to the present moment.

The scene was replayed for his uncle, and again for his cousin, but the sense of grief and loss had dulled him so that he seemed to see little of his surroundings.

When the ceremony closed, they all went out into the hot, still air. The wreaths which had been placed on the coffins had been rearranged on frames on the shaded side of the building, and Vanmore stood looking at them. Bees were already threading their way from flower to flower, some of them moving from one to another of the yellow flowers, others preferring the white.

"Life goes on," said a voice beside him. It was Rajendra Naryan.

Vanmore turned to him. "I should have seen more of him, Raj."

"I know. It was the same with my parents. Did you wish to be alone for a time, Max? Or would you prefer to talk?"

"Perhaps it's better to talk."

"I'd like to see you later today, Max. I've come across some very interesting information."

"Oh?"

"Yes. My boys managed to pick up a vortex beam broadcast from this Alcenar ship. I believe you knew Ferris, the Australian who's returning on it? Am I right in that?"

"I knew him." Vanmore looked back at the wreaths.

"Good. I won't worry you with the content of the broadcast at a moment like this, but I needed to see you alone for a short time. May I call on you tonight?"

"I'd like that, Raj." Making an effort, Vanmore turned away from his absorbed concentration on the bees exploring the flowers, and looked at Rajendra's dark eyes. "Say about eight? I'm in the penthouse on top of the Titanium Tower. Floor 50."

"I'll be there," said Rajendra quietly. They both looked back towards the others, who were standing near the exit from the chapel, under the shade of the line of jacarandas that formed a contrast to the dark cypresses. The three women had formed a little group of their own, and Gannon was standing talking with Kranzen and the chaplain.

Seeing that Vanmore was no longer in conversation with Rajendra, Gannon excused himself from the others and went across to him.

"Pardon me a moment, Max, but Captain Kranzen has just brought it to my attention that we have a quorum here for a Board meeting. While he and Dr. Lester both happen to be in Amadeus—"

"Is she on the Board?"

"I thought I told you that."

"You didn't. Well, that makes Kranzen, Dr. Lester, you, me—"

"And they can get hold of Marsh."

"That's five—of whom two, we two, are new arrivals on the Board. That means effectively a meeting of three people. Does that sound like quorum to you?"

"Apparently it does to them."

"When do they want to hold the meeting?"

"They suggested this afternoon."

Vanmore drew his lips back from his teeth in a grimace of irritation. "If we don't go along, they'll probably hold their meeting anyway. Let's find out what they think is so urgent." He turned momentarily to Rajendra Naryan. "I'll see you later, Raj."

With Gannon beside him, he walked over to where Kranzen was standing. The chaplain had now left him, and was talking to the three women.

"You'd like a meeting this afternoon?" queried Vanmore.

"If you feel up to it—it'd be convenient for us. Dr. Lester has come up here from Adelaide, and I've come a fair distance."

Vanmore nodded. "Say four o'clock? In the Board Room?"

Kranzen nodded. He walked over towards the little group formed by the chaplain and the three women. The chaplain had his back to Kranzen, but Dr. Lester was facing him, apparently listening, like the others, to what the chaplain was saying. Kranzen pointed to his wrist watch and held up four fingers, and Georgia Lester gave a barely perceptible nod, whereupon Kranzen looked back at Vanmore and Gannon, and nodded.

7

Just before Vanmore was ready to leave the penthouse for the Board meeting, Rona went up to him and put her arms around him.

"Be careful, darling. I don't trust any of those people."

He smiled. "You too, now? Join the club, honey." He kissed her, gave her a quick hug, then stepped back. "I'll stall as much as possible—until I have more time to get a working knowledge of the setup."

On the way down in the elevator, he wondered whether he had sounded more confident than he felt. To Rona, probably, no. She knew him very well by now.

When he arrived in the board room, ten minutes early, Gannon was already there, with another man who was carrying a device that looked like a metal detector. He was sweeping the walls systematically in arcs, with a flat, circular head of the instrument just clear of the panelling. Once, it emitted a sharp beep, and the operator scanned the same area again.

"What's that?" asked Gannon, who was standing on the far side of the room.

"Only part of your normal wiring. See? Runs right up."

Gannon grunted. As Vanmore walked around to him he gave an apologetic gesture. "Just checking for audio pickups. I know, not many people have access to this room, but it pays to be sure."

"Of course. Carry on."

The man with the detector was thorough. At last, he switched it off and turned to Gannon. ''The place is clean, Boss. Unless someone uses a parabolic mike from a distance.''

''We're safe from that, I think. The rest of the offices on this floor are vacant at the moment, and no one can get to the rooms above and below.''

''Right. I'll get along.''

''Thanks. I'll mail you your cheque.''

When he had gone, Vanmore looked at Gannon in some surprise. ''You get your checking done by someone outside the Company?''

''Just a double check. It's already been covered by a Company man.''

Vanmore walked round the long, oval table. ''Who usually chaired these meetings?''

''K.J.—when they were held here.''

''You always take the minutes? Or whatever?''

''I record them, yes. Later, I make a summary of the points raised, from the tapes.''

''Could I see a summary of the previous meeting?''

''I don't have it here—this was an informal meeting they arranged, remember.''

''Yes. Can you get it?''

''I haven't run the last set of tapes through, yet. With the explosion, and one thing and another. . . .''

At this point, Kranzen arrived, followed shortly by Dr. Lester and then Ashton Marsh. Vanmore had taken up a position at the head of the table, but when they were all seated he said, ''Normally, I'd be taking the chair, but in view of the fact that I've just come on to the scene, and haven't had time to build up a full mental picture of the Company's ramifications, I'd like to call for nominations for a chairman for this meeting.''

''I nominate Captain Kranzen,'' said Marsh.

''Seconded,'' said Dr. Lester.

''All in favour? Right.'' Vanmore stood up, but Kranzen, who was sitting halfway down the table on the right, waved his hand.

''No need for that much formality, Max. I'll stay here.'' He looked at Marsh and Dr. Lester. ''For the benefit of our two newcomers, especially for Max—since Quade has been present to record our previous meetings—I'll run over our history.''

He turned to face Max directly.

"You're probably wondering why some of the people who were most active on the National Stability Council have reappeared on the Board of Vanmore Titanium."

"I had," admitted Vanmore.

Kranzen seemed to speak as if he were on an electioneering platform all the time. "Stability is our overall goal. Stability for the country, and stability for the Company. There's no conflict there. What's good and stabilising for Vanmore Titanium is good and stabilising for Australia. Agreed?"

"Sounds logical," said Vanmore with tempered enthusiasm. He had the feeling he'd heard something like this argument before, but he wasn't sure where the reasoning led.

"Stability," went on Kranzen, "is part of a world-wide trend. We've eliminated war over much of the Earth—totally, in the case of the Northern Alliance—for four or five generations. But the Universal Peace has another side to its coin—stagnation."

He remained silent for a few seconds to let Vanmore consider the point, while Marsh and Dr. Lester both nodded as if he had stated an axiomatic truth.

"In Northworld," went on Kranzen, "both the Universal Peace and the stagnation appear to be permanent. The next century there is likely to be very like the last one, as was the case for hundreds of years in ancient Egypt or old China. Now, in the case of past empires or cultures with long periods of peace and stability, the end came sooner or later in disintegration—either that particular civilisation was overwhelmed by another, or it lapsed into barbarism."

Vanmore nodded without comment.

"Now," said Kranzen, "much as we prize peace and stability, none of us wants to see the whole of our civilisation run gradually downhill to a general collapse. When that happened in past ages, whenever one civilisation collapsed, another, somewhere else, was on the way up. Today, however, we have a world in which the various cultures are at about the same level.

"Clearly, though, the last quarter-century has shown us that it would have been possible for us to have gone on to greater heights. The Alpha Centauri colony has done that. It has produced an interstellar drive that we are unable to match. And if young Ferris was speaking the truth about an economy that can afford to pave its roads with sapphire—we may have lost the race for the Galaxy."

The man was obviously a fanatic, thought Vanmore. His own fragmentary knowledge of history was sufficient to give him several examples of the immense force some fanatics had exerted to change the world about them.

"We should know more about that in ten days' time," said Dr. Lester in a cool voice. "When Rik Dane has his face-to-face interview with Ferris. In the meantime, though, we have plenty of evidence that the Alcenar people have outstripped us in my particular field—biological research."

"In what way?" asked Kranzen.

"I was talking today with Bianca Baru. Her physique interested me—her adaptation to nearly twice our force of gravity. But more than that, I was impressed by her intelligence, her vast range of general knowledge, and—well, what I could only describe as wisdom. Also, her courage in coming to live for sixteen years in a civilisation so different from her own. If we'd started generations ago, we *might* perhaps have been able to evolve a subspecies as adaptable as that—but the point is that we never tried. These people did.'"

"I'm against that type of experimentation," said Ashton Marsh. "We don't know exactly what we're doing. We may evolve some type of being who replaces us."

"I agree," said Kranzen. "Earth is the original home of man. It should remain the centre."

"I'm not sure of that," said Dr. Lester. She tossed the hood back from her head, and her ivory-tinted scalp gleamed like polished marble. The bald head contrasted incongruously with the vivid scarlet mouth and the bluish eye shadow. "The greatest advances don't necessarily come from the centre of a civilisation."

"Give me an example," said Kranzen, unconvinced.

"All right. Men like Shakespeare, Newton, Copernicus produced the greatest flights of Western European thought in the north of the continent, at a time when the centre of Western civilisation was still in the city-states of northern Italy. And again, the highest achievements of Scandinavian political and literary development didn't come in Sweden, Denmark, or Norway, but in Iceland, away out on the fringe."

There was silence for a while, and Kranzen looked slightly irritated, a flush across his cheeks and forehead. It looked as if he didn't know whether Dr. Lester was stating facts or not, and didn't have time to check up without losing his "flow."

He seemed to come to a decision, after looking intently at Vanmore and at Gannon in turn.

"I'm going to trust you with highly sensitive information," he said. "I mentioned before that the Alpha Centauri colony had produced an interstellar drive that we had not been able to match. That was true at the time. It is not true today."

"You mean you've built a similar ship?" asked Gannon.

Kranzen nodded. "We didn't steal their drive from them, but once we knew it was a possibility, our backroom brigades went ahead and duplicated the idea within ten years."

"So you've had an interstellar drive for six years?" queried Vanmore.

"The drive, yes. The ship—that's only recently completed."

"Could it compete in speed with the Alcenar ship?"

"We believe it can. Probably better it by a small margin."

Vanmore thought of what Rajendra Naryan had told him. He'd have to tread carefully, here. "Captain Kranzen, the whole world knew the Alcenar ship came here sixteen years ago. They all knew about its drive at the same time. Could anyone else have produced a ship comparable with yours?"

Kranzen was emphatic. "No. I keep up with American and Japanese developments, and they seem to have lost the momentum they once had. The other parts of the Northern Alliance—United Europe, Russia, China—have been stagnant for generations. To them, the Universal Peace is more of a god than it is to the Americans, because they have more history of war on their own soil than either the Americans or Japanese."

"Anyone else a possibility?" persisted Vanmore.

"Who? Brazil? Argentina? The Indian states? Africa? I can't see it."

Vanmore nodded, and said nothing.

"What do you intend doing with the ship?" asked Gannon.

"We wait until the *Alphard* comes here in ten days—see what else we can learn from it. Then, around the time of its departure, *we* leave. We believe we can get to the Alpha Centauri system before they do."

"Are you certain of that?" asked Vanmore. "If it comes to a race like this, it's better not to compete than to come second."

"We'll be there first!" thundered Kranzen, stepping up the

volume of his voice at least a hundred per cent. His eyes looked very light and hard, the pupils contracted to points that were hardly visible from across the table. The long silence that followed was broken by Dr. Lester.

"Have you settled on a name for your ship?" she asked.

Kranzen turned to her. "The *Endeavour II*—after Captain Cook's ship." He looked around the table with a hard, brilliant smile. "The voyage will be primarily a matter of 'showing the flag'—showing Alcenar and other human settlements in the Centaurus system that Northworld is not the only force remaining on Earth—in fact, not even the most advanced one. It's insurance for the future. Trading contracts will be cemented between Australia and Alcenar, not between Alcenar and the Northern Alliance."

"Have you any other goals in going there?" asked Vanmore.

As Kranzen hesitated, Georgia Lester cut in. "It should be an excellent chance for the scientific personnel on the ship to gain new biological knowledge. I really feel that the Centauran people represent the next step upward in human evolution."

"That may be putting it too strongly," said Marsh, who had been sitting with his eyes closed during Kranzen's harangue as if he had heard it all before. "As an ecologist, I see it differently. Man is part of the total environment, and too sudden a change in the species may have disastrous overall effects."

Dr. Lester seemed to whiten with controlled anger. "That's the kind of attitude that explains why we've lost the lead to the Centaurans in biological research."

"I wouldn't accept that," snapped Kranzen. "They have a few highly developed techniques, that's all. And techniques are easily learnt."

In the pause that followed, Vanmore glanced around the table. "One point," he said. "What's the link between National Stability and the production and sale of titanium—which after all, is our business?"

The others seemed astounded for a moment at the introduction of so basic an idea. It was Ashton Marsh who answered.

"This happens on the boards of most of our key industries. It's a way of making democracy work—and keeping it working indefinitely into the future."

"I always thought the definition of democracy was government by the people—one vote, one person."

"*We* are the people," said Marsh.

"I know. But a very small percentage of the population."

Kranzen gave a short laugh. "Government is *always* by a small percentage, whatever your system. Even in a so-called free vote, people tend to group themselves into blocs to save the trouble of individual thought. Then, in each bloc or group, a small, vocal faction, or even an individual, tells them how to vote. Even within family groups, this happens."

Vanmore nodded without speaking. Then the curiously calm, cool voice of Dr. Lester broke the silence.

"It's the way it is, Max. The way it's been since people lived in caves. It's probably the way it'll be as they reach out across the stars."

"Quite," agreed Marsh, looking at Vanmore. "All we're doing is trying to assure that the more able people make the decisions."

Vanmore nodded. *Able by whose definition?* he thought, but he didn't say it. Perhaps he had said too much already. After the pause had prolonged for a few seconds, he nodded again as if deep in thought. "I see," he said. "There's logic in that."

"There is, when you think it through," said Marsh.

"Well," said Kranzen, "that wraps it up for now. As to the next meeting—" He looked around the table.

"Could I make a suggestion there?" broke in Vanmore.

"Yes?"

"I don't know your usual interval between meetings, but I'd like to move that we make it coincide with the satellite telecast of Rik Dane's interview with the people on the *Alphard*. That's ten days off, and it'll give me time to get a better grasp of the workings of this firm."

"I'll second that," said Dr. Lester.

Kranzen looked at the others. "Right, everyone? Then that's settled. We'll watch the telecast from the Roundhouse, get the Council to defer any voting until they've thought over the implications—say for twenty-four hours—and have our own meeting immediately afterwards—perhaps here, if you're agreeable, Max."

"Fine," agreed Vanmore.

"Then that's it for now," said Kranzen. When they stood up, he whispered something to Marsh, who nodded. As Marsh was passing Georgia Lester, Vanmore saw the movement of his lips and although he heard nothing he had the impression the lips had formed the words "twelve o'clock tonight."

Vanmore walked out with the others as far as the elevator. On the way, Kranzen said to Dr. Lester, "Heading straight back to the Institute, Georgia?"

"Yes. I'll fly on automatic most of the way and catch up on a bit of sleep."

"We'll see you in ten days, then, Captain Kranzen—Dr. Lester," said Vanmore, and they gave him a formal acknowledgement without much warmth.

"I'll be around, of course," said Ashton Marsh, and the three of them entered the elevator and descended, leaving Vanmore and Gannon.

"How did you think they took my point about the definition of democracy?"

"Hard to tell. I don't think they liked it much. Still, I wouldn't worry about it." Gannon glanced at his watch. "Nothing else we need to fix today, is there?"

"No. See you tomorrow, Quade."

As the elevator slid down the shaft, Vanmore went into his office suite. Elsa Perry was still in the reception office.

"I think we'll make it an early night, Elsa," he said. "It's ten to five, anyway."

"I suppose it's been a heavy day for you, Mr. Vanmore. By the way, I wanted to come out to the funeral, but Mr. Gannon thought it better not to have too many people."

"There were very few there, Elsa. Count them on your fingers. I think it was a sound idea to keep the number down, after what's happened." He put his hand to her shoulder, and she gave a slight start as if unused to physical contact of any kind. "I'll see you in the morning, Elsa. I'll lock the office as I go out."

After the sound of the elevator had faded down the long shaft, a profound silence settled over the twenty-fifth floor. The tower, built in the boom period when Amadeus City was in vigorous growth, had always been half empty. It had been built fifty storeys high for prestige, and some of the offices and even whole floors had been rented out to other organisations—a couple of real estate firms, a finance company, an advertising firm, an office equipment distributor, and similar establishments—but still, after forty years, half of it was vacant.

When Amadeus City had been built, it had been projected that it would have a million people by now. In reality, in spite of its impressive clump of skyscrapers, its population still fell short of the hundred thousand. Most of the outside firms who were tenants in this building had taken up the lower floors, and a few high up in the tower, leaving the middle twenty-odd floors deserted, except for the twenty-fourth, twenty-fifth, and twenty-sixth, which Vanmore Titanium had kept for its own use, and the twenty-seventh, where the cafeteria had been located, together with two or three small outside offices whose tenants had been attracted by proximity to an eating place.

Vanmore heard some sounds from the cafeteria floor, then the hum of elevators, and finally—a little after five o'clock—an abysmal silence. His footsteps echoed along the empty corridor as he walked to the elevator shafts and then back to his office.

Locking the outer door, he went straight through to the inner office and unlocked the hologram room. He stood looking into its cavernous darkness for a few moments, for the automatic light switch was still disconnected. He found the torch he had placed just inside the door, then switched it on and threw its beam around the empty room, with its hooded hologram alcoves.

Twelve o'clock tonight. If his lip reading had been correct, that was what Marsh had said to Dr. Lester. That was the time the three of them, including Kranzen, intended to make contact.

By then, Georgia Lester would be somewhere down in Adelaide, more than a thousand kilometres away. Marsh would be somewhere here in Amadeus City, and Kranzen would be in some army base which might be almost anywhere in Australia. If they made contact tonight, clearly it would be through this type of hologram installation.

Switching on the overhead lights manually, he closed the door, then set out the tools he had asked Rona to bring him from the hardware department of the supermarket. First, the floodlights that would automatically light up anyone in front of the TV camera. He found the wires that fed power to them, cut them, and put his own switch in the circuit, so that *he* could decide when they functioned and when they did not. Then he did the same thing with the camera. Then he went back to the camera which could record, through a wide-angle lens, everything on the eight hologram alcoves. He left its wiring intact, but took out the small red light on top of the camera which showed when it was operating. He taped the central contact of the globe and then screwed it part-way back into its socket, so that it looked intact but did not function.

Now, when anyone used the hologram rooms, this one would appear empty and in darkness, should they be able to look through its cameras. And anyone who sat here, in the dark, could watch the others conversing from alcove to alcove.

But wait! Even with the lights out, the small amount of light thrown out by the holograms themselves would show that he was there. His figure would be lit badly, perhaps be unrecognisable, but would still be visible as an intruder.

He walked around behind the recording camera, which stood high up on a black, pyramid-like base made of timber covered with black-painted hardboard. He removed the sheet of hardboard from the back of the base, and found he could sit in the space below the camera. From the front, the base would appear as before. He pried a piece of beading loose at the top of the sheet in front of the base, and pared the edge of the hardboard down so that when the beading was replaced there was a small, horizontal slit left below it. Through this, he could see all the hologram alcoves without there being any possibility that the people at the other terminals could see him.

Something in him revolted at this type of eavesdropping, but he felt that he simply hadn't time to play the game straight. He smiled to himself as he worked. How many other people in the history of the world had thought that way? Politicians, bank robbers, anyone in a hurry who could mentally justify cutting corners.

Satisfied at last with his preparations, he locked the hologram room, locked his office, and rode the elevator to floor 50.

When he went into the penthouse, Rona kissed him a little absentmindedly.

"What's wrong?" he asked.

"Maybe nothing. Someone just tried to ring you up about a quarter of an hour ago."

"Who?"

"That's just what's bothering me. He didn't leave any name, and I didn't see who it was."

"You mean he had the visual turned off?"

"No. That was clear enough, but all I could see was a wall—at an odd angle. As if someone were using an ordinary hologram booth, but holding a mirror in front of one of the cameras, and blocking the others altogether. What I could see of the image was monochromatic—all green."

Vanmore thought for a while. "And he just asked for me?"

"Deep, husky voice. Said 'Is Max Vanmore there?'—and when I said no, just rang off."

"Odd. Because not many people know we're here." He walked to the window, and looked out. The sun was low in the reddening western sky. "Want to eat out?"

"I'd rather not, Max. I can fix something here."

"Good. Listen, I'm slipping down to the office for a while. Be right back."

He went down to the twenty-fifth floor, and in to his inner office. He sat in his father's chair for a while, looking down at the unobtrusive pedal projecting from the right bank of drawers. At last, he put his foot on it, and when the silent drawer slid open he took the laser pistol from its clips, checked the safety catch, and thrust it into his belt. It was small, and his jacket hid it.

Then he went back up to the penthouse.

8

JUST ON EIGHT o'clock, the bright landing lights of an airkar flashed across the windows, and they heard the machine landing on the flange at the back of the tower.

"Should be Rajendra," said Vanmore, but before he went to the door he felt the compact little laser pistol in his belt.

"Be careful!" urged Rona.

Vanmore looked out through the window. "It's all right," he said, and opened the sliding door as Rajendra Naryan strode out of the breezeway leading from the landing flange to the roof garden.

"Excellent view you have from up here, Max."

"Yes. A bit warm, though, for my liking. Come inside. Here's Rona."

Rajendra pressed his hands together in the traditional Hindu namaste.

"Max has told me quite a lot about you," Rona said. "I believe you knew each other in America and Japan?"

"Yes. We had some very interesting times together—eh, Max? We did courses where we were the only two who didn't come from some part of the Northern Alliance. We stuck together as a threatened minority."

"Max tells me you're the—President, is it?—of Nu Karnatika."

"Actually, some of my people have suggested resurrecting the old title of Maharajah."

Vanmore, who was returning with drinks, looked up in surprise. "What's this maharajah bit? I thought the last maharajah went out of circulation in the Gandhian period."

"Ah, we've travelled in a circle since then. Have you ever heard of Stottle's theory of political cycles?"

"Stottle's . . . ?"

"I heard it only once, on an old tape. I've never been able to get the tape again, but it made a profound impression on me. It set out the theory that there is no ideal form of government, but different types of government follow each other in a roughly predictable cycle."

"How d'you mean?" asked Vanmore.

"Well, you can start looking at the cycle anywhere you wish. Say we begin with a period when there's been a breakdown. Anarchy. Utter chaos! Now at this point opportunists —warlords, if you wish—tend to take control, and then you have the rise of princes and similar leaders."

"What happens then?"

"You have the emergence of a supreme ruler—let's say a king, rajah, sultan, or whatever. The names will vary from culture to culture, but the principle is the same. The next stage is a sacred ruler who can do no wrong in the eyes of his subordinates—or at least, that's the image he projects."

Vanmore nodded. "There have been plenty of those scattered through history."

"Quite so. Now, the next stage is government by an aristocracy—that's about where we are in Nu Karnatika now. If Stottle's theory is right, this should develop into an oligarchy—government by a few top men. That, if I may say so, seems to be where *you* stand right now."

"Could be. Go on."

Rona began rubbing the back of Vanmore's neck. "This all sounds very depressing, doesn't it?"

Rajendra flashed her a smile. "Wait until you hear the rest of it. The next stage is a widening of the power base—democracy. Government by the people. Sounds ideal, eh? Trouble is, the power base goes on widening out, so that power is scattered between more and more people: trade association members, union organisers, consumer groups, religious pressure groups—you name it, until eventually the situation becomes chaotic. You get an ultimate breakdown."

"Not a happy picture, Raj," said Vanmore. "What happens then?"

"Next, you again get opportunists picking up the fragments —charismatic leaders, minor warlords bringing some kind of hard order—and the whole cycle goes round again. And again. Perhaps forever."

"Sounds a real barrel of fun," murmured Rona.

Vanmore stood up and walked slowly across to the window, staring down at the lights along the Esplanade for a while before turning around. "Who was this fellow Stottle?"

Rajendra shook his head. "I don't know. I heard the tape only once. It was based on material collected a long time ago by something called the Hudson Institute, in New York. Far as I know, the man's name was Harold Stottle—I think they called him Harry. He was probably an American who worked with the Hudson Institute."

Vanmore paced back across the room, looking down at the lime and red carpet. "You know, I've heard something like this before. But I think the fellow was called Aristotle. A large-scale Greek shipping magnate, back in the twentieth century."

Rajendra shrugged. "Could be. Doesn't matter much who he was—it's the theory we're looking at."

"Sure. You know, I think we might have broken out of the cycle."

"How?"

"With the National Stability Council. I know, you'd call it an oligarchy. But it's added something new. It keeps very good control over the media. It vets any new idea *before* it releases it for the national networks."

"So what's new? Most countries have censorship."

"Yes, but this is done so smoothly the population as a whole don't realise their news is being pre-digested."

"How did *you* find out what's happening?"

"I've just recently been accepted on the Council. Now I see how it operates, I can recall plenty of incidents in the past that must have been "handled" by the Council. Attempted charismatic leadership, new philosophies, presented in such a disjointed order that all the magic was taken out of them."

"But do you think that technique will work forever?"

"Frankly, no. Like another coffee?"

"I'll fix them," said Rona, and went over to the auto-kitchen.

"Anyway," said Vanmore, "you mentioned you'd picked up a telecast."

"We did, indeed. A vortex beam from the Alpha Centauri ship to the transfer station."

"But I thought the signal travelled along the one tight beam?"

"It does. Hah! You're like the so-called experts of North-world, Max. You can't grasp the fact that technology marches on, even if your own country is marking time. That's what Stability and Universal Peace do to you."

"But how did you do it?"

"My boys have had a lot of experience in space the last cou-ple of decades. It was easy enough for them. A probe located in space on an exact line between the approaching Alpha Cen-tauri ship and the transfer station."

"But how did you keep it there?"

"Lasers, and positioning jets. It picked up signals from the vortex beam, and transmitted them to another probe outside the beam. This one redirected the signals to us."

"And the people on the transfer station never detected it?"

"They were so secure, in their view, it never occurred to them to look for any leak."

"So much for the security of the vortex beam." Involun-tarily, Vanmore chuckled. "Anyway, what did you pick up?"

"Hah!" Rajendra took a small video cassette from his pocket. "Have you a set here where we could run this through?"

"Sure."

A minute later, the three of them were watching once again Rik Dane's long-range interview with Frank Ferris. Rajendra stood back, and Rona sat in a chair immediately in front of the hologram. Vanmore stood a little to one side, where a sidelong glance could show him Rona's reflection in a wall mirror.

Watching the picture for the second time, he concentrated on Ferris' expressions as he spoke. There was no doubt he be-lieved everything he was saying. His eyes shone with an almost religious fervour as he tried to make certain Dane believed what he said.

". . . technology they have developed on Alcenar is fantastic! They have matter converters which can turn one element into another. . . . I saw a whole road paved with sapphire—real sapphire! I broke some of it off, and I have it with me. . . ."

At the mention of the sapphire road, Vanmore glanced covertly at the reflection of Rona. She did not express immediate surprise, but glanced sidelong at Vanmore, who was able to swing his gaze back from the reflection to the hologram as she began to turn her head.

He was sure, then, that he had *not* talked in his sleep of the sapphire road. Then where had Rona really heard of it? Obviously, when she had been out with Bianca. But how? Where?

"What do you think?" asked Rajendra. "You knew the fellow. Is he telling the truth? Or is it all fantasy?"

"He believes he's telling the truth, I'm positive."

"I'd agree with that," added Rona. "I knew him quite well —and he hasn't had time to change much. He's been in cold storage almost all the time since we knew each other."

Rajendra said nothing for a few seconds, his attention switching between Vanmore and Rona. "Do you know what I propose to do, Max?" He seemed to hesitate for a moment, then went on. "You may wish to join me in this project—I don't want you to make up your mind straight away, but the offer stands.

"I plan to fly our new ship, the *Mohenjo Daro,* to Alcenar."

"You? Yourself?"

"With a trained crew—who have had more, and wider, practical experience in space during the past ten years than any other team in the Solar system. I can leave my associates to run the State until I return—most of them are members of my family, in any case."

"But it'll mean sixteen years of your career, Raj!"

"Somewhat, less—perhaps no more than fifteen years. But I think the time and the temporal dislocation will be well compensated for by the techniques I learn on Alcenar."

"Perhaps."

"Think this over, Max. Remember what we learned from our studies in Northworld? We've made better use of our knowledge than the local 'brains,' because we had superior motivation. We're not crushed by a system made stagnant by its Universal Peace.''

Vanmore looked at Rona. "It's a tempting offer, Raj, but I couldn't leave Rona for fifteen years."

"I'd say not!" flared Rona. "I wouldn't mind waiting a year or two, darling, but fifteen years? Do you think I'd be here when you came back?"

"Sorry, Raj," said Vanmore. "That's a good enough reason in itself."

"Another thing," said Rona. "You'd still be only thirty-six, while I—hell, I'd be nearly fifty!"

"Unless we took you with us," suggested Rajendra.

"What?" Rona turned to face him, her eyes wide. "You're not serious, are you? You can't be!"

"Why not? I know Max. I know his ability to absorb ideas. Of all the people I know, he's the only one I rank with myself in that faculty. Of all people, I'd choose Max to accompany me on a voyage like this one." He smiled. "And I wouldn't want to separate him from his lady."

Vanmore looked at Rona. "It's a new thought, isn't it? But impossible, I'm afraid. There's the Company, for one thing. And we don't really know much about Alcenar, do we?"

She smiled. "Perhaps when we hear this next telecast of Frank's—the face-to-face one. . . ." She broke off and looked back to Rajendra. "I think it's the most exciting offer anyone's ever made to me, Raj. If Max should change his mind. . . ."

Rajendra shrugged. "Nothing is certain, yet. But should events indicate that it's advisable to make the voyage, I think we might learn enough to make the proposition pay. Don't you agree, Max?"

"I agree that it's a possibility. But let's wait."

"Of course." Rajendra looked at his watch, then stood up. "I must get back to my hotel. My people might be trying to contact me."

"I'll keep in touch, Raj," said Vanmore.

Rajendra again pressed his hands together with a slight bow.

When he had gone, Rona seemed more excited than Vanmore had seen her for a long time. "Do you think it might really be possible?" she asked him.

"Possible, yes."

"Another world. Different customs. I might even make *my*

trip pay—bring back different fashions." She looked around the room. "Different ideas of interior decoration—things like that."

She was still trying out a succession of ideas when she went to bed.

About eleven thirty, after Rona had gone to sleep, Vanmore took the elevator down to the twenty-fifth floor. He removed the light-tube in it so that no one would notice the movement of the lift down the transparent shaft on the outside wall of the building. Stepping out, he held the door for a moment and reached in to press the button for floor 50. Then he let the door shut, and stood in almost total darkness in the deserted corridor while the lift slid its way upward.

He went into his office, through the outer room without switching on the lights, and into the inner office, before even risking the use of his small torch. He opened the hologram room, went in, and closed the door behind him, shone the beam of his torch around, then took up his place sitting behind the panel supporting the TV camera, his eyes level with the narrow slit.

He put the torch out, and waited.

And waited.

His watch, with its luminous dial, seemed to move with appalling slowness. On two occasions, he actually held it to his ear to hear if it was still functioning.

Approaching midnight, he found himself wondering whether his hunch had been farfetched. Then, suddenly, one of the green globes lit up. Number 2. Almost simultaneously, Kranzen's image appeared in one of the hologram alcoves. A few seconds later Szabo appeared in number 5, then Marsh in 3, and finally Dr. Lester in 8.

"Good," said Kranzen. "We're all here."

A murmur of assent came from the other three. Vanmore started his sound-recorder running.

"Right," said Kranzen. "I called you together because I want to put you in the picture in regard to the *Endeavour II*. This is emphatically not for general release, but we have actually made a test run with the new drive, and we're all delighted with its performance. I'm holding the crew on a twenty-four-hour alert, so we could take off at a day's notice any time events dictate quick action."

"What kind of action?" asked Szabo.

"We could begin the journey to the Alpha Centauri system the day after tomorrow, if necessary."

"That's a bit sudden, isn't it?" asked Dr. Lester, "in view of the fact that the voyage will take something like eight years?"

"Less," said Kranzen, "but we might be engaged in a race against the *Alphard*. A day or two might make a vital difference to the result."

"You spoke before of 'showing the flag,'" said Marsh. "If that meant what I think it did, how are you going to back it up?"

"The *Endeavour II* has teeth, just as her namesake did. The old *Endeavour* carried cannon, some swivel cannon, some truck cannon. We carry laser armaments, and twenty-four bombs."

"What type of bombs?" Georgia Lester's voice sounded higher-pitched than before.

"A new development," said Kranzen. "Not large, but they have unbelievable power. I estimate two of them, at the most, would suffice to force the capitulation of a planet, should it be resistant to the idea of Earth domination."

"How are they delivered?" asked Szabo.

"They can be fired from silos built into the ship, and directed by laser to the target. The silo area is kept out of bounds to most of the crew, since the detonating mechanisms of the bombs are vulnerable. In fact, most of the crew don't know the bombs exist."

"I don't like this," said Georgia Lester. "I think it's one of those decisions that's so important that it should be put before the entire Council."

"What? You might as well leave the decision to a nation-wide referendum." Kranzen packed savage scorn into his words. "And you know what the result of that would be: When in doubt, vote *no*."

There was a general pause; then Szabo said, "You're right about that, anyway."

"You'll be away nearly sixteen years," said Marsh. "That's a long time out of the scene."

"I'll be leaving it to you to maintain stability until I get back," said Kranzen. "*Then* we'll see what sort of world we can build."

9

DURING THE NEXT ten days, Vanmore learned more about the titanium industry than he had absorbed in the previous thirty-six years of his life. He had thought he had known all anyone needed to know about titanium—that it was a grey metal with a relative density of 4.5, melting at 1690 degrees Celsius, atomic number 22, atomic weight 47.90. He had all this kind of information available because he used the metal in his own business of producing synthetic sapphires.

As a result, he had approached his analysis of Vanmore Titanium with the easy confidence that he could unravel it all in a couple of days' concentrated effort. At the end of the week, he was just beginning to get some overall idea of the full complexity of the field.

Some of the titanium came from rutile extracted from the sands of the Queensland coast, some of it from ilmenite, some of it even from the spacemining operations of Nu Karnatika. The last was a more expensive source, but from time to time the Company had been forced to use it when industrial conflict in Australia tied up both the rutile and ilmenite supplies in protracted strikes.

In fact, at the end of the first week, after processing mountains of data, Vanmore was beginning to feel as if he didn't know much about *anything*. The links between the Company and Nu Karnatika were intricate and subtle, maintained against everchanging outside pressures from the National Stability Council, the Amalgamated Titanium Workers' Union, the Arbitration Court in Canberra, and the embassies of the countries of the Northern Alliance.

Around sunset on the tenth day, he went up to the penthouse, kissed Rona, and flopped into an armchair where he could look out at the flaming sky reflected in the lake.

"The bastards are mad," he said with an air of sudden cognition.

"Which bastards, darling?" asked Rona, bringing him a drink.

"All of them! The whole bloody human race! Except us, of course, and possibly Rajendra Naryan. You know what the trouble is? They've inherited power systems built up over generations, without having the ability to control them. Too much power for their brains. Like a three-year old kid at the controls of an army helicopter." He swallowed a large part of his drink at a single gulp, and sat looking at the glass. He raised it towards Rona. "Thanks, honey. I needed that."

"Why are they mad?"

"Perhaps that's the wrong word, if you apply it to most of the human population. But they haven't evolved fast enough or far enough to keep pace with the techniques available to them. They can't see the total picture, because the picture has become too big and too complicated for anyone to grasp it any more. I'm running into that myself, the last few days."

"Still," she said quietly, "at least you're trying."

"There's that, I suppose. Most of them don't try to get the overall scene. They just aim at what's good for them right *now*, and to hell with next week or next year."

Standing behind him, she began massaging the muscles at the back of his neck and shoulders. "You've got that meeting at the Roundhouse tonight, haven't you? Why don't you have a bath now?"

He swallowed a little more of his drink, then gestured with the glass. "They're like beginners playing chess. The opponent pushes some pawns out, and they seize the chance to grab each one as soon as they can, without realising they're leaving themselves open to a 'fool's mate.' "

"Weren't you ever caught with a fool's mate?"

"Yes, but only once. I think I was six at the time." He sighed. "Keep on doing that for a while, honey. Just *there*. It's really relaxing."

"All right. But not for long. You have to go to that meeting, remember."

"How could I forget it?"

Rona saw him off at a quarter to eight. She waited at the window as he circled the top of the tower once in his airkar, and waved as he swept past. Then she went to the visiphone and tapped out a number. Bianca appeared in the hologram.

"Max has just left," said Rona. "I'll pick you up in five minutes."

"Right. I'm ready. I'll give Charl a call while you're coming over."

Rona locked the penthouse and rode the elevator down to the forty-fifth floor, where the second landing flange of the building was located. She walked quickly out to the airkar she had rented that afternoon in an outer eastern suburb of Amadeus City, and took off quickly, swinging down towards the Point. Bianca was already waiting for her under the carport, and she quickly sprang in beside her.

"No bugs in this thing, I hope?" she asked.

"Couldn't be. No one saw me bring it home."

She headed out along the line of the irrigation canal towards Charl's place.

The meeting of the National Stability Council began like the first one Vanmore had attended. The only other people physically present were Ashton Marsh and Quade Gannon, but Max had the impression of being in an assembly of ninety, so complete was the realism of the holograms.

The chairman was elected—a white-haired man called Vic. He plunged straight into the business at hand.

"We have the face-to-face telecast here, made less than an hour ago, from the orbiting transfer station. It shows Rik Dane in a direct interview with Captain Rance and with Frank Ferris. To save our time, I propose to delete the interview with Rance—we can't alter that in any way, and it's perfectly innocuous from our viewpoint. However, here's the Ferris segment."

This time, an isolated hologram alcove at one side of the room lit up, as a similar one would be activated in all the other Roundhouses throughout Australia. It showed the smooth-walled, clinical purity of the quarantine section of the orbiting station in its synchronous orbit.

Rik Dane's tall figure was on the left, as always in his telecasts—he felt he presented a better image with his right profile—and this time his hair was vividly red. The young man sitting opposite him showed up far more clearly than in the previous long-range telecast. He looked exactly like the Frank Ferris Vanmore had known sixteen years ago—even younger, somehow. Dane was in the middle of a sentence as the sound came on.

". . . long were you on Alcenar?"

"Only a few of their days, actually." Ferris' voice sounded higher and younger than Vanmore remembered it. "But we saw enough to realise that most of their techniques are way ahead of ours."

"What techniques, Frank?"

"Well, making different materials. They make some tremendously strong metals."

"So do we—at a price."

"But they use more of them. They have a thing called a matter converter."

"A what?"

"A matter converter. It can turn one sort of material into another sort."

Dane seemed to be considering his next question. "You mean it could turn lead into gold? Iron into silver? Something like that?"

"Well—yes."

Dane turned towards the camera for a brief aside. "Something I've always wanted." He turned back to Ferris. "What's it look like?"

Ferris shrugged. "Oh, I've never actually seen one."

Dane grinned wolfishly. "I see. Just heard about it from the local boys?"

"Well, more than that. I've seen a road paved with real sapphire."

"You mentioned that in our long-range interview, Frank. *Sapphire!* That's very expensive stuff, isn't it?"

"It is here. But they had a road of it. A wide road. Long. I couldn't see the end of it. All sapphire."

"But that's rather hard to believe, Frank."

"Well, it's true. Sapphire's a very hard material, nearly as hard as diamond. Good for making a road surface—except that *here* it would cost the whole planet. But they must make it through their matter converters."

"I see. Are you sure it wasn't some kind of pavement that just looked like sapphire?"

"I don't think so. Gopal Aiyar and I found a place where the road was being extended, and we broke a couple of pieces off the edge of it. Everyone we've shown them to says they're sapphire. Corundum with a little mixture of titanium. I've got one of the pieces here."

"Could we see it?"

"Sure." Ferris bent down and took something from a bag, placing it on the table between himself and Dane. Dane picked it up in his large hands. The fragment was as long as his hand, and as wide, and nearly as thick as its width. Dane looked upward at someone out of the range of the picture.

"Can you get a blow up of this?" he asked.

"Right," came a muffled voice, and suddenly Dane's hands and the piece of blue, translucent material grew enormous in the alcove, filling it. Vanmore could see the tiny reddish hairs and pores on Dane's skin, and the blue object still looked like a huge piece of sapphire.

"My mate Gopal has a bigger piece of it," came Ferris' voice.

"How big?"

"Long as his forearm."

"Is it here?"

"No. He left on the shuttle down to Nu Karnatika about an hour ago. Took it with him."

The figures in the alcove returned to normal size. Dane hefted the piece of sapphire in his hands.

"Do you mind if I have an expert look at this?"

"Go ahead. But a geologist on the ship said it was sapphire."

The image flicked out.

"There's more, later," said Vic. "But I can summarise it for you. Expert checked it. He said sapphire. Pure sapphire." He paused. "Any comment?"

Kranzen was the first to speak. Watching him, Vanmore saw him press a button on the console in front of him while Vic was finishing speaking. Apparently it showed a numbered signal on the chairman's desk, because he indicated Kranzen straight away.

"First," said Kranzen. "I think we're agreed that we kill all reference to the matter converter or the sapphire road in the general telecast. I think the next step is to try to verify what we've heard. If they're really so far ahead of us that they can pave their roads with something we regard as a precious stone, the implications are frightening."

"Could I make a suggestion here?" said Vanmore. He had the impulse to rise to his feet, but realised that would have put his head out of range of the hologram cameras. "I think I have two qualifications that might help us all in this matter. First of all, I'm an expert on sapphire—I've been making synthetic sapphire, mostly for industrial uses, in my plant in Queensland for the past ten years. Second, I used to know Frank Ferris personally, and so did my lady, Rona Gale. I'd be happy to have young Ferris stay with us for a while, until he gets his bearings. That way, I think we might be able to get a very clear picture of the developments they've made on Alcenar."

Before the chairman could put the suggestion formally to the meeting, Kranzen broke in. "Vic, I think we could handle this better. An army psychologist would be the best person to find out how reliable Ferris' report is." He gave his cool smile. "Once we have him on a lie detector, the picture might change."

"I disagree with that," said Vanmore. "I know Ferris. Try to force him, and you'll get nothing out of him. On the other hand, Rona and I were his close friends. I'd suggest we try my way first. Then, if nothing emerges, Captain Kranzen can try his electronics."

"Let's get some semblance of order into this," said Vic, as a murmur of voices swept through the alcoves. "Someone like to move a motion?"

Rather to Vanmore's surprise, it was Quade Gannon who spoke. "I move that our first contact with Ferris be Max Vanmore, for the reasons he suggested."

Vanmore didn't catch who seconded the motion, but in the ensuing voting the green lights made up over sixty per cent of the total array.

"Carried," said Vic. He looked at Max, his eyebrows raised. "How do you propose to arrange your contact with Ferris?"

"My Company imports some ores from the asteroid belt. We have our own spaceport for shuttle landings down at Island Lagoon. I could arrange to have Ferris brought down in a shuttle and meet him there."

"Sounds logical," said Vic. "Any disagreement?"

"I think the army should be there as a backup," said Kranzen.

"That's fine," answered Vanmore. He looked at Kranzen a few seconds later, and saw that his eyes were bright with suppressed fury.

Back at the penthouse, Vanmore was jubilant. He embraced Rona and swung her round.

"I've fixed it for us to meet young Ferris before anyone else—even the media," he said.

"How'd you manage that?"

"Just by saying the right things at exactly the right time. Anyway, the Council has agreed that it's best, in the interests of national stability, for us to contact him when the shuttle lands at Island Lagoon, and bring him directly here."

"You want me to come down with you?"

"Sure. Two familiar faces will be better than one." Thoughtfully, he pulled the front of her dress downward. "Rona—try to dress 'young.' The way you looked at the time he went away."

"God, Max, I was only eighteen!"

"So? If you want to, you can look almost exactly the same."

"How about you?"

"That's harder, but I'll do what I can."

The shuttle came down steeply and quickly, to a spectator used to watching the landing of other aircraft. To Rona's eyes it looked thick and chunky, and didn't seem to have enough wing surface for its bulk. Its computer-controlled flight slowed and levelled startlingly close to the ground, and the shriek of oxyhydrogen jets heralded the vast, boiling dust cloud that almost hid the lime and red machine as it skimmed in for a smooth landing.

There were no windows along most of the length of the shuttle, for it was primarily a freighter. A door swung open near the windowed cabin, and a jointed metal ladder unfolded to the ground.

Vanmore and Rona stood near the small terminal building, and a short distance away was Captain Kranzen with two of his aides. Their dull-green, two-rotor helicopter stood just around the corner of the building, near the Vanmore Titanium Company jet.

Ferris followed one of the shuttle crew down the ladder, and walked towards the terminal building. He seemed to be having a little trouble with the rhythm of his stride, walking as though slightly drunk—no doubt an effect of his sudden adjustment to the gravity.

He recognised Max first, and hurried towards him with his hand outstretched, as Max went to meet him.

"Good to see you, Mr. Vanmore. How's Max?"

"Hey, you've skipped a generation. *I'm* Max. We've been getting older while you've been snoozing across the light years."

"God, of course!" Ferris threw his arms around Max in an uninhibited embrace.

"I've got Rona waiting over here."

"Where?"

"Right there. In lilac. Silver hair."

"*What?* Rona!" He ran towards her, lurching as he stepped a little too high, but soon picking up the changed rhythm needed. He held out his arms to embrace Rona, then seemed to hesitate.

"Frank! It's been a long time!" She put her arms round his neck and kissed him. He responded at first, but then a shocked expression came into his eyes for a fleeting moment.

"What is it?" she asked.

"Nothing. It's just—nothing. It's only—I don't know, you feel different, somehow."

"Nobody stays the same for sixteen years, Frank. But I'm still me."

"Sure, Rona." He had control of his expression again, now, and his smile seemed natural. But it was obvious to Max, standing a couple of paces away, that something had changed inside both of them.

Rona suddenly took Ferris by the arm, and the gesture seemed almost maternal. "Come on, Frank. We'd better get you straight to our place where you can rest for a while before the media boys get hold of you.''

Ferris looked around the bare, sun-drenched spaceport. "I was more or less expecting them here. You know, cameras, microphones, the lot.''

"That comes later," said Max.

"If I might intrude—"

They turned to find Kranzen standing there.

"I'm Captain Kranzen. There's been a slight change of schedule, Max," he said in a lowered voice to Vanmore, then went on. "Our top brass have arrived at the decision that it would be best to interview Mr. Ferris while his memories of Alcenar are still fresh.''

Ferris looked at Rona and at Vanmore. "Well, if there's anything I can tell you that's of any help—"

"There may be. It won't take very long."

"Where did you want to hold this interview?" asked Rona.

"We have a base with a suitable room just on the outskirts of Amadeus City," said Kranzen.

"I know it," said Vanmore. "We'll bring him along there after he's had a bit of a rest."

"We'd prefer it *before* he's been anywhere else—so his memories of Alcenar are as clear and uncluttered as possible. You're welcome to come along, if you like. Follow us, and land where we land." He turned to Ferris. "Coming, Mr. Ferris?"

Ferris hesitated. "If it's all the same to you, sir, I'd rather ride with Rona and Max. I haven't seen them for a long time."

To Vanmore's surprise, Kranzen accepted this. "Fair enough. You follow us in, then, Max."

"Right." Max watched Kranzen stride away towards the army helicopter, his two aides joining him as he passed them and falling into precise step with him, a pace or so behind. The three of them marched to their machine like automata. He turned to Rona and Ferris. "Come on," he said, and led them over to the Company jet. Because of the risk of security leaks, he had flown it down to Island Lagoon himself.

He had thought the jet would outdistance the helicopter easily, but as he flew along at his normal cruising speed the twin-rotor machine kept ahead of him. It was not easy to see against the reddish landscape, flying on an exactly straight course, like a monstrous insect.

"What's the army got to do with this?" asked Ferris.

"Well, national defence, you know," said Rona. "They tend to be a bit paranoid, I think."

"Can't see they're in any danger from Alcenar," mused Ferris, "seeing the place is eight years away at half light speed."

"Well, there's nothing to worry about—or they wouldn't have invited Max and me along."

"Suppose so," said Ferris. He looked down from the window at the red sand and spinifex. "You know, this doesn't look much different from some of the dry parts of Alcenar."

"What was it really like there?" asked Rona. "What were the people like?"

"Oh, they varied a lot. Some of them like us. Some very different."

"How different?"

"Well, they have settlements on four or five different planets in their system. Not like our settlements on Mars and the Moon and the asteroids. They change the people to fit the environment, instead of making a sealed Earth-type environment inside a dome, the way we do. They don't seem to have our feelings that Earth-type living is the only natural living. See what I mean?"

"I think so."

"They fly from planet to planet in their system almost as easily as we fly from continent to continent, so at their major spaceport you see all sorts of people. You wouldn't believe some of them unless you saw them."

Rona apparently didn't want to pursue this line of conversation any further. "How does it feel to be back?"

"Great! Good to see you again, Rona. Although—"

"Although what, Frank?"

"It's strange to see you—older. Not that I mean you're actually *old*, but—sorry, I'm not getting this across the way I meant it."

Rona laughed. The rest of the way to Amadeus she kept the conversation light and shallow.

As the city came in sight, she pointed out the Titanium Company tower and some of the other landmarks. Max cut the power back and followed the helicopter down over the eastern end of the lake, landing where the helicopter pilot indicated—he did it by flying along a runway made for jets, then swinging up and to one side as Vanmore touched down.

He reversed the thrust of his jets to slow the machine, then looked around. "Where did he go?"

Rona pointed. "He's just landing over near that green building."

Vanmore swung the jet off the strip and taxied across the hard, yellow ground. Kranzen met him as he pulled in beside the helicopter and led the others out. In spite of himself, he was impressed by Kranzen's organising smoothness as a dark green bus glided to a stop besides them just as they met.

"This'll take us to the psych. lab.," said Kranzen.

The bus travelled between rows of dull-green buildings, finally pulling up at an isolated house-sized structure. Kranzen led the way inside, where the walls were pale green and the decor stark, almost Spartan. A stocky man in a white coat and glasses came through an inner door, and Kranzen introduced him as Dr. Orr.

Orr spoke briefly to Ferris, then led him through the door, closing it after him. Kranzen turned to Rona and Vanmore.

"Come through here—there's an observation room." He led them into a room where a large, tinted window took up almost the whole of one wall. The only light in the room came through this window. On the other side, Dr. Orr and Ferris were walking in to a lighted room with a table placed between two chairs.

"This is a one-way screen," said Kranzen, indicating the window. "We can see them, but they can't see us. From there, it looks like a wall. Fairly soundproof, but best to keep our voices down." He indicated chairs facing the one-way glass, and they sat down. Orr started a tape recorder running, and as he did so the sounds of the lighted room came through to the darkened one through a loud speaker evidently linked with the recorder.

"I don't get this," said Ferris suspiciously.

"I just want you to undergo a little test, is all. This business of the sapphire road could be very important. So important that we want to make absolutely certain you weren't the victim of some kind of delusion, or hypnosis, or whatever."

"What's this thing? A lie detector?"

"You might call it that. I want you to hold these two cans. A very small electric current passes through, and your reactions to questions will vary the resistance, depending on the emotional charge. Basically, the thing's simply a Wheatstone bridge, with a controllable circuit balanced against the one passing through you. At the same time, I'm going to pick up variations in heart rate and blood pressure. Right?''

"OK, if it makes you happier.''

"Good.'' Orr took some time setting the apparatus up. "Blood pressure's good. Hundred and ten, seventy. Pulse around sixty-four.''

"That's slow, isn't it?''

"Yes, but that's good. Squeeze those two cans a moment. That's right. A good, hard squeeze. Right. Now, how do you feel about being back home?''

"Good.''

"Find what you expected to find on Alcenar?''

"Not what I expected, no. Interesting, though.''

"Just relax," said Orr easily. "That's it. What's the place like?''

"Slightly heavier gravity than ours. Oh, it was around mid-year, as they call it, so you had no real night there. There are two suns in the Alpha Centauri system. Well, three—but two that matter. One yellow, one orange. . . .''

The questions went on. Vanmore touched Kranzen's arm, and whispered to him, "These questions don't seem to be getting anywhere, do they? You could find out this stuff without asking Ferris.''

"True. But he's just getting him settled down. Look through the glass down here—you see the three pens leaving a trace on the roll of paper? Red, green, purple. They show heart rate, blood pressure, electrical resistance. Watch.''

The pens wavered only slightly from their straight lines along the unrolling tape. Orr fed Ferris more irrelevant, innocuous questions, then without altering his voice he slipped in a punch line: "Did you really see this road made of sapphire?''

"Yes. I broke a piece off it. Rik Dane had it examined.''

The needles hardly wavered. Orr remained deadpan. He was too experienced to show any reaction that might have produced feedback. A little later, though, he did get a violent reaction on the needles.

"Bit unusual for a fellow of twenty to make a two-way journey that would take sixteen years, wasn't it?''

"Maybe," said Ferris, still relaxed.

"Because of a woman?" asked Orr in the same even voice. The needles surged. The one linked with the electrical resistance ran right off the dial, and Orr had to turn a knob to bring it back again.

"What were the people like on Alcenar?" asked Orr.

"Well—they varied." The red, green, and purple lines slowly straightened out again.

"Did you see their main city? Astralon?"

"No. I didn't get there."

"That where they have their matter converter?"

"I guess so." The traces of the pens had now smoothed out into their normal rhythms.

"Did you feel things were being hidden from you?"

Ferris thought for a few seconds. "Not really. Not conscious of anything being hidden. Of course, I saw some pieces of equipment that were simply too advanced for me to understand."

"Too advanced for you to grasp? Like what?"

Slight movement on the needles. "The way their fliers worked. They flew with very fast acceleration, and stopped quickly, yet you didn't feel it. They called it antiner—short for anti-inertia, I think. They seemed to take it for granted, as if they'd had it for generations."

"I see. Aside from purely technical things—anything bother you?"

This time, there was a pronounced surge on the dials. "Some of the people. They were mostly like us—many a bit shorter, maybe because of the heavier gravity. Then others were much taller. They have their legs rebuilt with a metal called vitallium, with electric muscles controlled by relays."

"Do they work efficiently?"

"Better than ours."

"Many of these streets paved with sapphire?"

"I saw quite a few." The needles remained exasperatingly steady.

"Meet any women you liked on Alcenar?"

A pause, then a deep surge of the needle. "Well, there was one girl—"

"Never mind," said Orr. "I don't want to dig into your personal life. Learn anything of their political setup?"

"Not much. There were tensions there—there always are when you get a lot of people together, aren't there?—but I wasn't there long enough to get the feel of different factions.''

The traces remained steady.

Orr kept it up for an hour, then signalled the interview was coming to an end. A few minutes later he met Vanmore, Rona, and Kranzen in a different room.

"See it all?" he asked. "He was telling the truth about the sapphire road—and the matter converter—I'm sure of that. He's certainly not catatonic. You saw the surge when I touched on his sex life."

"You didn't follow it up," said Rona.

"Nothing to do with me. All I wanted was strong reaction about *anything*, so we know he's *capable* of strong reactions. That way, the absence of any surge when he talked about the sapphire road meant he wasn't lying about it. It means your road's real."

Vanmore nodded. Kranzen grunted.

"I wonder what woman," mused Rona.

"Listen," snapped Orr, "what'd you want? You want me to get the information you asked for, or do you want me to play around digging into his love life?"

"Sorry, no. You did an excellent job," Vanmore broke in.

"It was just idle curiosity in my part," admitted Rona. "I used to know him."

Orr nodded bleakly, then looked up at Kranzen and at Vanmore. "Well, you can take it your road of sapphire exists —but a hell of a long way away." Unexpectedly, he gave a guffaw of raucous laughter.

It was just a short flight in the jet from the army base to the Company airstrip, and Vanmore, looking in the rear mirror, was irritated to see that they were being shadowed by one of the dull-green army jets.

"You know," he said to Rona, "I think it might be a good idea if we moved out of the penthouse as soon as possible."

"Perhaps we could look for a place to live this afternoon," she said, "with the excuse that we're showing Frank the town. Tell you what! We could use the other little airkar I rented. Nobody would connect it with us—I'm still keeping it down on the flange at the forty-fifth floor."

"Good idea. Feel like seeing a bit of the town this afternoon, Frank?"

"Well, if it's all the same to you, Max, I feel like a bit of a rest. I don't know whether I'm in space or in the middle of Tuesday night."

"All right," said Rona. "We have a spare room in the flat all ready for you."

"Long as it's got a bed in it, that's fine," said Ferris. "I thought that guy'd never finish with his questions. Ninety per cent of them didn't have any point, as far as I could see."

Vanmore landed the jet, and they rode up to the penthouse in the outside elevator. They stood in the scorched roof garden for a few minutes pointing out features of the landscape to Ferris—the jumbled rock domes of the Olgas, far across the

lake, and the giant, rounded monolith of Ayer's Rock, the
sacred Uluru of the Aborigines. Then they went in to the air-
conditioned coolness, and, while Rona showed Ferris his
room, Vanmore rang down to his office.

"Any calls come in, Elsa?"

"Yes, there was a person-to-person call from Nu Karnatika."

"Thanks. That'd be Rajendra Naryan. I'll call him back
from here."

He looked at his watch. Two thirty. It would be about ten in
the morning for Rajendra. He put the call through, and in
quite a short time the Hindu appeared on the hologram. Behind him was a vista of the interior of some kind of automated
factory, as if seen through the glass wall of an elevated office.

"Ah, Max!" He pressed his hands together. "I tried to
reach you a short time ago. I've just learned some interesting
facts from young Gopal Aiyar."

"Yes?"

"Among other things, I've seen the piece of sapphire he
brought back. Some of my boys have examined it at a
laboratory right here. It's genuine sapphire, and the piece is
nearly forty centimetres long."

"I've just been present at an interview between Frank Ferris
and the army—they used a lie detector. They're convinced he
isn't lying."

"I see. It might be interesting if we could share our data,
Max."

"It might. I have an idea. We've produced some new extruded sections of titanium alloys. Perhaps I could fly some
over to you—in person."

"I'd like to see them—very soon."

"Tomorrow?"

"That'd be excellent. I have some other things I'd like to
show you. You know the way to find our private airfield? One
moment." He held a map up to the cameras so that it seemed
to be just in front of Vanmore. His long, brown forefinger indicated a spot on the map, and he kept it there as Vanmore
made a hard two-dimensional copy of the hologram. He ran
the sheet out of the slot and looked at it.

"Got it," he said. "Tomorrow, then."

"Tomorrow," agreed Rajendra.

•   •   •

Vanmore walked towards the bedrooms, but Rona met him in the passageway with her finger held against her lips.

"What is it?" whispered Max as he drew close to her.

"Our interstellar pioneer—he was sound asleep as soon as he stretched out on the bed. Didn't even have time to get undressed. I think he's been wide awake for the past forty or fifty hours."

"Come back into the living room. There—I'll close the door. Now, how would you like a quick trip to India tomorrow?"

"What?"

"To see Rajendra Naryan. I'm taking some samples of titanium alloys across to him."

"Do you have to do that personally?"

"In this case—yes. He's learned more about Alcenar from young Aiyar—Frank's pal who made the trip with him. Listen, Rona, things are shaping up. I think Kranzen's planning to take a ship to Alcenar, and so's Rajendra."

"And you want to be on one of them?"

"I've no chance of being on Kranzen's ship, but remember the offer Raj made us?"

"It kept me awake half the night." She smiled. "It's the sort of offer that comes once in several lifetimes." Then her face changed, and she pointed towards the bedroom. "What'll we do with Frank?"

"We wouldn't be away long, but we'd have to get someone to babysit."

"He has some relations on the irrigation area over near the Alice—or had, sixteen years ago. He told me while you were calling Rajendra."

"That's a long shot. They mightn't even be there, now. Anyway, the guy'd think we were nuts."

Rona grimaced. "I get the feeling he's beginning to think everyone on Earth is nuts. After the army's performance, I don't blame him."

Vanmore looked at his watch. "I want to go down to the office in a few minutes, but there's a newscast I want to catch, first. Might be some mention of the Alphard. The Stability Council were going to kill at least part of the segment with Frank on it, but they were letting an interview with the captain go over the network untouched."

The newscast contained a direct interview between Rik Dane

and Captain Rance of the *Alphard*. It was preceded by some pictures of the ship taken in space, but the sharp contrast of blazing sunshine and ebon shadow gave it a slightly unreal look, like that of most objects in space. It was an enormous cylinder of bright metal, with a meteor shield at the forward end and a battery of immensely potent-looking drive units at the rear. Hatches were already open, and space shuttles were loading and unloading, dwarfed by the size of the interstellar ship.

Rance was a big, tanned man with bleached yellow hair and a massive jaw. He had an aura of authority that somehow made Dane the subordinate figure in the interview, quite a different person from the Rik Dane who had so easily manipulated Frank Ferris.

"Our voyage is purely a trade mission," Rance said, looking straight out of the hologram at his viewers. "We bring you mainly machines and electronic equipment. We take with us seeds, plants, and some animals for breeding purposes—not only domestic animals, but as wide a range as possible to enrich our ecology."

"Will the equipment you mentioned be for sale?" asked Dane.

Rance gave a tolerant shake of his head. "With our two civilisations separated by more than forty by ten to the twelfth kilometres, an exchange of currency would be useless. What we are engaged in is oldfashioned barter. We give you a machine you can copy as often as you like, and we take in exchange seeds that may give us forests of useful trees for an indefinite future."

"Which cities are you visiting, Captain Rance?"

"Last time we confined our itinerary to the northern hemisphere of your world—New York, Mexico City, Tokyo, and some other cities. This time, I intend to visit Melbourne, Sydney, Amadeus, Sao Paulo, Buenos Aires. . . ."

"Amadeus!" exclaimed Rona. "What would bring him here?"

Vanmore shook his head. "Damned if I know. Hardly the wildlife."

The interview was short, with a promise of others to come. There was no mention of Frank Ferris or Gopal Aiyar.

Vanmore went down to his office and checked on the availa-

bility of one of the Company jets for the following morning.
There was a twin jet with long-range tanks fitted, which would
enable him to reach Nu Karnatika with one refuelling stop in
Singapore. He then went down to the sales department and
made a collection of sample sections of extruded titanium
alloy. He called in to Quade Gannon's office.

"Quade, Rajendra's been in touch with me. He's got some
new project going—wants some samples of our alloy sections.
Think I'll fly them over myself, tomorrow—have a look at
what he's doing while I'm at it. That should give us an edge on
any competition."

"What are you taking?"

"The Skyhawk. I'll get it fuelled up in the morning."

"Need a pilot?"

"No. Raj has something hush-hush, I think."

"Well, in that case, the fewer who know the better. Have a
good trip. By the way, what's happened to your guest?"

"Sleeping at the moment. I'm going to have a talk with him
about Alcenar, and sapphires, and a lot of other interesting
things this evening, after a meal."

Quade seemed to tense suddenly as a thought came to him.
"Say, you haven't told him the Stability Council killed his
telecast, have you?"

"Hell, no. That'd only come out later when the media boys
really get to him."

"Mind if I call over there tonight? I'd like to be in on your
session with him."

"Suits me. Come for a meal?"

"Later, Max. Say eight?"

Frank Ferris obviously enjoyed the meal Rona cooked for
him.

"Long time since I've tasted something like this, Rona."

"I suppose the meals on the ship were limited," said Rona.

"Not only on the ship. The food was odd on Alcenar. Varied enough, but I didn't have time to find the dishes I liked.
Their stuff was hard to identify. Synthetic, a lot of it. Odd
colours. Had all sorts of vitamins and trace elements in it, protein
and whatever you needed—but how do you get enthusiastic
about eating food that's bright blue?"

"Exactly how long were you on Alcenar, Frank?"

"About ten of their days, that's all. Of course, their days

are nearly twice as long as ours. And while I was there they had only a couple of hours of night. The yellow sun was up for twenty hours or so, and the red one nearly all the rest of the time. Sometimes you had a sun on each side of the sky.''

''Confusing?'' asked Rona.

Ferris helped himself to some more lemon chicken. ''Look, everything was confusing about that place. The books I read before I went there called it an Earthlike planet, but I bet the fellows who compiled them had never been there.''

''You mentioned one thing that interested me a lot,'' said Vanmore, topping up Ferris' glass with wine, ''that anti-inertia system on their aircraft. How did it operate?''

''The antiner? Like one of their gravity fields turned in the direction of the axis of the aircraft, or whatever. They can make localised gravity fields, you know. Step into them, and you can be lighter or heavier than in the surrounding area, depending on what you want.''

''How did they work?''

''I'm not an engineer, Max. You'd have had a better chance of figuring it out. They were built in, so I never had a chance to examine them.''

''Are you taping all this?'' asked Kranzen's aide in a room high in an adjoining building.

''Yes,'' said the technician. ''Not very clear, is it? The pick-up's on the roof of their penthouse, so the signal varies as Ferris moves about. Orr injected the 'bug' on the left side of him, so the signal's better when he turns his left side towards the pickup. But we'll be able to process the tape later to get a fully audible signal.''

''Take long?'' asked the aide.

''Few minutes. Do it before I leave here.''

''Their voices sound clearer than his at times. But what's that pounding noise?''

''That's nothing. Only his blood.''

''Have you got that lump of sapphire with you?'' asked Vanmore.

''Only a little piece. They kept the bigger part of it for examination. But here's the smaller bit.''

Vanmore took it and walked across to hold it close under a reading lamp.

"I suppose it's real," said Rona.

Vanmore grunted. "No doubt. Seems to be made of a lot of big sapphire crystals fused together by heat and pressure. I can see the pattern of the titanium crystals, always 60 degrees apart. These crystals are not only sapphires. They're star sapphires."

"Yuk! Want to change your business before word gets out?"

Vanmore lifted her sapphire pendant and let it drop against her creamy skin. "Not much good making star sapphires when someone else can pave blasted roads with the things!"

"Well," said Ferris cheerfully, "the competition's a hell of a long way away, like the doc said at the army centre."

"That's beside the point," said Vanmore. "It'd hardly be a paying proposition to import the sapphires from Alpha Centauri, but it *would* be feasible to import the idea. The technique."

About eight o'clock, Gannon's airkar came past the windows on its way around to the landing flange. Vanmore opened the door for him and introduced him to Ferris.

"You didn't bring Bianca?" he observed.

"No. We're having a slight—ah—difference, you might say."

The three of them—Vanmore, Rona, and Gannon—talked with Ferris in non-stop relays, but as the evening crawled on it became evident that they were not going to learn as much about Alcenar as they had expected. It was not the fault of Ferris. He was co-operative enough, but he simply did not know any facts about Alcenar that would have been of any use to them. He knew there was something called a matter converter, but he hadn't the faintest notion how it worked, what it looked like, how big it was, how expensive, how numerous. It was the same with the antiner device—it remained for them a tantalising mystery just on the hazy edge of credibility.

In the end, Gannon stood up, flexing his arms. "I have a solid day coming up tomorrow, Max. Better head for home." He extended his hand to Ferris. "It's been very stimulating talking with you, Frank. You've certainly had an overwhelming experience. But I must say good night. And to you, Rona—many thanks."

Vanmore went out with him to his airkar. "Are we wasting our time?"

"Possibly," said Gannon. "He's absorbed a lot of dazzling ideas, but he doesn't like to confuse himself with facts, does he?"

"I think he's confused himself with too many facts. Given himself mental indigestion. Anyway, see you tomorrow before I leave."

"Ciao," said Gannon, and got into his airkar.

Next morning, just as they had finished breakfast, Rona went to the visiphone. Her first call was unproductive, and they heard her making a note of another number to ring. She sounded jubilant as she waved the piece of paper.

"I've traced Frank's cousins—and guess what? They've moved from the farm near the Alice and come to the irrigation area north of here—the one fed from Lake Amadeus. They're not as far away as I thought. You ready to speak to them, Frank?"

"Sure, Rona."

She tapped out a number. A brown-faced woman of about forty appeared on the hologram.

"Mrs. Baker? I understand you're the cousin of Frank Ferris, the man who's just come back from Alpha Centauri?"

"Are you from the television?" asked the woman.

"No, but I have a surprise for you. The people who make the decisions thought it would be better for Frank to have a few days' rest after his journey before fronting up to the news people. He's here in Amadeus City. Would you like to speak to him?"

Ferris suddenly moved alongside her. "Lillian! It is you, isn't it?"

Rona tiptoed back into the living room and let the two of them adjust to the time dislocation that had put their lives sixteen years out of phase.

"What are they like?" asked Vanmore quietly.

"Only saw her. Looks all right. Successful farmers, I'd say. Look, darling, while you're getting the jet ready, and your samples, or whatever else you're taking, I'll fly him out there in the brown airkar. No one should know it. It's still on the flange five floors below us."

"Sound them out about him staying the night there. We'd be under less pressure if we could leave it until tomorrow to pick him up."

• • •

By nine thirty, Vanmore had the Skyhawk fuelled and warmed up on the airstrip. He saw Rona's brown rented airkar alight on the second top flange of the tower, and walked over to the two mechanics who had brought the jet out of the hangar and checked it over.

"I'm having a look at our plant up in the Kimberleys," he said. "Might be back tonight, possibly tomorrow—it depends on what I find to look at up there." He grinned. "Don't anyone wait up for me."

He taxied the jet down to the end of the runway, then brought it part-way back. Rona, in a loose pink tunic over yellow pyjama-like trousers, with a wide-brimmed yellow hat, came through a gate at the side of the field and ran across to meet him. He opened the door of the jet, gave her time to climb beside him and put on her seat belt, then gave the jets full power and raced down the runway towards the lake. He pulled the wheel back and climbed almost vertically to fifteen thousand metres, then rolled the jet on to a level course and pushed it to Mach 1.4.

"God, if anyone wanted to follow you in this thing they'd have to move," said Rona.

"The army boys could do it, but they'd have to make it very obvious," he answered, and switched on the radar screen. "Everyone except Quade Gannon thinks I'm heading up to one of our installations in the Kimberleys. We have several there, and I didn't say which one." He pointed to the little chart table between them. "I'm heading over them, then to Singapore, then India. Nearly a straight line."

Rona settled happily back in her seat. "Nu Karnatika, here we come."

Vanmore glanced at her. "Soon, it might be a case of Alcenar, here we come. Could you take it?"

"I don't know. You'd have to try me."

KRANZEN WALKED BRISKLY into the office set aside for him at the Amadeus army base, and immediately called one of his aides.

"What're the latest movements, Earl?" he asked.

"We have contact with Ferris again—"

"Again? You lost it? How?"

"Well, Vanmore went down to his Company airstrip around nine, and had a twin-jet Skyhawk brought out and made ready for a flight. We picked up some conversation near the hangars on the parabolic mike. He said he was going up to the Kimberleys."

"That checks. The Company has some installations up there, and he's been doing a lot of ferreting since he took over." Kranzen thought for a moment. "Never mind about him right now—what happened to Ferris?"

"Shortly after Vanmore left the flat, we lost contact with the implant in Ferris. Not a sudden cutoff—a quick fade, like he'd gone down in the elevator. The pickup's on the roof, of course. A couple of minutes later, a brown airkar left the flange on the forty-fifth floor of the tower, heading north. Jake was trying to get a direct reading from the bug, using maximum gain, and he picked up a short, garbled trace just as the airkar was passing the building where we were doing the monitoring."

"Was Ferris flying the airkar?"

"No. Ms. Gale, I think."

"What happened then?"

"I raced up to the roof and found I could still see the airkar in the distance. I got a fix on the point on the horizon where it was last visible. I picked up Jake and his gear, and we flew out along the same course. About forty kilometres out, the same airkar passed us on the way back. Ms. Gale flying it. Yellow hat on."

"Never mind her bloody hat—was Ferris with her?"

"No. We were both sure of that. We were looking slightly down into her car."

"What'd you do?"

"Kept the same course for a few kilometres. She'd been flying low, and gaining height, as if she'd taken off not far away. Jake kept listening, as I flew over a number of buildings—farmhouses, mostly, because it's an irrigation area. We finally located the farm where Ferris was hiding. It belongs to a couple called Baker."

"Take any action?"

"Left Jake and his equipment on a ridge about a kilometre away, then flew over the farm and dropped a scatter of pickups. One landed against the wall of the house, another lodged in the roof guttering. Jake's been picking up conversation, but so far it's just family stuff—Ferris is some relation of the Baker woman. Jake's taping it all, but says nothing matters yet. What do we do?"

"We wait. I can always get the AI7 boys to pull him in." Kranzen sighed. "If it's necessary. I'm beginning to think he's not worth the trouble. But *don't lose him again!* Right?"

Bianca Baru found out from Charl, who seemed to listen in to everything, that Captain Rance of the *Alphard* was staying at the Ulbunali, the best hotel in Amadeus City. After wearing down the resistance of several people on the visiphone, she eventually came face to face with Rance's hologram.

He looked exactly the same as when she had known him—perhaps younger. Before, he had seemed old enough to be her father, but now they were contemporaries. He didn't recognise her at first, until she reminded him that she had been one of his passengers on the first voyage of the *Alphard*.

"Of course!" he said. "Young Bianca!"

"Not-so-young Bianca, now, Don—I suppose it's all right

to still call you Don?—could I possibly see you for a few minutes?"

"Where are you?"

"Right here in Amadeus. I could be there in five minutes."

He glanced at his watch. "Come right over. Room 901."

She put on a white, hooded sun cape, and glanced at herself in the mirror. She looked broader than she was tall, but Rance was used to seeing Chironian women on Alcenar. She put some gold eye shadow under her brows, and vivid lipstick on her wide mouth. Then she went out to her van, and within five minutes she was in the foyer of the Ulbunali.

Some of the guests glanced at her curiously as she waddled briskly through to the elevators, but she was used to that. She rode one of the lifts to the ninth floor, and knocked on the door of room 901.

It was Rance who opened the door. As he stepped aside and waved her in, he seemed taller than she had remembered him.

"Hot out there, Bianca. Bad as Astralon in the early afternoons."

"You don't get the same range here, Don." She tossed back the hood of her cape. "Gets cool at night, but not to the point of snowing. Say, you know, you look fantastic! That green uniform picks up the colour of your eyes."

He laughed. "Let me take your cape. Ah, you've kept your muscle tone, I see."

"This light gravity *is* a temptation. But if I let myself go soft, I'd never readjust to home."

"You intend to go home, then?"

"That's why I'm here." Bianca patted a stray lock of hair into place.

Rance did not speak for a few seconds, but sat down in an armchair and waved towards another one facing it. Bianca sprang up into it, and it creaked under her weight as she sat with her round, blocky legs straight forward.

"Did you plan to go back with us?" asked Rance, and the tone of his voice made her suddenly cold.

"You have room, haven't you?" she asked.

He looked at her for a long time before he slowly shook his head. "Unfortunately, my dear Bianca, I'm leaving only two passengers this time—Ferris and Aiyar, the Earth fellows—and I'm taking on three for the return. The biologist and the historian who came out with you, and an Earth biologist who's going back with them. So I'm already overloaded."

"But Don!" She leaned forward, her eyes wide. "What'll I do? My God, it could be years before a ship comes here!"

Rance stood up. "I think we both need a drink," he said. He walked with long, easy strides across to a sideboard and took out a couple of glasses and began looking at the labels on bottles. "I'm not very well up in these Earth wines," he said. When she didn't volunteer a reply, he opened a bottle at random and began to pour. He began to speak soothingly.

"There's a second ship of ours on the way here now, I believe. It was scheduled to leave about four Terran years after the *Alphard*, so it should be here in another four."

"Will *that* have room for me? Don, it *must!*"

"There's one thing you can do. You can apply for a berth on it as soon as it gets within vortex beam range." He held a glass out to her. "Here. Drink this, girl—you look white."

"God, I *feel* white! I'm going to be stuck on this bloody planet for another sixteen years! I could die here!"

Rance glanced out of the window. "Why do you describe the planet as bloody?"

"Oh, that? Just a local expression. They say something's bloody when they want to get rid of emotional tension."

"I see. Look, I wish I could take you on board, Bianca, but we have to plan these missions a long way ahead. All I can definitely promise is to reserve a berth for you on our next voyage."

Her eyes didn't seem to focus on anything within the room. "Sixteen frigging years!"

Suddenly, she sprang from the chair more than halfway across the space between them, landing with her body leaning forward and her right hand slamming the floor. Somewhere down in the subconscious levels of her mind she may have expected the apelike violence of her movement to throw a momentary fright into him, but he gave no sign of it, except that his eyes never looked away from hers.

"It may not be that long," he said, sipping his drink. "On the way back, we'll pass the other Alcenar ship—not close, but within radio range. We'll be broadcasting a taped message to it, which it'll automatically pick up and adjust for doppler effect, then play back to the crew when they come out of hibernation. I'll include a mention of you in my report, and ask them to give you priority on their return trip. So it may be only four years.''

"Thanks," she said in a dull voice. Again, he held a glass towards her, and this time she took it and drank a little.

"Feeling better?" he asked.

"Oh, delirious. I feel like a prisoner who just might have a sixteen-year sentence reduced to four years for good behaviour.''

He rested his hand lightly on her shoulder, then went over and sat opposite her. She looked at him with slightly moist eyes. "You are taller, aren't you?" she asked irrelevantly.

He glanced down in surprise, then crossed one leg over the other. "Yes. Something new since you were in our system. A bio-engineering firm in Astralon, Zondra and Komordo, made rather a breakthrough. They rebuild limbs and muscles to take care of different gravities. Replace the long bones with vitallium, and build in electromagnetic and hydraulic muscles. Komordo's an Astralon engineer, and Zondra came from Chiron.''

"I taught a small girl on Chiron called Zondra," said Bianca thoughtfully. "Only about ten. Blonde, blue eyes, very bright.''

"Could be her. Remember, she gained eight years on you during the trip here, and, if you add the sixteen you've been here, that'd make her thirty-four.''

"And by the time I get back, she'll probably be in a geriatric hospital," said Bianca bitterly. "Forty-two even if I started now.''

Rance laughed. "I've been living with time dislocation for a long while. It has one advantage: you see changes in cultures happening at a speed that makes them real to you. Like a moving picture, where most people see stills.''

He stood up, and stroked Bianca's shoulder with surprising gentleness.

"I'll do what I can, about that other ship," he said.

"Thanks, Don," she said in a hollow voice.

He helped her on with her sun cape, and before she went out she pulled its hood well forward over her face.

She drove home and repaired the damage to her makeup, then sat in front of the visiphone alcove trying to get her thoughts into order. She had always assumed that she could have a return flight on the *Alphard* to her own system merely for the asking, and the sudden collapse of her plan was a disaster unspeakable.

She waited quite a while, until her pulse rate was fairly normal and her slow, deep breathing was even again. Then she looked up the number for the Amadeus army base.

"Could you put me through to Captain Kranzen?" she asked, when a young man with patent-leather hair and an army shirt appeared on the hologram. "It's Ms. Baru here."

"One moment, please."

She waited for a couple of minutes, and then Kranzen was there. "What may I do for you, Bianca?"

"I understand the army has a spaceship capable of interstellar flight. Is that right?"

"Where did you hear that?"

"Oh, several places. It's one of those rumours that floats about, but I've heard it so often I began to wonder whether there might be something in it."

Kranzen's replies were careful, like those of a man who is putting an interview on tape. "Well, let's say it's a possibility. We have the capacity, but as yet, we don't have the motivation. Does that answer your question?"

"Perhaps. Captain Kranzen, if you did at any time make an interstellar flight, I assume the target would be the Alpha Centauri system. Am I right?"

"That's a reasonable guess."

"Could I come to the point straight away? I came from that system, and I'd like to go back there. I assume you'd head for Alcenar. Is that right?"

He nodded almost imperceptibly. "That's a fair guess, too."

"Now, I know Alcenar. I've lived there. I could act as a very useful guide, in return for my passage there."

"Perhaps—but our ship is set up for a limited number of highly trained personnel. It carries no passengers. In fact, in your case we wouldn't have a suitable spacesuit for transfer from shuttle to ship."

"I still have a spacesuit I brought with me from Chiron."

"I see." Kranzen appeared to think for a few seconds. "What's Alcenar actually like? Similar to Earth?"

"No—different in a lot of ways. Tremendous mountains,

often in circles like the impact craters on the Moon. Alcenar was hit by a number of asteroids in relatively recent times, and the ringwalls haven't had time to erode down.''

''Do you still have asteroid impacts there?''

''Not now. Any bodies that are a threat, they simply blast into a safer orbit.'' She hesitated. ''The weather there might be a problem for your people, if they had no one with them who was used to it. Long days, hot in the middle, snowing at night.''

Kranzen nodded. ''I'll keep in touch with you, Bianca.''

She nodded. ''You mean—don't call me, I'll call you?''

He gave a frosty smile. ''Don't make it sound like that.''

She switched off. ''Bastard!'' she said to the empty room with pent-up venom.

Kranzen sat motionless for a minute, then buzzed for his aide.

''Earl,'' he said, ''get the AI7 boys to pick up Ferris. Now!''

12

RAJENDRA NARYAN'S PRIVATE airfield was a long way from the building described as his "palace." Vanmore, as he came in over the Coromandel Coast near Madras, began sending a signal on the special waveband Rajendra had told him about, and soon he established contact, not with Rajendra himself, but with one of his aides.

"We know about you, Mr. Vanmore," said the man in a precise diction. "We will meet you at the airfield and bring you straight to the Palace." Something in the way he said Palace demanded a capital letter.

The airfield was on an area of level plain inland from the Western Ghats north of Old Mysore. They were met by two of Rajendra's men, who had brought along a large electric car painted in the crimson and saffron that Nu Karnatika had adopted as its state colours.

One man drove, silent and absorbed, while the other talked, sitting beside the driver and leaning an arm on the back of the front seat, so that he could keep up that tireless flow of conversation that seems to be a specialty of many Indians.

"Our new capital is Nu Mysor," he explained. "A little northwest of Old Mysore on a large lake formed by damming the Cauvery River."

His travelogue went on like an endless tape. The road on which they were travelling ran southward, through villages that had remained the same as Indian villages had been for hundreds of years, perhaps thousands. The only new note was struck by the occasional nuclear reactor or chemical installation, huge, silvery, unreal in the distance. Here and there along the road, in ancient contrast, were "load takers," made of a horizontal slab atop two vertical ones, put in centuries ago so that a man carrying a load on his head could rest without putting his burden on the ground. Strangely, there were still some women carrying loads on their heads along the side of the road. The space age and its spinoffs had not had much influence yet on village life. There were still countless cows wandering along the roads, and pie-dogs in the villages which seemed to Vanmore exactly the same as the Australian dingo.

Rajendra's Palace, looking across a level stretch of ground and on over the lake, was a very impressive building. Its style owed something to the old Palace of Mysore, which in turn rivalled the Palace of Versailles. The traditional style had been maintained in the architecture—actually, like the old palace, a blend of Hindu and Moslem.

An immense durbar hall, like a grandstand built into the front of the palace, looked out over the great outdoor court, but their self-appointed guide led them through a huge pillared banquet hall lit by green and violet stained glass windows, and along into tiled passageways. At last, Rajendra met them in one of the small inner halls of the building, still with a ceiling two storeys high and lit by a violet and green clerestory.

"I'm extremely sorry I couldn't meet you at the airfield, but things have been happening very rapidly in the past few hours."

"Here, too?" asked Vanmore. "Kranzen and his army crowd are definitely going to make a flight to Alcenar, leaving very soon."

Rajendra looked thoughtful. "We could probably beat them for speed."

"I'm not sure of that. Kranzen says he can make the voyage in a substantially shorter time than the *Alphard*."

Rajendra looked worried. "I wonder what he means by substantially shorter?"

"Who knows? A month? A year?"

"Well, I'll show you the *Mohenjo Daro*. Not in actuality, but in a model—the real ship was naturally assembled in orbit."

He led the way into a room dominated by a large glass showcase. Inside it were the models of two spacecraft.

"The small one is the *Chandragupta*, one of our shuttles.

We included that to give scale."

"How long is the shuttle?" asked Rona.

"About sixty metres."

"Then the big ship must be enormous. Why is it black?"

"Reflects no light in space. We didn't want to advertise its existence too early. You'd see a silver ship in orbit going across the sky—no doubt you've seen many—but a black one's harder to spot."

"It's like some of your asteroid ore freighters," said Vanmore, "but on an increased scale."

"That's exactly it—built by the same people, with the same equipment. Only the propulsion units are quite different."

"Is it armed in any way?"

"Armed? This isn't the eighteenth century, dear boy. I may take a couple of pistols on board, in case of unforeseen eventualities. But that's all."

Vanmore hesitated for a long time, and Rajendra, sensing that he was struggling with some piece of data, said nothing.

"Kranzen's carrying twenty-four bombs," said Vanmore at last.

"*What?* What sort of bombs? Nuclear? Neutron?"

"I don't know, but he described them as having inconceivable power. He could have had nuclear or neutron bombs if he'd wanted, which suggests that these are something even more deadly."

"He's mad!" said Rajendra. "He's like something from the time of Attila the Hun!"

"I think you were right about your cycles. Something like that seems to come up every few centuries."

Rajendra nodded. "All we can do is get there well ahead of him and put the Alcenar people into the picture."

"How soon can you leave?"

"Couple of days."

"You still have space for us?"

"Plenty of space. I expect to bring a lot of cargo back, so we're not pushed for room." He looked from Vanmore to Rona. "Could you join us?"

"I think it's the most exciting offer anyone ever made to me," she said.

"I'll be with you," said Vanmore. "As soon as I've tied up some loose ends at the Company."

"Can you be ready in two days?"

"If you are."

Rajendra stepped forward, and they clasped hands.

"Like the old days in Northworld," he said.

"Are we doing the right thing?" asked Rona as they flew homeward.

"I don't know, honey. But when I look back, I find the only things I regret are the things I *didn't* do."

"Yes. I suppose you're right."

It was late afternoon when Vanmore swung the Skyhawk down over the lake and headed in for a landing on the Company strip. They rode up in the elevator and Rona went straight to the visiphone.

"Must see how Frank Ferris is," she said.

When Vanmore emerged from the bathroom, she was standing in the middle of the living room floor. She said nothing.

"What is it?"

"He's gone!"

"Gone? How?"

"The Bakers say two men in grey uniforms came along and said he was needed by the army to answer some questions about Alcenar. They flew off in a grey airkar—with one-way windows."

Vanmore went to the visiphone and called the army base. After much delay he got through to Captain Kranzen.

"Are you holding Frank Ferris?" he asked.

"Frank who? Oh, the fellow from the *Alphard*? Why, the last I heard he was with you."

"Was it them?" asked Rona as he rang off.

"I don't know," he admitted. He looked at his watch. "I'm going down to the office for a while."

After he had gone, Rona called Bianca. "I have some news. Can I drop over?"

"Certainly, kitten. Might cheer me up a bit."

Rona flew across in the brown airkar, which she had still kept parked on the lower flange.

"What's the matter?" she asked as she walked in to the living room of the green brick house on the Point.

"Had a rough spot, today. Saw Rance, the captain of the *Alphard*, about getting back. He can't take me."

"Why not?"

"Says he's overloaded. Might be true."

"But that doesn't seem fair."

"Huh! I don't know how I'm going to get back home, but I *must*."

"What about Quade?"

"That's what bothers me most. We've had good times together, although he's become very busy lately. I've written several letters to leave for him, but somehow I always end up tearing them up. I mean, what can you say?"

"You really want to go home very badly, don't you?"

"Look, I even phoned Kranzen this morning to see if I could hitch a ride on his ship, in return for acting as a guide when he got to Alcenar."

"But you're not supposed to know about his ship, are you?"

"I know. I don't doubt he's figured that out."

"Listen, Bianca, Max took me over to Nu Karnatika today to see Rajendra Naryan. He showed us a model of his ship. He's got plenty of room in it, because he's a lot of space to bring stuff back from Alcenar. We may be flying on it."

"Yes. Would there be a possibility . . . ?"

"I think there would. On the basis of you as a guide."

At that moment, a shadow flicked across the window.

"What was that?" Bianca moved quickly to the window. "Grey airkar. Isn't that like the one that followed you?"

"And the one that picked up Frank Ferris this morning."

"What?"

"I left him with some relatives of his on a farm out in the irri area, and two characters in a grey airkar took him in to answer questions about Alcenar."

"Frankly, he didn't seem to me to know much about it."

Two large men in grey came to the outside of the sliding glass door and rang. Bianca slid the door open.

"Yes?"

One of the men flashed a badge briefly. "AI7," he said, and stepped in. He had a thin, sharp nose and a straight slit of a mouth.

"Ms. Baru?" he asked, and when she assented he turned to Rona. "And you'd be Ms. Rona Gale? I'm afraid we're going to have to ask you both to come to our headquarters."

"And if it isn't convenient?" asked Rona.

"It's convenient for headquarters. That's all that concerns us."

The second man had moved across the room and stood near

Bianca. He had a sullen expression emphasised by a bulbous lower lip.

"But I don't see how I could help you, whatever you're inquiring about," said Rona.

The man with the sharp nose took a pair of handcuffs from a back pocket of his uniform, and held them up. "Now, I take it you're not going to force us to use things like these?"

"No," said Rona. She looked across the room. The man with the bulbous lip was standing with his feet apart, his right hand resting on the butt of a pistol in a small scabbard. Bianca, looking straight at Rona, flexed the fingers of her right hand and moved it behind her, feeling the edge of a small, heavy table.

"All right," said Rona. "But we'd better take the sapphire with us."

"What sapphire?" asked the first man.

"A big lump of sapphire Frank Ferris asked us to mind for him. I wouldn't want to leave it in an empty house."

"Where is it?"

Rona let her eyes stray to the top of a high bookshelf, and immediately the man moved a chair across to the shelves. He stood up on it, looking on top of the shelving, and at that instant Bianca acted.

She made no move at first towards the man standing right beside her. Again, Rona had the impression of watching a trick film. The table, turned over with its legs upward, spun across the room and struck the man standing on the chair, so that he was thrown off into the corner of the room, striking the wall and sliding down.

The second man drew his pistol and whirled, but Bianca had been waiting for him. She gripped his wrist with her right hand and slammed his forearm down over the edge of a sideboard. He screamed harshly, and the pistol dropped out of his hand. Bianca picked it up in her left hand.

The man reeled away towards the middle of the room, his right arm swinging as if an extra joint had been formed between wrist and elbow.

The sharp-nosed man was beginning to stir, and Rona moved towards him, picking up the chair he had used to stand on. As his eyes opened she held the chair above her head. But at that moment Bianca moved past her. The man made a sudden effort to get to his feet, but Bianca slapped him openhanded across the side of the face with a sound like a pistol shot. The slap shook him, but didn't immobilise him, so she brought her clenched fist back. He dropped back into the corner.

Rona picked up the handcuffs. "He was going to put these on me," she said. They were designed to fit a variety of wrist sizes. She snapped one of them over the sharp-nosed man's right wrist, and the other over his left ankle.

The man with the broken forearm was sitting on the sofa, white-faced. He, too, had a pair of handcuffs in a back pocket, and Rona handcuffed him in the same way as the other man, although she used his left wrist. His right arm was useless, in any case.

"What happens now?" she asked, looking at Bianca.

"They'll have more people here as soon as they realise these two are not showing up. And we can't get away with this kind of thing a second time."

"I'd better call Max," said Rona.

She went to the visiphone, while Bianca began taking objects from the pockets of the two AI7 men.

"Max," she said, as he appeared on the hologram, "two men who said they were from AI7 tried to pick up Bianca and me at her place."

"What happened?"

She told him. He thought for a moment, a deep vertical furrow between his brows.

"We'd better take Rajendra Naryan up on his offer. Now. Can you be ready to leave in a few minutes?"

"Yes—but can we take Bianca?"

He hesitated, then nodded. "Tell her to get her things together. I'll meet you at the penthouse, then we can pick her up."

"Where will we go then?"

"I'm just going to arrange that now. Not sure, yet."

He rang off. When Rona went back into the living room she found that Bianca had put strips of adhesive plaster over the lips of the two men. She had taken their pistols, small two-way radios, and the keys of their handcuffs.

"Max thinks he can get us out of here. He's picking me up at the penthouse, then coming on here for you. You'd better write that letter to Quade."

Vanmore sat for a while in front of the inter-office VDT, then

punched out the code for the movements of the Company's
ore shuttles. One of them was now unloading at Island
Lagoon, and would be ready to lift off in a couple of hours to
rendezvous with another ore freighter from the asteroid belt.

Island Lagoon was a thousand kilometres away. He could
phone them to delay the takeoff of the shuttle, but the army
could find out about the call and intercept him on his arrival.

He thought of contacting Quade Gannon, then decided to
do it later by radio.

On the way out, he said to Elsa Perry, "I'll be out for a
while, Elsa."

The understatement of the century, he thought as he rode
down in the elevator.

He reached ground level, and walked through to the loading
bay where the Company's airvan came in for merchandise to
be delivered to areas at a moderate distance. He borrowed a
medium-sized van, filled it with fuel, and flew it up to the top
landing flange on the tower. Rona's brown airkar was already
there—she had evidently thought there was little point now in
hiding it on the lower flange.

"Packing didn't take long," she said. "I still have most of
my holiday things packed."

"You may need something warm where we're going," he
said.

"Have to worry about that when I get there."

He gathered his own gear together, looked briefly around
the penthouse, then carried the bags out to the airvan. Before
he took off, he looked around the sky, but saw nothing suspicious.

He took the van down towards the Point, and landed just
outside Bianca's front door. She brought out a number of
bags, then a bulky object in a plastic bag.

"What's that?" asked Vanmore.

"My spacesuit. I'd never get one to fit here."

She tossed something into the corner of the van.

"What's that?"

"Handcuff keys belonging to the boys inside, and their
radios. I took the batteries out in case there's an automatic
location trace."

"Right. Let's go."

Vanmore headed eastward at first, until he was out of sight
of Amadeus City, then swung southeast, passing close to

Mount Conner. He kept on a southeasterly course over the eastern end of the Musgrave Range, and on down over the margin of the Victoria Desert.

"I'll contact Rajendra once we're in space," said Vanmore.

"I still don't see why you need the space shuttle to get to Nu Karnatika," said Rona.

"We're not going to Nu Karnatika. We're going direct to the *Mohenjo Daro*."

When they came within sight of Island Lagoon, the lime and red Company shuttle was still there, with its hatch open and a mobile crane standing over it like a giant insect, lifting boxed packages of ore into a waiting truck. Vanmore flew the airvan around the perimeter of the area, but could see no sign of AI7 or any other suspicious intrusion.

Island Lagoon was a vast area of white, hard salt, with three islands scattered across its expanse, and some water concentrated in a small part of it which had been artificially deepened to drain the rare rainfall off the salt, leaving a natural landing field. Vanmore landed the airvan close to the terminal building, which was painted lime and red like the shuttle.

"Wait here," he said to the two women, and walked to the building, which was surmounted by a radome.

An iron stairway led to an upper floor which evidently served as a control tower and radio room. A man met Vanmore near the head of the stair.

"Where's Stan Cook?" Vanmore asked. He had been introduced to Cook a few days ago by hologram, and he was the only person at Island Lagoon he knew.

"In here," called a voice from an enclosed office at one side of the room, and Vanmore went to the door of it. A tanned, balding man whom he immediately recognised as Cook rose from behind a desk.

"Mr. Vanmore. This is unexpected." He extended his hand, and Vanmore shook it.

"I've been in touch with Rajendra Naryan, and I want to inspect one of his spacecraft. The simplest way to do it was by the Company shuttle."

"That's right. It's going up in half an hour or so."

"Do you know about this new ship of theirs?"

"Heard rumours. Believe it's bigger than anything they have at the moment."

"So they tell me. Anyway, I know where the coordinates are. I can get the shuttle pilot to drop me off at the ship, then go back to the ore freighter he was going to unload."

"How do you get back?"

"Rajendra Naryan was going to arrange that."

Cook took Vanmore out and introduced him to the pilot of the shuttle and his co-pilot.

"By the way," Max said to the pilot, "you're running empty on the way up, of course?"

"That's right."

"Just as well. I have two women with me, and one of them will be going down to Nu Karnatika later—she has quite a lot of luggage."

"No problem. If it'll fit in your van, it'll fit in the shuttle easily."

As he walked back to the airvan, Vanmore looked towards the northwest. There was no sign of any pursuit, although the hot, shimmering air could have hidden a machine at a distance of only a few kilometres. Then it occurred to him that the threat might not necessarily come from the northwest. The army had bases all over Australia, all linked by radio. Trouble could strike at him from almost any direction.

He drove the van over alongside the shuttle. The operator of the mobile crane gave him a flexible metal net, which he spread on the ground. He put all their luggage on the net, then lifted the corners and fitted their rings over the crane hook as the crane driver brought it down within his reach. A few seconds later, the baggage was disappearing into the hatch of the shuttle.

Within minutes, they were strapping themselves into the acceleration seats, and the oxyhydrogen jets of the shuttle were warming up.

The shuttle was able to take off under its own power, like an ordinary aircraft. Vanmore was sitting near one of the small, thick ports, and he was able to look out as the machine raced across the salt with ferocious acceleration. Just as it nosed upward and the ground sharply away, he saw a fast-flying, dull-green helicopter coming in towards the terminal building.

For both Vanmore and Rona, it was their first experience in spaceflight, and they found it hard to repress their excitement. For Bianca, of course, this liftoff was relatively mild—she had already blasted off from Alcenar and against the appalling gravity of Chiron.

"Where is this ship?" the pilot asked Vanmore, as they

cleared the thin upper atmosphere.

"In a synchronous orbit above the equator on meridian 80 east."

"Right," he said. "No problem."

"Will it take much extra fuel?" asked Rona.

"No," said the pilot. "Most of our fuel goes in take-off and landing. Once out in space, we use very little." He looked curiously at Bianca. "By the way, we'll have to wear spacesuits to transfer to the other ship—you realise that?"

"Yes, Stan Cook told us there was a selection on board."

"I brought my own," said Bianca. "It's in the hatch. Can we get in there from inside the ship?"

"Yes. There's an airlock back here. One of us can put a suit on and go back and get yours."

When they eventually came near the *Mohenjo Daro*, they picked it up on their radar before they could see it visually. The dead black of its surface hid it effectively until they were close enough to see its shape outlined by eclipsed stars.

"Damn funny colour for a spacecraft," said the pilot. "You could easily fly into it."

Closer up, they could see that the ship was enormous. They put on spacesuits which the pilot selected for Max and Rona, Bianca using her own suit, and they carefully checked them for pressure.

The pilot got in touch with the big ship by radio. "Permission requested for three passengers to come aboard—Max Vanmore and two companions. Can you check with Rajendra Naryan?"

"That may take a few minutes," said the man in the *Mohenjo Daro*. "We'll call you back."

While they waited, Vanmore said thoughtfully, "I'm surprised we didn't get some contact from the army."

"Why?" asked Rona.

"I saw one of their helicopters landing at Island Lagoon just as we lifted off. Perhaps they figured we'd have to come back in the shuttle, anyway. Or—there's another possibility —Kranzen may have decided to leave for Alcenar already!"

13

VANMORE CAME OUT of hibernation to find Rajendra Naryan looking down at him.

"Where are we?" he asked.

"We made it. We're on the outskirts of the Alpha Centauri system. Elapsed time for the voyage, 2830 Earth days—I think that's about ninety days shorter then the *Alphard*'s time."

"All right for me to get up?"

"Yes, but be careful. There's no gravity here." Rajendra reached over and removed a couple of straps that held Vanmore to his bunk.

"You seem to have adjusted well enough."

"Ah, I've been out of hibernation for a few days. You'll feel better when you've had some food—but not too much at first."

Vanmore carefully sat up, holding the edge of the bunk. "How many of us are awake?"

"You're the fourth—the first one not part of the crew."

Rajendra led him into the control room, and showed him the main vision screen.

"As you see, the primary sun looks like ours, even to the greenish corona. There's the red component over there. We came in away above the ecliptic, to avoid any of the meteors or other debris that might be circling around. Of course, there's no real 'up' or 'down' here, but you can think of this as looking down on a plan view of the system from above."

135

"Where are the planets?"

"I'll show you. There's a fixed picture of what you've just been looking at." Rajendra pressed some keys. "Now, there's a similar picture taken about an hour ago, when the ship was about a hundred thousand kilometres back along its course. Now—" He began adjusting some dials. "I superimpose one image on the other, exactly, so that the background starfields match. Then I alternate them—you see?—so everything that appears to move backwards and forwards is within this system."

"I see," said Vanmore.

"Now, the next step is to use a negative of one image to cancel the other—like this—and you're left with a picture of the Alpha Centauri system against a black background. I'd say that would be Alcenar there. Three moons, you see?"

"What are all these small points of light around here?"

"Yes, we'll have to be careful of those. This system has an inner and an outer asteroid belt. One between Alcenar and the sun, one outside its orbit."

"I don't suppose there's any way of telling whether Kranzen and his team arrived ahead of us?"

"Not from here. Look at the size of the image of a planet. Now imagine looking for the image of a spacecraft."

"Can we get the two women out of hibernation?"

"If you wish, Max. But it's going to take us days to get down in close orbit around the planet. Can't rush it. We don't know where their meteor swarms are."

"Better let the girls sleep for a while, I suppose. Say, isn't there a third sun in this system?"

"Proxima? Yes, but it's about 9000 astronomical units out, and only radiates about seven ten thousandths of the light of the sun. Hard to find it against the background."

Vanmore continued to look at the screen. He knew he wouldn't be able to see Kranzen's ship, even if it were somewhere there—but something impelled him to look.

By now, the *Endeavour II* was already in a wide orbit about Alcenar, fifty thousand kilometres out and spiralling inward. Already, it was well within the orbits of the three moons, which looked like captured asteroids, pockmarked with craters to an even greater degree then Earth's Moon.

Alcenar itself Kranzen had been led to look upon as a twin

to the Earth. Seen this closely, however, it looked shockingly alien. It was about the size of the Earth, or a little larger, but its surface had been scarred by appalling meteor impacts, some of them leaving craters hundreds of kilometres in diameter. Its landscapes looked raw and young, with snarling peaks that had not had time to erode.

Once, while he was watching it, a brilliant point of green light shone three times from a mountain top in the southern hemisphere, about twenty or twenty-five degrees south of the equator. Three short flashes, at intervals of about one second. Seen from fifty thousand kilometres, the light must have had an incredible power—unless it were a tightly focused laser deliberately directed at the ship.

Either way, it was disturbing. If it had been a focused laser, that meant that the people on the planet had some way of detecting the precise location of his ship at an immense distance.

Kranzen had just settled down for his rest period when the alarm bell sounded, and he sat up irritably.

"Yes?" he said, looking towards the voice-activated mike. Barton's face appeared on the screen.

"Something on our forward screen, Chief. Think you'd better see it."

"Right." Within seconds, Kranzen was down the short passageway and into the control room. "What is it?"

Barton indicated the forward screen, with its diamond dusting of stars cut off along one side by the magnified crescent of the planet.

"I don't see it," said Kranzen. "Give me a comparator flash."

"Right. Hundred second interval to now."

The screen flickered for a moment, then steadied as Barton adjusted the projection so that the two images coincided exactly, one showing space as it was now, the other a hundred seconds earlier. Kranzen at once picked out the tiny point of light that moved against the background, flicking back and forth over a short distance.

"Sure the interval's only a hundred seconds?" snapped Kranzen.

"Check."

"Then the thing's moving damn fast."

"I know, Chief. What d'we do?"

"Get the higher magnification on it. High as you can go."

The stars on the screen seemed to move apart, as if the ship had leaped forward at an impossible speed towards the centre of the field of view. The moving point of light grew, central on the screen, but no detail showed up.

"Carrying its own light," said Barton. "That's not just reflected light."

Kranzen grunted. "Got it on radar?"

"Yes. Just the blip. Oh, here's something: we've got a temperature reading. The thing's cold. Very cold. Only a few degrees above zero K."

"Distance?"

"Two hundred fifty thousand metres. Closing more slowly, as if it's beginning to match speeds with us."

"I don't like it. Get the laser guns ready."

"Right."

"Don't do anything else, yet. Wait for them to make the next move."

"Something coming over the radio," said Jones. "On several different wave bands. Just a continuous hum, like a carrier wave."

"Directional fix?"

"Yes. It's from that thing." Jones nodded at the vision screen. "I think it's being beamed at us. The sound wavered at first, as if it were scanning near us. Then it seemed to lock on."

Abruptly, the sound from the loud speaker cut off, and a voice came clearly, although with a strange accent.

"This is a relay from Astralon Control. Would you please identify yourself?" The message was repeated three times. Then followed a series of wavelengths, in metres, on which a reply could be made. After a pause, the same frequencies were repeated in kilocycles.

"Do we answer?" asked Barton.

Kranzen thought for a moment, rubbing his chin with his hand. "No need to rush it just yet. How far away is the thing now?"

"Only 10,000 metres—and it's matched our speed and direction, exactly."

"Dimensions?"

"Quite small. Too small to hold a man. Can't get any shape to it, yet, but its maximum measurement would be less than a metre."

Somewhere back in the ship came a sharp report, like a rifle shot, and following it came the sound of the alarm siren that signalled an air pressure drop. The sound dwindled as airtight bulkheads closed automatically between the source of the trouble and the control room.

"Where was it?" shouted Kranzen.

Chung snapped switches on one of the control panels. A red light shone. "Leak behind the right airlock. Slight loss of pressure—not much. Must have been a small meteorite."

"Get a suit on and see what damage it did. You too, Jones."

The two men climbed into their suits and fitted on their bubble helmets, checking the suits for pressure. Chung took a final look at the panel where the red light was showing.

"That's odd." His voice came metallically through the helmet microphone and external speaker. "The pressure in there is holding. It dropped for the first half minute or so, then stayed at the same level. Someone in there must have plugged the leak."

"There's no one in there," said Kranzen decisively.

Chung looked as if he were going to argue. Then he shrugged his shoulders and went off with Jones towards the sealed-off zone.

When they opened the bulkhead, the pressure in the affected section had already been brought to normal by automatic compensating mechanism, so there was no rush of air in or out. Nevertheless, they closed the bulkhead again behind them. Jones switched all the lights on, and they stood looking about the room.

"If a meteor came in, it must have gone out somewhere," said Jones.

"I haven't figured where it came in, yet." Chung began to move along the outer wall, which was curved with the sweep of the hull. "Aha!" he said suddenly.

Jones went across beside him, and they stood looking at the thing on the wall. It was within easy reach, a disc of dark metal, about four centimetres in diameter. It was made of a number of overlapping segments of thin metal, radiating out from a central boss. They were like the blades of an iris-type shutter in a camera, except that, instead of swinging in and out about a central opening, they were pivoted at the inner ends.

"What is it?" asked Jones.

"Don't know. But I think it's plugging the leak. Just a minute." Chung took a thin screwdriver from a set of tools at his belt, and eased the edge of one of the metal blades away from the wall. There seemed to be some rubbery substance on the inner side of it, towards the wall, and as he forced it back there was a fierce shriek of air blasting through to the external vacuum. Chung withdrew the screwdriver and the rush of air stopped, as the pressure again forced the segmented disc flat against the wall.

"But who put it there?" asked Jones.

"Yes, who?" Chung looked around the room. "Anybody there?" he called. His voice echoed emptily around the metal walls. They exchanged glances, doubt and a hint of fear in their eyes.

"Another thing," said Jones. "Where did he get it?"

"Huh?"

"We use much bigger patches. Nothing like that."

"I'm going to have a look at the hole," said Chung. With the screwdriver he forced the disc away from the hole, allowing air to scream out for perhaps ten seconds before he replaced it. He turned to Jones, his forehead corrugated.

"It's nothing like a meteor hole. It's a perfectly round hole, as if it's been drilled. Or burned—the edges of the metal are blue. There's a boss on the other side of this thing that centres it in the hole. It looks as if it were made for just this size of hole."

Jones looked around. "The bulkheads closed automatically as soon as the pressure began to fall. So whoever made the hole must still be in here."

"How do you know it was made from the inside?"

"How else did he get that thing in place?"

"That's right. But why?"

Jones spread his hands. Systematically, they began to search.

The zone was D-shaped, the curved wall following the hull, the straight one running across the middle of the ship, deviating to avoid the central shaft. The place was actually an emergency workshop, with a couple of lathes, a milling machine, grinders, and more sophisticated equipment based on the use of lasers. Not a very large space, but there were plenty of places for a person to hide.

"What was that?" asked Jones sharply.

"What?"

"Just the movement of a small shadow—near one of the lights."

They went across in the direction he indicated, but a close search revealed nothing. Jones was unable to explain what he had seen. Chung reached the conclusion that he must have imagined it, and for a while there was an irritable quietness between them.

The disc was holding the pressure satisfactorily, so they decided to return to the control room. Jones operated the control that opened the bulkhead, and as the door slid open he turned to switch off the lights. At that moment, he was startled by a sharp cry from Chung.

"Look there!"

Jones reached Chung's side as he pointed down the short corridor leading to the metal stairway, but he saw nothing suspicious. "What was it you saw?"

"Thing like an insect. Buzzed past me and along the corridor, then up the stairwell."

"An *insect*? How the hell could an insect get in here?"

"Eh? Look, it was a thing like a small dragonfly. Flying very fast."

Jones looked at him with an expression of disbelief that gradually faded, leaving his eyes dark and void.

"That could fit in with the shadow I saw," he said.

"Sorry," said Chung awkwardly. "I thought you'd imagined it at the time."

"What'll we do about it? If we tell Kranzen he'll think we're nuts."

"Well, I saw it, and you saw its shadow. Let's see if we can find where it went."

But a quick look around the stairwell showed nothing. The other bulkheads had been opened by now, and the insect—or whatever it was—could have travelled anywhere in the ship.

"We'd better tell him," said Jones. "This could be connected with the thing patching the hole in the hull."

Kranzen listened to them with his face devoid of expression. "Show me," he said, and after a glance at the panel showing air pressures he led the way to the punctured zone.

He stood looking at the disc for a long time. "Get one of our patches," he said. When he had it, he borrowed Chung's screwdriver and prised off the disc. He took a brief look at the clean, circular hole, then slapped the standard patch on to it.

"The hole's about two and a half centimetres in diameter, and these blades spread out to about four." He turned the swivelling, overlapping blades so that they formed a smaller circle, no larger than the boss, which apparently fitted the hole. This made the device small enough to have been forced through the hull from outside, if it could have been pushed in against the pressure of air rushing out to the vacuum.

"The hole was cut through the hull from the outside," said Kranzen. "You can tell by the arras of molten metal left around the inner edge." He looked at the others. "I think what happened was this. Something bored a hole in the hull, came inside, then plugged the hole with a disc specially made for it. Obviously, whoever planned it didn't want us to lose too much air."

"Then they're probably friendly," said Jones.

"That doesn't follow at all," objected Kranzen. "They might have thought we wouldn't notice a small loss of air, so we might never know this had happened. Meanwhile, they've got something loose in our ship—the thing you thought was an insect."

"It was very small," said Chung.

"That means nothing. It could relay data outside—probably to that probe that's matched speed with us."

"What d'we do?" asked Jones.

"We find it. As soon as someone sights it, we seal off the section where it is, then concentrate our search there." Back in the control room, he asked Barton, "What's the distance of that probe?"

"Holding steady at 10,000 metres."

"I want a closer look at it. Send out one of our survey probes."

"Right." Barton turned to a control panel with a number of small visual display screens above it, and punched a number of keys. "Probe away," he called. "Locking on target. Locked."

As the *Mohenjo Daro* drew steadily closer to the planet, it seemed to the people aboard that Alcenar took on a more and more sinister appearance. The vast, broken ringwalls stood as monuments to unthinkable cataclysms of the past, and to judge from the jaggedness of some of the peaks, not so very distant a past.

Its proportion of land and sea was not very different from Earth's, but the distribution was quite dissimilar. There was no polar continent at either pole—only what may have been a pair of huge ice rafts. The land was mainly concentrated around the areas which on Earth would have included the tropic and temperate zones. There were many land masses—no single area of the size of Asia or even Africa, but more than a dozen as large as Australia or Brazil, and countless smaller fragments.

While several people on the ship were watching the mottled surface of the planet, a brilliant green light flashed three times in the southern hemisphere. Its intensity suggested a laser beam directed towards them.

A minute or two later, a blue light shone above the radio board. The radio man twiddled some dials, then turned to Rajendra. "There's a tight beam signal coming through from *Endeavour II*."

"Put it through the speaker," said Rajendra.

A sustained hum came from the speaker for perhaps half a minute. Then it suddenly cut off. The voice of Captain Kranzen came through clearly.

"Come in, *Mohenjo Daro*. This is Kranzen of the *Endeavour*."

"I didn't know he knew the name of our ship," mused Rajendra. He leaned forward and pressed the call button.

"Rajendra," he said curtly.

"Did you see three green flashes of light from down on the planet?"

"We did."

"We saw the same thing earlier. Since then, there's a probe been shadowing us about 10,000 metres out. We sent two of ours to have a look at it, but they both malfunctioned when they got close to it. The probe identified itself as a relay to Astralon Control, whatever that is."

"Did you reply to it?"

"No."

"Why not?"

Kranzen ignored the question as if the answer were self-evident. "Some time ago, something penetrated our hull. Neat hole, about 25 millimetres diameter. Something came in, sealed the hole, and is loose inside our ship.''

"I suggest you contact their probe," said Rajendra. "It looks as if they might have a technical edge on all of us."

"That would give them the initiative," said Kranzen.

"If they contact me, I'm going to answer them," said Rajendra.

"I think we'd better discuss this fully before we do anything as rash as that," said Kranzen.

"Has it occurred to you," said Rajendra, "that they're probably listening in to every word we say?"

Apparently this thought had not entered Kranzen's head, because his only response was a prolonged silence. Vanmore moved alongside Rajendra.

"Raj, have you a shuttle that could take me over to the *Endeavour*?"

"Yes, but why?"

"I'd like to talk to Kranzen, not over the radio. I think his whole approach to this thing is wrong. You're carrying out a trade mission. You've brought along billions of seeds of Earth plants. I doubt if he's brought anything at all to exchange. He used to talk about 'showing the flag,' and he's taken along an arsenal of bombs."

"Do you feel you could talk sense into him?"

"Frankly—no. But I have to try. Otherwise, you might finish up with a long-range war that could set the pattern of human development for the next thousand years. We've had dark ages before. We don't want another."

"I think you're doing a risky thing."

"If there's one chance in a hundred that it comes off, it's worth it."

"But what are you going to say to him?"

"I'm not sure—yet."

When Kranzen opened the channel again, Rajendra said, "Captain Kranzen, I have someone here who'd like to talk to you. Max Vanmore." He stepped aside, and waved graciously to the mike.

"Captain Kranzen? It's Max Vanmore here."

"What the devil are you doing there? Never mind—what did you want to say?"

"I think we should have some kind of conference about our methods of contacting these people."

"That's possible."

"We'd all agree that radio is the wrong medium. Anyone could listen in."

"So?"

"They tell me our ships are only 35,000 metres apart. As long as we maintain position with each other, I could go across there in our shuttle. Would you be agreeable to that?"

"Well, we might as well pool the data we have on these people."

"Right. I'll come across to you within the next half hour."

As the channel closed, Vanmore looked around. Rona was standing behind him, her face white.

"I think you're mad," she said. "You can't trust him. But I want to go with you."

He held her tightly. "You can't do that, honey. But wait here for me. I'd feel better knowing you were safe, than if we were both running a risk."

"I think he's right," said Rajendra with surprising gentleness. He took Rona aside, and Vanmore didn't hear what he said to her. But after a minute or so she seemed calmer.

The shuttle was quite small. It was flown by a young man called Das. While he and Vanmore were putting on their spacesuits, Bianca Baru appeared.

"I just heard what you're doing," she said to Vanmore. "I'm coming with you."

"Sorry, Bianca. I've just knocked Rona back."

"So she told me. But with me, it's different. I *know* this planet. I've lived on it. I know the people. And I know what kind of an idiot Kranzen's going to look when he tries to throw his weight about with them."

"I don't think you'll convince him with that kind of reasoning." Vanmore gestured with an outward sweep of his arm. "Anyway, you'll have to get Rajendra's OK to come with us."

"I've got it. He's agreeable."

Vanmore shrugged, and Bianca padded off. She returned in a couple of minutes with her strange, drum-like spacesuit, with its assymetrical arms and short, concertina-like legs. Without a word, Vanmore and Das helped her into it—an easy enough task in the ship's light gravity—and fitted on the domed, transparent inner helmet.

They checked their suit radios, and tested the suits for pressure. Then Das led the way through an internal airlock into the shuttle bay. The shuttle looked like a thickened version of an oldtime fighter aircraft of the late twentieth century. Just before he stepped aboard, Vanmore glanced up at the window of the observation room, and saw a number of people standing there. One light-coloured face among the dark ones— Rona. She gave him a tense little wave. He waved back, smiling broadly so that she could see the smile through his helmet visor, then followed the other two into the shuttle.

It was built to hold only six people, with three pairs of seats. Space was limited inside—there was no aisle, for instance, and you reached some seats by folding the backs of others down. Das did this to climb in to the lefthand front seat, and indicated they take the two behind him. Bianca moved across to the far side, on the right, and Vanmore climbed in next to her. She had difficulty bending her legs forward sufficiently to sit.

"In our spacecraft we stand," she said through her radio. "On Chiron we stand in all our vehicles."

"The bottom part of the seat comes out," said Das. He showed her how to release it. "Now, stand there and put the belt around you. Right?"

"Right. What do I do with this seat? We don't want it drifting loose."

Das took it and secured it by the belt on the seat next to him. Vanmore felt a little irritated that both of these people obviously knew more about spaceflight than he did.

After an elaborate check of his instruments, Das opened the radio channel to the ship's. "All clear for takeoff."

"Right," came a voice, "opening the hatch."

The large door of the shuttle bay swung out and up, showing a spangling of stars and one of Alcenar's corroded-looking moons in a ragged crescent phase. Das used the shuttle's nitrogen-operated positioning jets to send it gently out of the bay and turn it, so that its main blast would not strike the *Mohenjo Daro*. He made another call on his radio.

"Will you patch me through to the *Endeavour*?"

"Will do. We'll monitor, OK? Coming through—now."

Das waited a few seconds. "Shuttle to *Endeavour II*. Can you hear me?"

"We read you, shuttle. We'll give you a beam of modulated light for guidance."

"Do you need that, Das?" cut in the voice of the *Mohenjo Daro*'s operator.

"Not really. I'll move across and get them between me and the planet. Then I can zero in on them visually without any signals."

"Did you get that, *Endeavour*?"

"As you wish."

Das began to move into the black abyss. The planet, in the crescent phase from their position, like its moons, looked a very long way away. Soon, so did the *Mohenjo Daro*. Used to either the ground under his feet or clean blue air around him, Vanmore felt his confidence waning slightly. In this immensity of stars and filmy, far-off gases in the limitless blackness, he felt crushingly unimportant.

As Kranzen was standing behind the *Endeavour*'s radio board, Barton came rushing in.

"Chief! We've found it!"

Kranzen turned. "The 'bug'?"

"Chung picked it up on one of the monitors—in the pump room. We've got it sealed off. Do you want to see a replay?"

"Yes." Kranzen strode ahead of him. Chung, still in front of the monitor complex of small video screens, pressed a number of keys, and pointed.

"I've slowed it to one eighth speed," he said. "There!"

The screen showed a distorted, fish-eye view of a room with a number of large pumps and a maze of differently coloured pipes. Something like a small dragonfly skimmed across the field of view, hovered quite motionless, turned slowly, then darted off in a different direction.

"Can you get a bigger magnification?"

Chung replayed a scene, stopping the motion at a few points, then increased the magnification until the somewhat blurred image of the thing filled the screen. Enlarged, it looked less like an insect and more like a tiny helicopter, with transparent wings blurred by such rapid movement that they couldn't see exactly how they worked. They did not rotate, but seemed to oscillate like the wings of a hovering hummingbird, although there were four of them.

As the thing turned, it showed an unbelievable complexity. There were hooded lenses in front of it, and behind—the tail of the dragonfly—something that looked like a minute laser tube, together with some hair-thin antennae of unknown purpose.

"Sophisticated," said Kranzen grudgingly.

"Will we try to get it without destroying it?"

"Could be dangerous. If there's the least threat, destroy it."

Barton, Chung, and Jones, armed with laser pistols, carefully entered the pump room, while Kranzen watched on the monitor. Barton was carrying a mobile TV transmitter, and when he switched it on Kranzen put its image on to another screen. The pump room seemed to lurch and sway as Burton moved around, the camera apparently slung against his chest.

Once or twice, Kranzen sighted the metal insect. It darted about in a complex pattern in the air, changing direction with bewildering speed. Barton and the others tried shooting at it as it turned, but with no result apart from blistering the paint on the walls. Kranzen hoped they wouldn't step up the power of their lasers.

Suddenly he sprang to the public address microphone.

"Stop shooting! Some fool's hit a water pipe."

"We'll turn it off," came Barton's voice.

"Hold it!" Kranzen's voice was ragged. "That pipe's violet! That's the supply of coolant to one of the reactors! Shut it down! And open the bulkheads."

"But if that thing gets out—"

"To hell with it. This is top priority. The reactor."

Minutes later, Kranzen had cut in the emergency flow of water to the reactor. Fortunately, there was a large head of water in reserve at all times to guard against such emergencies, but his forehead was glistening with sweat.

The sound of firing and the shouting of voices came from somewhere further back in the ship. Kranzen began running, ice in the pit of his stomach.

He ran through two open bulkheads.

"Hold your fire!" he shouted. "Through there are the bomb silos!"

In the shuttle, the three occupants watched the slowly growing speck of the *Endeavour II*, black against the bright crescent of the planet, except where the sun silvered one edge of it.

"How far are we?" asked Vanmore.

"Difficult to estimate, because I don't know the dimensions of their ship," said Das. "I don't want to use a radar bounce, because my signal would go on down to the planet—and that might be unwise." He thought for a while. "Would you say their ship is as big as the *Mohenjo Daro*?"

"Probably not. Since it started later than us and got here before us, it's probably built mainly for speed."

"If it's half as long, I'd say we were still 8000 or 10,000 metres out."

"Notice that bright wedge of cloud showing along the edge of the planet," said Vanmore thoughtfully. "There's a sharp point along the line of the equator, pointing around towards the dark side."

"Except the dark side isn't really dark," said Bianca. "It's red and black, blotchy. That's the light of the other sun. The black is probably ocean and forest, which doesn't reflect the red—"

All three of them shouted at once, as a terrible light flooded in through the forward windows. They automatically closed their eyes, and the ferocious light beat redly through their eyelids, so that they had to raise their hands as a shield. They could feel heat—radiant heat.

"My God," screamed Bianca, in a voice shaken ragged. "What is it? Something's gone nova!"

"It couldn't," said Vanmore. Still shielding his face with his hands, he opened his eyes slightly to look down at the floor, which should have been in near darkness. Every detail—matting, struts, rivets—everything was lit brilliantly by reflected light from the roof of the cabin.

"It's the *Endeavour*!" shouted Das. "The bastards must have blown it up! But how? From this distance?"

"Have you got some kind of sun shield?" asked Vanmore.

"Yes." Groping, head down against the glare, Das felt above the forward window and pulled down an amber-coloured sheet of plastic. It made little difference, and he substituted a deep ruby screen, then another of dark cobalt blue. Finally, he used all three.

The speck that had been the *Endeavour II* had been replaced by a swelling fireball so enormous that it already hid the crescent of the planet beyond. It was losing some of its blinding brilliance as it expanded, dimming and reddening at its edges, and within it were dark, jagged little shapes of outward-whirling debris.

"Do we head back to the *Mohenjo*?" asked Das uncertainly.

"No!" Vanmore's reply was emphatic. "We could lead them back to it, and they might give it what they gave the *Endeavour*."

"Some of those pieces might hit us," said Bianca. "Look! They're spinning like boomerangs."

"Das," said Vanmore. "I have an idea. Put all the lights out on this shuttle—turn *everything* off. Then use your positioning jets to spin us."

"Why?"

"The people down on the planet are probably looking this way. If we're showing no lights or radio output, and spinning slowly, we'll look just like some of those pieces of debris from the exploded ship. They're not going to watch for long. They'll assume there's nothing left around here but blown-apart fragments of hull."

Das fired the forward nitrogen jets to the right, and the tail set to the left, and the shuttle began to turn at a slowly increasing speed. "How fast do you think? About one turn every two or three seconds?"

"Should do it. Most of the pieces are spinning faster than that, but they vary."

When the shuttle was revolving like a grotesque merry-go-round, Das shut off the nitrogen jets, and snapped off switches, the last one putting out the lights of the instrument panel. The glare of the expanding fireball was far less brilliant now, and he was able to dispense with the coloured filters on the window. In any case, the glare of light was moving around them, now, actually taking about five seconds to complete its full circuit, passing down the righthand ports, then coming from behind, then up the left side and across the front again.

"Better keep our suits on until we're through the site of the explosion and out the other side," said Vanmore. "We might be hit by something."——————

"We're not going *through* it?" Bianca's voice seemed to crack like a teenage boy's.

"We have to. It'll be cooler by the time we get there. We're several thousand metres away."

"Would there be any radiation?"

"No. Why should—" Vanmore hesitated. "Hell's delights! The bombs they were carrying! I forgot that. That's why they made such a spectacular finish. They were carrying twenty-four bombs!"

"What sort?" asked Das.

"Something new. I never found out."

"Neutronic?"

"No. If they were, we'd be dead by now. Well, there's nothing we can do about that."

"Listen," said Bianca. "Remember we're heading straight towards the planet. Have you any heat shielding on this thing?"

"Yes," said Das. "It's made for planetary landings."

"Where you have a properly equipped spaceport," said Bianca. "How about a possibly hostile countryside?"

"It's quite manoeuverable, in atmosphere," said Das.

"Listen," said Vanmore. "We're still hundreds of kilometres—thousands—away from the planet. Whatever blew up the *Endeavour* probably came from that land mass where we first saw the flashes of green light. Now, the rotation of the planet is slower than Earth's, but it's still going to carry that place around into the night side, and away out of sight of us, in the next twelve or fifteen hours. *Then* we can turn our power on and go where we like."

"True," said Das. "Back to the *Mohenjo Daro*—or down there."

"Let's take a vote on it," said Vanmore.

"I'd say back to the ship," said Das.

"I'd say down, to the planet," said Vanmore. "Think of the people on the ship, and think of what happened *there*." He pointed to the right, where the fireball appeared at the moment. "One each way. How about you, Bianca?"

"Down to the planet," she said without a moment's hesitation. The speed and certainty of her reply startled Vanmore, and something in his glance made her explain it. "I know some people down there," she said. "We might be able to sort things out before anyone else gets hurt."

The dead silence of space outside was broken by an eerie, whistling sound that brought them all to a stunned silence. Soon the whistle grew into a sound like a howling gale.

"The gases," said Das. "We're hitting the gases from the explosion."

Soon, there was flecked, reddish light all around them, and once something metallic clanged lightly against the outer skin of the shuttle. Almost imperceptibly, at first, they felt the temperature rise.

14

As the glowing gas blanketed the windows on all sides, Vanmore felt himself sweating inside the spacesuit. He noticed that Das had taken off his helmet, and he did the same. The air of the cabin, though scorchingly hot, was fresher than the bottled atmosphere inside the suit.

"We'd better get out of these suits," said Das. "They're meant only for ship-to-ship transfers. Not intended to cover emergencies like this."

They helped each other out of the suits, Bianca emerging last, because her suit had a more elaborate life-support system. The glare of orange light from the windows was almost intolerable, and Vanmore felt rivulets of sweat running down the whole surface of his body. Das indicated an internal temperature gauge, which was reading 58 degrees Celsius and still climbing.

"Isn't this gas outside getting redder?" wheezed Bianca.

Vanmore had to make an effort to speak, and his voice didn't sound to him like his own. "If it's getting redder, that means the expansion is making it cooler."

Sure enough, the thermometer levelled off just on 60 degrees Celsius, then began to fall. From time to time, more small metallic objects struck the outside of their hull—probably things like rivets wrenched from internal structures by the explosion—but they did not seem to have much impact. The shuttle had been close to matching speed with the

Endeavour. The real danger would have come earlier, from the fast-flying, massive fragments torn with appalling violence from the very heart of the explosion area. These others were the mild result of secondary disintegration as the rest of the wreck had simply vibrated apart.

"We're coming through it," shouted Das suddenly.

It was true: the reddening fire-mist was breaking into boiling swirls of gas, through which they could glimpse rifts of blackness, and, finally, the battered crescent of Alcenar. But the shuttle remained hot for quite a time.

"Could we kill the spin, do you think?" asked Das.

"I wouldn't, yet," said Vanmore. "We don't know how good their observation systems are. They don't have to be watching from telescopes on the ground, you know. Remember the thing that got inside the *Endeavour*?"

Das looked uneasily around. "I don't suppose that one of those things we heard hit our hull back there—no, that'd be ridiculous, wouldn't it?"

Vanmore slowly shook his head. "Not at all. But unlikely. Anyway, we'll know soon enough."

Ultimately, they hit on the idea of reducing the spin of the shuttle very slowly, so that a distant observer, human or electronic, would be unlikely to notice the change. In any case, the real debris thrown out from the *Endeavour* must be scattered through an enormous volume of space by now, probably subtending an angle of at least a degree from the surface of the planet.

They all felt a sense of relief once the spin had completely gone, and the shuttle was in line-of-flight position. Even though there was no risk of striking the atmosphere for a long time yet, they felt that when the moment of entry came the machine would be fully controllable.

"We'll land around the sunward side," said Das. "West to east, near the equator, to minimise the momentum loss needed. Does anyone remember how long it takes to rotate on its axis?"

"Just over 2300 Earth minutes," said Bianca promptly. "That's a bit over thirty-eight of your hours."

"And the circumference around the equator?" asked Das.

"I think the diameter was 14,000 kilometres. That'd give you an equatorial circumference of—er—nearly 44,000 kilometres, wouldn't it?"

"Rather bigger than Earth. Aha. That means a spot on the equator will be moving at—ah—about 1150 kilometres per hour. That's what I've got to match, near as possible."

"Can you get down to that?" asked Vanmore.

"Have to do it in atmosphere."

Hour after hour, they watched the slowly distending crescent, lengthening as they drew closer, and thickening in its brightly sunlit part as they swung round between the planet and the sun.

"Can't see any sign of civilisation, yet," said Vanmore.

"You wouldn't see any this distance from Earth," pointed out Das.

"Could we risk a tightbeam radio call to the *Mohenjo Daro*, do you think? That point where the green flashes came from is away out of sight, now."

"They have people all around the planet," said Bianca. "Thinly scattered in some places, but there'd be no side of the globe that's uninhabited."

Vanmore grimaced. He wanted to let Rona and Rajendra know they'd survived. They must have seen the disintegration of the *Endeavour*, and they might well have assumed that the shuttle had vanished with it. On the other hand, the Alcenar people—he caught himself thinking of them as Kranzen would have done, as *enemies* of fantastic ability—these people may not yet have realised either the *Mohenjo* or the shuttle existed. In this case, radio might well open up a fresh attack.

"How do you think they did it?" mused Das. "Blow up the ship, I mean?"

"Possibly an immensely high-powered laser. Perhaps some kind of guided torpedo. Maybe even something introduced inside the hull, like the thing Kranzen spoke of."

"Perhaps they found out he was carrying bombs, and decided—" Das made a slashing movement with the edge of his hand across his throat.

"That could well be."

Bianca had been silent for a while, standing looking out of one of the side ports. "There's home," she said suddenly. "Look!" She pointed to the red sun, burning in space like a strontium flare, and Vanmore was able to pick out a red, starlike object near it.

"That point of light to the right of it?" he asked.

"That's Chiron." She went on as if talking to herself. "It'd be terrible to get this close, and. . . ." She let her voice trail off. In the reflected glow of the planet below, Vanmore noticed her eyes were wet. He decided to leave her with her thoughts.

Closer down to the planet's surface, their view of it began to take on a dimension of depth. The atmosphere lay below them like a blue veil, with white and grey clots of cloud masses deep within it, concentrated along the equator. Perhaps because of Alcenar's somewhat higher gravity, the atmosphere seemed to have a more sharply defined surface than Earth's, and here and there a number of harsh, gigantic mountain peaks snarled above it like broken fangs. From down here, the circular pattern of the vast, ancient impact craters was less evident.

They strapped themselves in their seats as they neared the tenuous upper surface of the atmosphere, and found themselves listening tensely for the first shriek of air against the skin of their craft, watching for the first sudden lift of the needles indicating external temperature.

The first impact was shockingly unexpected. Heat built up so quickly that Das was forced to bring the craft upward again. He skipped it over the level upper surface of the gas like a flat stone skipping over water.

Eventually, he killed enough forward speed to be able to dive deeper into the alien air. Vanmore began to wonder if it were really breathable. Ferris had been here only a few days, and they might have kept him in enclosed buildings and vehicles—Vanmore couldn't remember anyone thinking to ask him questions like that.

They broke through a layer of cloud that looked like cumulus, except that by Earth standards it seemed much higher than cumulus should have been.

Below was a great river system, draining a wide valley walled in on the right by towering mountains, possibly fifty kilometres distant, and to the left by a series of mesas and buttes of quite different formation, almost as though the land became drier across that way. Then Vanmore noticed they were in the rain shadow of a really tremendous mountain mass ahead.

The land below seemed largely covered in dense, viridian jungle, with open stretches of yellow grassland, and flat plains of lime green. Ahead, the river widened out into a complex delta, with estuaries opening on to the lime-green plains. They couldn't see where the water went at first.

"Look!" shouted Das.

Vanmore had seen it at the same moment, a line of dark indigo blue, like a knife-cut across the plain. At the end of it was something metallic.

As they drew closer, they saw that it was some kind of surface ship—apparently a large hovership or hydrofoil. It was abruptly clear that the lime-green areas were not plains, but sheltered stretches of sea covered with a dense carpet of floating weed. The ship had cut a temporary track through the weed, leaving a dark line of water visible.

"Think they saw us?" asked Das.

"Mightn't mean much to them. Just a passing aircraft."

They crossed an area of ocean where the water was weed-free and dark blue, but studded with jagged chains of islands and other looped, low-lying, complex reefs built up on a sinking sea floor by something like coral. They were losing speed all the time.

Das kept veering to the right, getting further away from the equator, where the cloud buildup seemed heaviest, probably because of the long hours of sunlight evaporating moisture from the tropical seas. Soon another land mass appeared ahead, with its mountains vanishing into a level layer of cloud.

They headed in over a wide river estuary with a brief glimpse of a group of buildings, perhaps a small port of some kind. They followed the river up a long valley.

The ground began to rise, forcing them up, up towards the cloud base. In every direction it spread away like a grey ceiling. Still the land came up, streaming past below them at a terrifying speed when seen this close.

"Have to go up in the cloud," said Das. The first grey wisps of vapour whipped past the windows on either side, flickering in changing patterns of light and dark.

Then, suddenly, there was something solid in the cloud. Spires of rock closing in on the left.

There was a sharp, jarring blow on the left wing, and the flying attitude of the craft altered. Vanmore heard Das begin to shout, and then things happened very quickly. Rocks filled the forward view, whipping out of the fog. Bianca screamed. Sitting on Vanmore's right, she suddenly twisted round and flung her massively developed right arm across his chest, sliding it up and gripping the back of his seat so that his chin rested against her thick forearm.

Then the impact came. His seat belt held him in the seat, but it was Bianca's arm that stopped his head whiplashing forward. There was a stunning farrago of sound, and light poured in through the left side of the hull, where a spur of rock had ripped it from bow to stern. Jets screamed, forcing the shattered nose of the craft into a cleft in the rock, their noise mingling with the roar of the storm outside. Rain beat in through the torn hull.

"God!" said Bianca. She was sitting with her eyes shut. Vanmore released his belt, climbed forward, and shut off the valves feeding liquid oxygen and hydrogen to the jets, and at least one stupefying sound died away.

Das was still in his seat, but he was not moving. His head was right forward on his chest, with his neck twisted to one side. Vanmore released his belt and lowered him carefully to the floor in front of the seats, but there was nothing he could do. Das' cervical vertebrae were dislocated, and his eyes were still slightly open, but not moving. With the rain pelting in through the rent in the hull, Vanmore crouched over the body to shield it from the storm, but he knew it was useless. He sat there for a time, the rain saturating him, then got up and went back to where Bianca was sitting.

"Das is dead," he said.

She looked up at him, her eyes dark.

He said nothing, and she glanced towards the body.

"He wanted to go back to his ship. You and I wanted to go down to the planet. We outvoted him, and now he's dead."

Vanmore shrugged. "It was a chance. . . ."

"Yes. But we took a chance with someone else's life."

He slid down into the seat alongside her. "What happened to him would have happened to me, if you hadn't put your arm across in front of my neck."

"Oh, that. It always seems to me that the original pattern of man isn't suited to resisting this kind of thing. Their necks are too vulnerable."

"Anyway—you saved my life."

"Perhaps," she said, her voice hardly audible against the thundering rain.

Vanmore went to the airlock of the shuttle, but the door was jammed and distorted. A new current of fear suddenly shot across him. The long rent in the hull was not wide enough for them to get through, and with the airlock inoperable they might be trapped here.

He began searching the inside of the cabin for some kit of tools, but found nothing apart from a set of small electrician's tools—screwdrivers, pliers, and so on.

"What's the matter?" asked Bianca.

"I'm trying to find some way of getting us out of here."

"The windscreen?"

"Moulded in, and very thick. First thing I thought of, but it'll be hard to get out that way."

The seats were bolted in place, and he was able to use the small tools to get one of them loose. Its frame was solidly made, and he was able to use it as a lever to force the torn skin of the hull aside. At last, there was room for them to get out, when the need arose.

There was a strong smell of damp vegetation. They were not Earth-type plants outside, although in some cases their different lines of evolution had parodied those of his home world. Putting his head out briefly in the hammering rain, he saw the trunks of great trees with what appeared to be scales instead of bark, and creepers with strange, vivid flowers. The understorey of lower vegetation had glossy, dripping masses of rubbery green leaves with large holes in them, and there were bright fungi growing below them in many spots. The whole scene looked grotesquely alien.

"How long does it last—this rain?" he yelled.

"I don't know. I've never been in the Wetlands before."

The rain seemed to become heavier, running in streams over the chocolate-brown soil and forming miniature rivers that grew and merged and captured tributaries from one another as they watched. It had an intensity Vanmore had never seen in rain before, even in the Earth's tropics, thundering down on them with a numbing fury.

"It's something to do with the slow rotation," Bianca shouted, coming close to him to make herself heard.

"How's that?"

"You get nearly twenty hours sunlight from the primary— enough to evaporate an awful lot of water from the equatorial seas. That builds up very deep cloud masses—we saw them from space, remember?—that big, white wedge more than halfway around the planet. By the afternoon, like this, it starts to come down again—and there's time for it *all* to come down. Next day, it does it all over again."

"That's great. Could go on for hours. If you knew about this, why didn't you warn us?"

"I'd forgotten. I'm only remembering it now from my geography lessons as a kid on Chiron. We did the geography of all the inhabited planets in the system."

"How long were you actually on Alcenar when you were here before?" he asked.

She hesitated, and he moved around so that he could look straight into her face. "How long?" he persisted.

A flush spread over her cheeks and forehead. "A few weeks," she said.

"What part?"

"In the dry belt, further south. The starport's located about twenty degrees south of the equator to get it out of the rain zone. It's in the rain shadow of a big range of mountains, with the sea on the other side of it. It doesn't rain there at all. The few clouds that come over the mountains are handled by cloud-breakers."

"How do they work, these cloud-breakers?"

"I never saw one close up. Some sort of beam, I imagine. Maybe charged particles. The visible beam might be just to warn aircraft."

"Where's the nearest town from here?"

"I have no idea. I saw maps, a long time ago, but I only remember their main cities. Astralon is on the same coast as the starport. In fact, you can see its towers in the distance from the port."

"Which town did you live in, when you were here?"

"Actually, as I said, I wasn't here very long."

He kept looking at her without comment, so that she was impelled to continue.

"You see, I came here from Chiron only a few weeks before the *Alphard* left. I'd made all the arrangements from Chiron, but these people had strict quarantine laws at the time.

"After I got off our ship at the starport, I was put on a hovercraft and taken straight out to sea to an island they used for a quarantine station. I was there until just before the takeoff of the *Alphard*."

"What was the island like?"

"Quite small. Coralloid reefs around it. Not Earth coral,

but similar formations. It was part of a long barrier reef that runs along the coast offshore from the starport and Astralon.''

''Could you see the mainland from the island?''

''Only the tops of some snow-covered peaks along the skyline. They were a long way inland, the other side of the starport.''

''Then all you really know of Alcenar firsthand was the starport and one small island.''

''That's about it,'' she said with a wry smile. ''And the island didn't help much. The only vegetation there was some grass and trees brought by the earlier settlers from Earth. Coconut palms, tamarisks, Australian tea-tree.''

''But I thought you were supposed to be an expert on Alcenar!''

''I know. Try to understand it from my point of view, Max. I'd been sixteen years on Earth, and I'd had it up to here. I wanted to get home. This was my last chance.''

''But you knew you wouldn't be able to get away with it once you reached the Alpha Centauri system.''

''Of course. But by then, I'd be *here*. They wouldn't send me all the way back to Earth. And from here, Chiron is only a short run—I'd manage that, somehow.''

He looked at her as if he had never really seen her before. ''Do you realise what you've done? You've put over the most gigantic confidence trick I've ever heard of!''

She said nothing.

''Tell me something,'' he said, ''have you ever actually seen a road made of sapphire?''

''What's that got to do with it?''

''Listen, two ships have made this journey of—what was it?—forty trillion kilometres, on the strength of young Ferris' story about a sapphire road. Now, I don't know about Kranzen, but Rajendra and I wouldn't have acted on Ferris' story if you hadn't supported it. Remember? You said, 'I must have driven over sapphire without knowing it.' ''

''But Ferris actually *had* a bit of the sapphire.''

''Yes, but how do you know it came from a *road*?''

''I see.'' Her voice had dropped so that he didn't actually hear it against the booming rain, although he could see her lip movements.

''Now, tell me—have you really seen a road of sapphires?''

A long pause. "No."

He looked out at the shimmering curtain of rain. There seemed to be nothing to say.

"Well, it might help you all in the long run," she said after an interval.

"How?"

"It might shake you out of your apathy."

He looked at her with a vertical crease between his brows.

"Yes, apathy!" she repeated with a flare of anger. "*Racial* apathy!" She gave a harsh laugh. "You people and your Stability Council. That was your god—stability! I suppose you'd have liked to be able to cover the whole country with quick-setting plastic to preserve it in a stable moment forever!"

Vanmore suddenly became aware of the sound of thunder above the endless roar of the rain, and the gloom above them flickered with reflected lightning. Once, there was a crash that temporarily deafened them, and a blinding white rope of fire linked trees and sky only a few hundred metres away.

The lightning became more frequent, and all at once Vanmore got to his feet.

"This thing's metal. We'd better get out of here."

"Aren't we safer inside of it?"

"Not if the liquid hydrogen goes up."

He got a small knife from the toolbox, and began slitting one of the seats, getting the vinyl covering off in a large sheet. He tossed it to Bianca. "Some protection against the rain," he said, as he cut out another sheet for himself. They had worn only light clothing inside the spacesuits.

"I'm going to wear my suit," she said. "It's got a life-support system in it that lasts a lot longer than yours."

"OK. But hurry."

He helped her into the thick, drumlike suit, and she put the domed, transparent helmet into place. She could withdraw her left arm inside the suit, and she used it now to adjust a small microphone in front of her mouth.

"Can you hear me?"

He jumped slightly as her voice boomed from an external speaker. "Fine. Better than directly, in this rain. Now, let's get out."

Lightning struck uncomfortably close as he was climbing

out of the shuttle. Bianca passed him out the seat frame, and he used it to lever the opening wider to allow her to get the bulk of her suit through the irregular gap. She widened it by thrusting it further open with her heavily gloved right hand, then he was able to haul her through.

"We'll follow the water downstream," he said. "We're not far from the river estuary we saw on the way here—and there were buildings of some kind."

"Might be no one there," she said. "Nobody would live fulltime in an area like this. There are plenty of mining installations that run automatically."

"Let's get moving." He headed off down the side of a stream, and after he had gone a hundred metres or so he looked back to see if Bianca was following. He was surprised to find that she had kept up with him in spite of her bulky suit with its life-support backpack, using her hand like a third foot to give herself length of stride. Holding the piece of vinyl over him as a halfhearted protection against the rain, he pushed on.

The estuary must have been much further away than Vanmore had estimated. After about an hour, he estimated they had covered between three and four kilometres. One thing that bothered him, when he thought about it, was the network of narrow tracks they had found which helped their progress through the streaming jungle. Too narrow and random for human tracks, they began to look to him more and more like the hunting circuits of predators. Twice, he glimpsed something dark bounding away through the undergrowth at his approach, although he saw no details.

"Any wild animals about here?" he asked.

"Yes. They hunt some when their numbers get out of balance," she said. "A lot of our women wear reptile leather that comes from here, in the Wetlands."

"Anything that'd attack man?"

"I don't know. Now that I think of it, most of the predators hunt in the redtime."

"The redtime?"

"When the primary sets, and the red sun is in the sky. Less light, but their eyes are adjusted to reach down into the infrared. Gives them an edge."

"That's great. Just great." The main sun was low in the west. He couldn't see it directly, but the light through the clouds had the orange tinge of late afternoon light slanting nearly horizontally through a great breadth of air.

Unexpectedly, the rain stopped, except for the sullen dripping from the trees. Breaks appeared in the cloud cover for the first time since their crash, showing glimpses of dark blue sky.

Shortly after the end of the rain came the end of the jungle, thinning out onto a terrain studded with jagged rocks like the ones that had crashed their shuttle. It looked like a relatively recent lava flow which had cut a broad swathe through the jungle, leading down to the sea. Vanmore suddenly felt overwhelmed by fatigue, so that he could barely lift his feet from the ground. He sat down with his back against a rock. Bianca moved alongside him, and took off her transparent helmet, clipping it on to her backpack and taking a deep breath of air.

"Good atmosphere here, anyway," she said. "Plenty of oxygen. More than yours, I'd say."

"I'm damned tired, I know that," he admitted.

"It's the gravity. Hundred and fifteen. Means you're going around carrying an extra twelve kilograms of weight." She extended her right hand. "Want a lift up?"

There was no point in maintaining an image of self-sufficiency here. He grasped her gloved hand with both of his, and simply by bending her arm she lifted him easily to his feet.

They headed off down the lava flow. The very next change in its direction brought them in view of the buildings.

They were about a kilometre away on the edge of the sea, protected from the surf by a rough stone wall. Beyond them, the primary sun was almost setting over the water, leaving a dappled track of light towards the shore.

They stopped in the shadow of a rock and watched the buildings for some minutes, but nothing moved about them. They looked as if they had been made by pouring concrete over inflated formes of different shapes. One was simply domed, another a mushroom shape on a cylindrical tower, with two sloping rods running down to form with the cylinder the legs of an asymmetrical tripod. Near it was a large, shed-like structure open at both ends—they could see part of the sea and sky through it.

"They're not houses," said Vanmore.

"No. Nobody'd actually *live* here, unless they liked to suffer."

They plodded down the lava flow. There was a road slanting inland from the buildings, but it was no help to them, because it was roughly at right angles to their line of approach.

As they walked, Bianca suddenly turned. "Ah, it's nearly their mid-year. When one sun rises as the other sets."

He turned. The red sun glared sullenly between slatted bars of cloud. It was quite small, but it gave more light on the landscape than he had expected. The sky near it looked green, and where its red light glanced off the vegetation the colours looked weirdly altered. Something flew past overhead in the darkening sky with a screech that sounded like maniacal laughter, and when he looked up Vanmore saw it was no bird, but some form of flying reptile like something out of Earth's far-off past.

Bianca put her helmet back on her suit. Looking back towards the ridge where the wreck of the shuttle lay, they saw several of the flying reptiles swirling like black scraps of burnt paper above a fire. Suddenly, one of them partly closed its wings and arrowed downward, followed by a couple of the others. Still more, attracted by their cries, skimmed across the gloomy sky from different directions.

"What are they doing?" asked Bianca, an expression of horror on her face. "Not Das—"

"Come on," said Vanmore. "Nothing we can do." He drew her on down the slope towards the river mouth.

The buildings proved completely deserted. Beyond the sea wall was a stretch of beach with orange sand. The waves showed a line of white far out, but closer inshore they were choked by floating weed.

As the last glow of the primary sun vanished below the horizon, the red companion lifted higher in a now ebon sky in the east. A bitterly cold wind swept in from the black water, and Vanmore found himself shivering.

"Might be some shelter in that shed," he said.

The shed was about a hundred metres long and a third as wide, with a roof of some corrugated, translucent material over triangulated metal trusses. Bianca switched on a halogen light in the front of her suit, and its broad beam swayed and bounced along the walls as she moved. Vanmore found a stack of some material like timber-based hardboard, and he leaned some sheets of it against the wall to form a shelter from the wind, which howled through the building from end to end.

There were coils of what appeared to be nylon rope, and woven sacks, stacked empty. Exhausted now, Vanmore made a crude bed out of the sacks, and lay down.

"I can see a ship in orbit," called Bianca from the doorway towards the sea.

"Can't be the *Mohenjo Daro*—that's black."

"True. This looks gold. But plenty of ships come and go here."

He closed his eyes. He had to get a radio, somewhere. Best to contact the first human being who came along. Obviously they wouldn't survive long here in the Wetlands.

Rona might still think he had been wiped out in the explosion that had wrecked the *Endeavour*. God! They might even have gone home without them! That might suit Bianca, but it would leave him stranded on a strange planet for the rest of his life. He would probably never see Rona again.

With the wind howling through the red-lit building, he drifted into dream-torn sleep. Once he found Rona lying beside him. Reaching across in the half-dark, he touched her left arm. He ran his hand slowly up the satin length of it, round her shoulder, breast—and then something felt wrong, bringing him wide awake.

"Don't stop," whispered a voice, and a finger stroked the front of his throat, from the chin backward and downward. . . .

Then he was fully awake, half a metre away.

"I'm sorry," he said awkwardly. "I thought—" He left the sentence unfinished.

"I know," she said quietly.

He got up and walked to the end of the shed. When he went back, he saw Bianca's empty suit standing like a silent sentry. She was still lying on the bags. He made another heap of bags a short distance away and lay looking up at the red-and-black pattern of the translucent roof.

He awoke with white sunlight streaming obliquely across the door. His mouth felt dry. He could hear Bianca's deep breathing a short distance away, and he got up quietly and went outside.

He walked over to the dome-shaped building, holding one of the bags around his shoulders. He tried the door, which was locked. He peered in a window, and saw what looked like a kitchen, with a hot-water urn of strange design, and a tap and sink. He had noticed a spherical tank on a tower on the other side of the building, so it evidently had its own water supply. Might be safer than the nearby river. He went back to the shed and found a bar like a crowbar among some other tools. He returned and forced the door of the domed building, then walked through to the kitchen. The water tasted delicious. He found a cup and took some back to Bianca, then he looked out at the bridge over the river, where the road ran from the complex of buildings out of sight.

He walked across to the end of the road, and suddenly the beat of his heart sounded loud in the morning quiet. The road was blue. It was made of what looked like millions of crystals fused together, and in the heart of each of them was the six-pointed star of titanium crystals.

"My God!" he shouted to the empty coastline. *"It's true!*

Bianca appeared at the door of the shed, a bag draped around her. "What's the matter?"

"Look at this!" He waited until she joined him.

"It can't be—can it?" she murmured.

"It is. My business is making synthetic star sapphires. But if I ran my plant for a thousand years, I couldn't make enough to pave from here to the bridge. And look at it! All the way to those hills!"

"Then it's all real," she whispered.

"I don't know. I'm not sure of *anything,* right now."

15

VANMORE WALKED A short distance along the road, looking down at it. The sapphires, some the size of golf balls, seemed to have been fused together to give a level surface, as if smoothed by a gigantic flat-iron.

"But how did they make them in this quantity?" he asked, partly of himself, partly of Bianca. When she didn't reply, he walked over to where she was standing at the end of the shed, holding the wall, her eyes closed.

"What's the matter?" he asked.

"I need food. Any sort of food." She opened her eyes. "I've burned up a lot of energy getting here, and I've got a high metabolic rate. If I don't get some carbohydrates into me quickly, I'll go into a coma. I could die—and that'd be stupid after all this."

"There was no food where I got the water. I'll break into the other building."

He picked up the crowbar again and ran to the tower-like building with the mushroom top. He tried to pry the door open, but this time failed. There was a window on the ground floor, and he decided to smash it with the bar. The bar bounced back, its vibrations numbing his hands. The window was not glass, but some tough plastic. He hit it again, harder, and one corner moved inward where he displaced some of the inside beading holding it in place. He hooked the claw of the bar into the corner and levered the window in until it suddenly gave way. It did not shatter, but clanged like a piece of metal somewhere within the building.

He sprang upward and squirmed through the opening, glad now that the pane had not been glass. Inside, he found himself in a bare, circular room with a functional metal stairway curving up the wall to the floor above. There was a locker, made of metal, inside the door, which contained a number of hooded capes of some heavy, plastic material.

He climbed the stairs. There was one intermediate level before the large room that mushroomed out at the top, and it seemed to contain an eating place. There was a table, sink, stove, and cupboards. The whole setup reminded him of a control tower at a small airport, with a place for a quick snack just below the operations room.

He opened the cupboards and found some kinds of processed food he did not recognise. He noticed a visiphone alcove at one side of the room, but hurried down with the food packets to the ground floor. He was able to open the door from the inside, and he ran with the packets to Bianca.

She recognised some of them, tore one open, and began eating with a wolfish ferocity. She looked up at Vanmore. "Thanks. God, I needed that!" She ate more, then indicated a similar packet to the one from which she was eating. "Try that stuff. It's got everything you need."

He opened the packet. The stuff looked like dog or cat food, but it tasted vaguely like steak, and he soon found that he was eating hungrily.

After experimenting with a couple of other packets, less urgently this time, she smiled at him, her eyes suddenly alight.

"That saved my life," she said. "Really. I couldn't have broken in there, the way I was feeling."

"Makes us even," he grinned. "Any time." He gestured towards the tower. "Look, there's a phone over there. Do they have a planet-wide hookup here?"

She looked up at the tower. "That's a microwave dish, isn't it? Pointing over the sea. I'd say yes."

"What was the name of that friend of yours you said Captain Rance mentioned?"

"Zondra? That's a long shot. She mightn't even remember me. She was a schoolgirl on Chiron when I last saw her."

"What's her other name?"

She frowned. "I forget, now."

"Rance said she had a partner. What was the name of their firm?"

"I remember that. Zondra and Komordo. I remember, because Komordo's not a Chironian name. Moreover, it's a man's name, and I couldn't see one of my girls in partnership with a man." She made a small gesture with her hand. "Could be purely a business association, of course."

"Yes," said Vanmore in a flat tone, uncertain of what sort of expression to put into his voice. "Can you call a directory on these phones?"

"Eh? Oh, yes."

He left her still eating voraciously, and went back to the tower. In the ground floor room he discarded the bag he was still clutching around his shoulders for warmth, and selected one of the loose, hooded plastic capes from the locker. Then he climbed the stairs to the visiphone alcove, looking and feeling a little less like a castaway.

He activated the unit and pressed a button marked DIRECTORY. The screen lit up with a series of what appeared to be regional names, with numbers alongside them. The first name, flanked by the figure "1", was ASTRALON.

He pressed the "1" on the keyboard, and another list appeared on the screen, headed ASTRALON DIRECTORY, with a series of groupings such as Information Index, Subscribers Private, Subscribers Business—he stopped at that one and pressed the relevant key.

After further step-by-step breakdowns, he came to a list of firms headed "BioEngineering" and on it was the entry he wanted: ZONDRA & KOMORDO, LEV 75, ALTAIR BLDG, 1601 OCEAN BVD. There followed a number with about fifteen digits, which he tapped out on the keyboard. It didn't occur to him to wonder what time-zone difference might be involved.

A receptionist with large, striking eyes and a weird hairstyle appeared in the hologram. "Zondra and Komordo," she said.

"I'm calling for Ms. Bianca Baru," he said. "She's a friend of Zondra's."

"One moment."

The girl disappeared from the hologram, and Vanmore found himself looking at a tank of bright, odd-looking fish, while soft, haunting music filled the interval. Then, in a few seconds, a man's face replaced the view of the fish.

"Zondra's in conference at the moment," he said. "I'm Ab. May I help you?"

Vanmore repeated Bianca's name.

"One moment," said Ab. He appeared to consult a VDT to one side, punching keys and alternating his sharp gaze between keyboard and screen. He looked back at Vanmore. "The last we heard of Ms. Baru, she went to Earth more than twenty years ago."

"I know. On a ship called the *Alphard*."

Ab looked at his terminal again. "That's right," he said.

"Well, she's back. She returned on an Earth ship called the *Mohenjo Daro*—have you heard of it?"

"Just a minute."

Again, the waiting interval was filled with sensuous music and a view of square-eyed, unintelligent-looking fish with blue and yellow stripes, gliding among leathery green water plants. It dragged on until he began to attach individual personalities to some of the fish. Then, abruptly, Ab reappeared.

"Putting you through to Zondra," he said.

Vanmore found himself looking into a room where four people were sitting around a circular, dark blue table littered with papers and small instruments that may have been calculator terminals. Three of the four were men. The fourth was a large, blonde woman in a blue cloak. Like Bianca, she had an asymmetrical look, her cloak curving out over an enormous right shoulder, so that her massive head seemed offset towards the left side of her broad body. She was speaking to the others as the picture came on, and with a sudden gesture she looked up at the camera.

"I'm Zondra." She touched something on the table, and the visiphone lens apparently zoomed in so that her face almost filled the hologram.

"Vanmore. I'm calling for Bianca Baru."

The woman looked at him searchingly. Her light-coloured eyes seemed disturbingly direct. "Can't she call for herself?"

"Unfortunately, no. We were the only survivors of a shuttle crash."

Her eyes seemed to dilate and darken. *"What?"*

"We lost our way making a landing in cloud."

"Is Bianca injured?"

"I'm not sure."

"Where are you?"

"Can't give you an exact location. It's on a deserted coast in the Wetlands."

A vertical crease deepened between the woman's thick blonde brows. "You're talking from a phone. They're all area-coded. Read me the number below your screen."

She reached for a keyboard and punched out a series of figures and letters as he read them out to her. "I'll have you picked up. Wait where you are. And thank you."

The hologram vanished. He went back downstairs, and on the way out took one of the plastic capes for Bianca. The morning felt warmer now, and as he looked up the slope of the lava flow he could see the shimmer of evaporating ground moisture in the air. In places, on the low hills, were white drifts of snow. He hadn't realised just how far the temperature had dropped during the "redtime."

The red sun had given light, but little heat because of its distance, and now it was setting in a blaze of sullen crimson. All the warmth in the air seemed to be coming from the rising yellow sun the other side of the sky. The light effects were uncanny. Most of the shadows appeared red.

"I got in touch with Zondra," said Vanmore as he returned to the shed. "She's having us picked up."

"Great! What's she look like?"

"About your age. Same build, as far as I could see. Same well-developed right arm. Long, blonde hair hanging over her left shoulder." He smiled. "Seemed concerned about you."

"That'd be her." Bianca looked thoughtful. "Long, blonde hair, you said?"

"Yes. Quite attractive."

"Often thought there was something odd about Zondra. Unhealthy interest in men."

"What's unhealthy about that?"

"It's unhealthy on a planet like Chiron, where no men live."

"Well, she's apparently made an adjustment."

Bianca frowned briefly. "Nothing to do with me, of course." But as they waited to be rescued she was absorbed and morose.

Vanmore looked out over the sea. The red sun had set, now, and as the yellow one rose slowly the sky was becoming an intense blue. He might almost have been on Earth. Then a ragged file of the flying reptiles skimmed along the line of the offshore reef, their long, crested heads moving sharply as they scanned the water for food. He went back to Bianca.

"I must find some way of getting in touch with the ship," he said. "Rona and Rajendra won't know if we're alive."

"You should be able to do that from Astralon." She didn't sound worried. Then he realised that she was practically home.

After what seemed to him an interminable time, an aircraft appeared over the sea, flying straight towards them. It swung around them in a descending spiral, thick, chunky, with blunt, triangular wings, more like a spaceshuttle than a plane. It was bright yellow, with an overall pattern of round, black spots. It hovered in the open space between the shed and the tower, throwing out dust as it settled down. Landing jets seemed to thrust downward from the wings.

"Quarantine!" said Bianca in a flat voice.

"What?"

"Those colours. It's from the quarantine station."

A door slid open in the side of the machine nearest them, and a voice with a strange accent boomed from a loud speaker within.

"Baru and Vanmore?"

"Yes," called Vanmore.

"Come aboard, please, with your objects."

There seemed no choice. Vanmore sprang aboard the machine first, and Bianca handed up her spacesuit. He put it on one of the seats in the machine and reached back to help her, but she simply gripped the edge of the doorway with her right hand and swung effortlessly aboard. The door slid shut, so that all the light came from small, round windows to either side. The voice spoke again from a grille on one wall.

"I'll take you to Astralon Quarantine Station for a scan. Take seats, please. Suggest left seats—better view."

Vanmore glanced at the grille. "He doesn't risk direct contact, does he?" he muttered.

"D'you blame him? We could bring in micro-organisms he's never heard of. Anyway, he's probably flying this thing by remote control."

"I am." They both started as the voice came again from the grille. "I'm operating the aircraft from the Station."

Exchanging glances, they fell silent.

They felt absolutely no sense of movement as the machine lifted off. Jets screamed thinly, but they seemed to float motionless, while through the window the outside scene fell away a hundred, two hundred, five hundred metres in a few seconds.

In uncomfortable silence, knowing that every word they spoke would be overheard, they flew south-westward over dark indigo ocean for hundreds of kilometres without seeing land. Then they began to pass over countless islands, some isolated, others in long, curving chains.

"Those islands form arcs of enormous circles," said Vanmore. Bianca looked down at them.

"Impact craters," she said. "That's where asteroids have crashed into the ocean. Thrown up ringwalls from the sea floor."

"God, this place must have taken a hammering. Doesn't make you feel secure, does it?"

"They've deflected anything on a dangerous orbit by now. It's not asteroids you have to worry about." She touched his arm and pointed upward and astern.

How long the thing had been there, he had no idea, as he had been looking downward at the ragged island. At first glance, he thought it was simply a distant aircraft flying a parallel course, but when he looked more intently he realised it was very small—far too small to contain a human being—and quite close. It was a cylinder of dull, white metal the size of a handheld fire extinguisher, with arrowhead wings and a cluster of lenses at its forward end. The air behind it shimmered from the thrust of some propulsion unit.

It had matched speed and course with the quarantine ship with flawless precision. Vanmore thought of what had happened to the *Endeavour II*, and felt suddenly cold.

He looked down again at the ocean. There were more islands, and among them shallow stretches of sea within sheltering reefs, a stained-glass pattern of emerald and jade and turquoise. No sign of human life, though, except that on one island he saw a silvery, metallic structure of unknown purpose, and in a channel he noticed a line of ten or twelve small ships following exactly the same course, as if one were towing the others. They looked as featureless as torpedoes.

"We're going down," said Bianca suddenly.

He could feel no downward movement, but the water below
was closer, so that he could see individual wave crests flecked
with white. Soon, they seemed to be skimming the surface,
then abruptly there was land underneath them, level grey sand
bordered by scrubby, unfamiliar vegetation.

Again, there was no sensation of inertial forces as the machine slowed. The sound of the jets died, and in eerie silence
they glided into an arched airlock at the end of a huge building, painted yellow with a spotted pattern of black.

"I've been here before," said Bianca without enthusiasm.

Hard violet light of fierce intensity played over the outside
of the aircraft, and then it moved through another doorway
into something like a gigantic car-wash, where it was hosed
with foaming liquid and dried by a tornado blast of air. At
last, the door opened and the voice from the grille said, "Go
out, please, and follow the red line."

The air in the building was cool and fresh. Vanmore stepped
down on to a hard, smooth pavement with a surface that
looked like yellow enamel. He saw now that they were in a
building with an arched roof of translucent yellow material,
like a gigantic Quonset hut roofed with yellow fibreglass. A
red, glowing line appeared in the air above him, leading to a
door in the side wall.

"There are no people anywhere," he said.

"Don't rush it. You mightn't like them when you meet
them."

Another door in the side of the building opened, and a
machine built of what looked like stainless steel rolled out on
three wheels. Basically, it was a cylindrical drum with a projecting column carrying a spherical "head" housing a TV
camera. It had jointed steel arms with three-fingered ma-
nipulative claws. Below the camera lens was a loudspeaker
grille made in crescent shape so that it seemed fixed in an
idiotic smile. As Bianca was picking up her spacesuit the
machine glided forward.

"I'll take that," came a voice from the grille. Vanmore
wasn't sure, but he thought it was the same voice they had
heard from the loudspeaker in the aircraft. The thing picked
up the suit in its metal claws and rolled away with it.

They followed the red line to the indicated door, the line

vanishing as the door slid open. Inside, instructed by another disembodied voice, they were separated, going through different passageways. Vanmore found himself in a white enamelled room with walls, floor, and ceiling meeting each other in smooth curves, presenting no corners where germs might linger. A sealed window along one side reminded him of the one-way window at the Amadeus army base where he had watched Ferris interviewed by Dr. Orr. Here, however, the window was not one-way. Behind it were two figures—a grey-haired woman in a white coat, and a stainless-steel robot like the one that had taken Bianca's suit. The woman seemed to Vanmore to have an unusually large head, but otherwise she appeared normal.

She spoke into a microphone, and her voice sounded from the ceiling. "I'm told your name is Vanmore. From Earth, and from our own Wetlands. Did you make a landfall anywhere else?"

"No. How long will I be kept here?"

"Perhaps a few minutes. Perhaps a few years."

He wasn't sure whether she was joking. For the next few minutes he followed her instructions, stripping off his clothing, giving it to one of the shining robots, who took it away for cleaning, taking a shower in a recess where a succession of high pressure sprays doused him with stinging foam and pure water, then drying in an air blast. He put on opaque goggles supplied by the robot, and was irradiated. Finally, his clothes were returned to him, warm, and he was allowed to dress.

The grey-haired woman studied dials and gauges the other side of the sealed window. At last, she pressed some control that opened a door at the far end of the scanning room.

"You're clear," she said into her microphone. "Go out that way. You're being picked up."

He walked out along a short passageway into what appeared to be the concourse of a small airport. It was obviously no part of the sealed environment of the quarantine station.

The far wall was entirely of tinted glass, and he was able to see now that the quarantine station and the airport stood on a plateau on the island, perhaps a hundred metres above the level of the sea. Apart from a few jagged rocks, there was no other land anywhere near. Far away towards the south, he

could just discern a gigantic range of mountains rising from
beyond the horizon, barely visible in the blue haze of distance.
An irregular band of white puzzled him for a moment. Then
he realised he was looking at snowfields on the slopes of the
mountains. The snow did not reach the upper peaks, which
evidently thrust high above the precipitation level, possibly
out of the atmosphere altogether, for the raggedness of their
outline gave no hint of the effects of erosion.

At one end of the concourse stood a series of automatic
dispensers of food and drink, and clustered near them were
several people—evidently recent arrivals who had just come
through the quarantine scan. They were the first people of the
Centauran system he had seen, apart from the woman behind
the sealed window, and even from a distance it seemed to him
that there was something strange about them.

When Bianca came out through one of the doors, he took
her by the arm and they went down towards the others. Some
looked like Earth people, perhaps a little stockier and shorter
in the legs. Others were very tall and slim, and most of these
wore an enclosing exo-skeleton of metal, with electric
"muscles" to amplify their strength. They moved about easily
enough, even gracefully, and Vanmore wondered how sufficient electricity was stored to energise their equipment.

Some of them appeared to be robots or androids—roughly
human-shaped figures of metal and plastic. One of these
began to walk along the concourse to meet them.

"This thing looks as if it's coming to us," said Vanmore.

Its body seemed to be of smooth blue plastic, a sculptured
parody of a female human torso, exaggerating the curves of
breasts and buttocks. The legs and arms were jointed metal
rods, ending in padded, oval feet and narrow, three-fingered
copies of hands. The spherical head carried a hooded lens sug-
gesting a television camera, and below the lens was an upward-
curving grille, white, red-outlined, caricaturing a smiling
human mouth. As it drew near, a female-sounding voice came
from the grille, not at all metallic.

"Are you Bianca Baru?"

"I am."

The head swivelled so that the lens surveyed Vanmore.
"And you?"

"Max Vanmore," he said, and the head swung back to
Bianca.

"Call me Ula. Zondra sent me to see you reach her without trouble."

"Thank you."

"Your aircraft arrives in ten minutes. Have you any objects?"

"Any baggage? Only that spacesuit over there."

The figure turned and walked away. Vanmore looked at Bianca. "Is that thing a robot? Or is someone working it by radio?"

"Frankly, I don't know. I think we'd better talk to it as if it's a person. Perhaps it is, you know."

"How d'you mean?"

"Sometimes, if a person here isn't going to survive, they put a brain in a life-support system, and build it into a machine so it can sense its environment and move around. Other times, the person stays in a room and controls things like this through video and all sorts of sensory feedback."

"Do Zondra and Komordo do that kind of work?"

"Well, they're listed under BioEngineering. I suppose they do. That might be one of their—achievements."

"God, it'd be better to let the things die."

When Bianca spoke again, her voice had taken on a hard note. "You're very much a Terran chauvinist, aren't you? If people don't do something the Earth way, they're wrong! Look, out in this system they're opening up whole worlds. It's human brains against environments your people would be afraid to live in! And how they cope with their surroundings is *their* business."

Vanmore found a sharp edge creeping into his own voice. "You mean the way they coped with the *Endeavour II*? That looked like sheer, paranoid savagery to me."

She was silent for a moment. "But we don't know the full story, do we? Suppose Kranzen threatened them with his bombs?"

As another thought came to him, he felt a pain like a knife thrust in the pit of his stomach. The *Mohenjo Daro*! For all he knew, the people who had destroyed the *Endeavour* might have located it with their instruments, assumed it posed the same threat as the other ship, and blasted it by the same method. Rona, Rajendra Naryan, and everyone else on the ship might have been wiped out of existence in a single flash.

"Bianca!" he said tensely. "If we don't hear anything

about the *Mohenjo Daro*, don't mention it to anyone!''

"But you said you wanted to get in touch with your people."

"I know. Now, I realise I can't risk it. It might lead to them being destroyed."

"But as you said before, they might assume you're dead. And that means you could be left stranded here on a planet you know nothing about."

"Better than risking all their lives."

She looked up at him as if seeing him for the first time. "You never looked like a self-sacrificing type to me."

He managed a mirthless smile. "Perhaps I'm growing up."

She suddenly moved a little closer to him. "Careful. Here's our friend."

He turned to see the blue, robot figure striding towards them on its stilt legs. Its upcurved mouth grille, frozen in its bland smile, suddenly looked sinister.

"I sent your suit on to Zondra and Komordo's." The inflection in the voice was not robot-like at all. Vanmore decided that a human brain—probably a woman's brain—was controlling the figure, but he was quite unable to determine whether the brain was within it or at the other end of a radio link.

"We came through quarantine much faster than when I was here last," said Bianca, as though forcing a conversation.

"We're developing new techniques all the time." Ula swivelled her lens towards the windows, and thrust one of her hands out like a spear, pointing. "Here comes our aircraft."

Vanmore had excellent sight, but it was some seconds before he picked out the tiny speck against the sky. "How did you spot that?" he asked.

One of the metal hands lifted towards the lens. "I can zoom this on to telephoto. Sometimes useful."

The aircraft came down steeply and neatly, evidently in a computer-controlled landing. It was medium-sized, short-winged, emerald green. It did not appear to use oxyhydrogen jets like Earth machines. There were tubular structures through the stubby wings that pulled air in and squirted it out, but he couldn't see how they worked, although as the aircraft turned on the ground he saw an electrical discharge like St. Elmo's fire playing around the outlet pipes.

"Come with me," said Ula, and they followed her towards

the door leading out from the concourse to the landing area.
When they reached the doorway, they found there was no actual door, only an insubstantial film that gave a light resistance as they pushed through it—some kind of weak forcefield
that stopped dust entering the building.

"They didn't have these when I was here last," said Bianca.

Ula's head swivelled. "We move a long way in thirty
years," she said.

"Do we need tickets, or something?" asked Vanmore as
they joined the strangely mixed group of people moving out to
the plane.

"I've arranged everything," said Ula, and her voice had an
air of calm efficiency.

The aircraft seemed to float a few centimetres clear of the
hard pavement. It had no visible landing gear. The styling of it
seemed odd to Vanmore, with the vivid emerald green of its
exterior carried through seats, floor and inner walls, and the
white ceiling softly luminous over its whole area. He had the
feeling that Alcenar's civilisation was going to be far more
outlandish to his eyes than he had expected.

The seats were ingeniously designed to be adapted to a wide
range of body shapes. He took one against a window, and Ula
showed him how to alter the seat height and backrest angle by
touching switches. Bianca took the place next to him, leaning
against the backrest with her feet on an angled footboard.
There were no seat belts or other restraining devices, and Vanmore realised why as the machine lifted off. The island and the
sea dropped away at a frightening speed, yet the anti-inertia
field within the cabin killed any sense of movement.

They flew southward towards the snowbanded mountains,
which seemed to rise steadily higher as they approached, rolling up from beyond the horizon, their bleached, pockmarked
summits sharp and hard against the electric blue of the sky.

They were still not in sight of the coastline of the continent,
but the sea was becoming dappled with islands, many with
fringing reefs.

"Those reefs look like our coral," said Vanmore.

To his surprise, it was Ula who answered. "It's different
from your coral, but an equivalent. I believe Earth's coral
built up when the seas deepened after the melting at the end of
your ice age. Here, the water level rose each time a large
asteroid fell into the ocean. Same result."

"You're very well informed," said Vanmore.

"Put it this way. I have quick access to nearly all the information people have ever collected."

"How do you store it all in your head?"

"I don't. I said I have access—but perhaps it's too hard to explain just now." She paused, then went on in a softer voice. "You'll find most of us very different from your own people. We've come a long way, very fast. You'll have to take us slowly, at first."

He turned to look at the dark lens, fixed on him like a Cyclopean eye. Just then, the fixed smile of the upcurved grille was momentarily horrifying.

16

THE COASTLINE HAD a wild, primordial jaggedness, as if the monstrous cataclysms that had formed it had happened only last year. Barren lava slopes climbed towards the sky, to drop sharply in great escarpments thousands of metres deep, banded with differently coloured strata.

The aircraft climbed all the way, with the titanic mountains filling the sky ahead. Soon, the slopes were covered with snow, and still they flew steadily upward. At last, when Vanmore was estimating their height at between fifteen and twenty thousand metres, they went through a pass, their shadow skittering over snow and rock.

Ahead, a staggering vista opened up with the suddenness of a thunderclap. They were looking down into an ancient, gigantic impact crater. From the curve of the mountain cliffs as they swept away towards the horizon in either direction, the crater must have had a diameter of three or four hundred kilometres. Straight ahead, vast central mountains towered in a jumbled mass at the edge of visibility, a hundred and fifty or two hundred kilometres away.

At some relatively recent time, another unthinkable impact had breached the ringwall away to their right, forming a smaller, overlapping crater filled from the sea, so that it made an almost circular harbour twenty or thirty kilometres wide. As they swung towards it, they passed over a variegated carpet of cultivated land, fed by a grid of irrigation canals that spread across the floor of the main crater as far as Vanmore could see.

"Welcome to Astralon," said Ula. "The airport is on the far side of the harbour, and that's the city spreading around the water. The starport—where you should have landed—is over beyond the airport—that flat, bare-looking area."

Vanmore studied the city as the aircraft swung round. "But those buildings are huge. They must be thousands of metres high."

"Some of them are," said Ula. "The air's better as you get higher up."

"But why not build the city on the mountain slopes?"

"Stability. When my people build, they build a thing to last forever."

Vanmore thought for a time.

"Stability," he said at length. "We make a god of it, too. But in a different way."

"I don't follow that," said Bianca.

"These people look for geological stability, so they can put up permanent buildings. We aim at keeping our whole lifestyle stable."

"That doesn't work," said Ula. "Some of our smaller communities have tried it. They forget that people keep evolving all the time."

"So I see," said Vanmore slowly, glancing at some of the other passengers in the aircraft.

As they neared the city, they were flying across the circular bay towards the airport, and the towering buildings gleamed in the morning sunshine against the brilliant sky—pinnacles of silver and golden and copper-coloured metal, with large areas of transparent material that Vanmore took to be stained glass.

He leaned forward to look across at Ula. "Lot of glass in those buildings. Isn't it fragile?"

"Glass? That's zannite. You could fly an aircraft into it without breaking it."

The scale of the city, the complexity, the dynamic style of it left Vanmore stunned. Insect swarms of aircraft streamed about the landing flanges on the upper towers, and at many lower levels the buildings were linked by a net of elevated roadways. Further around the white curve of the beach, the height of the structures became progressively less as they neared the airport.

They flew lower, until they appeared to be almost skimming the water. Below them, its deep cobalt blue lightened, and they flashed over turquoise and emerald shallows, then over the broad, white beach and level, bare ground that seemed to reach to the horizon. It was intersected by many parallel runways in each of three major directions, sixty degrees apart, reminding Vanmore of the titanium crystals in a star sapphire. Or was it the colour? The shining runways were blue.

Their aircraft did not actually make landing-gear contact with the surface, but skated along just clear of it, supported by the tight, localised force field at its base. Although Vanmore was waiting for just the faintest trace of deceleration inertia, he didn't feel it, even when the craft swung sharply off the runway across a flat area towards a long line of terminal buildings.

There was no airbridge like the ones used in Earth airports, no doubt because the aircraft sat so close to the ground, and could be manoeuvred quite close to the gateway through which the passengers would exit. The nearest gate carried the number 89.

"What happens when it rains?" asked Vanmore as they moved towards the door.

"It's never allowed to rain here," said Ula, "except occasionally in the middle of the night."

When the passengers emerged from the plane, they stepped on to a moving beltway that carried them smoothly through the gate. Looking to either side as they moved along, Vanmore saw that the low terminal building was of enormous length, either end of it lost in the distance. Its windowed facade seemed to be of green-tinted metal, and an endless vista of numbered gates looked as if they went on to infinity. When he glanced back over his shoulder, he saw another such building far away across the field.

Other aircraft were nosed in to the buildings, some of them gigantic. He turned to Bianca.

"I've never seen anything on this scale," he said.

"Well, it's the main interchange for the whole planet," she said. "The spaceport's somewhere over there, the container seaport that way, and Astralon's their biggest city. You're going to get the full impact of their civilisation in one stiff crunch."

The breeze carried the smell of the sea, but it was subtly dif-

ferent from the odour of seas Vanmore had known. Then, as
he was still trying to analyse the difference, they passed
through an open door filmed over with another of the weak
force fields. Inside was a brightly lit concourse that extended
out of sight in either direction, with clusters and crowds of
people at various points along its length. A tall, blonde
woman arose from a seat opposite the gate.

"Bianca!" she called in a resonant voice.

"Zondra! It *is* you, isn't it?"

Vanmore recognised her as the woman who had spoken to
him on the visiphone. She strode quickly forward, leaning
slightly to the left. She wore a hip-length coat of what looked
like yellow leather, and her long legs were encased in close-
fitting black boots. Bianca went to meet her, and as they came
together the tall woman bent her knees and threw her gigantic
right arm around her. Straightening her legs with no visible effort, she strode to one of the seats and stood Bianca on it.
They hugged each other.

"Women!" said a quiet voice alongside Vanmore. He
turned and found Ula standing there. The blank lens and the
fixed smile of the grille seemed even more chilling now than
before.

"Oh, Zondra," said Bianca, "this is Max Vanmore. He
saved my life."

Vanmore moved forward. "In fact, we saved each other's
lives."

Zondra extended her right hand. Twice the size of a normal
human hand in every direction, it enfolded Vanmore's in a
soft, firm grip that he realised uncomfortably he could not
possibly have broken.

"Did my daughter make things run smoothly for you?" she
asked, looking from Bianca to Vanmore.

"Your daughter?" echoed Bianca in obvious bewilderment.

Zondra looked down at Ula. "Didn't you introduce yourself to Bianca as my daughter?"

"No, Zon. I thought it wiser not."

"Well, perhaps you're right." Zondra grimaced. "Trouble
with having a daughter who's all brain. If I argue, I generally
lose."

"He's from Earth, Zon," said Ula. "Just arrived. He
doesn't understand *anything*." She turned to Bianca. "I'll get
that suit of yours."

"Take it straight out to the flier, Ula," said Zondra. "I've brought the red one."

The blue robot figure walked briskly away on stilt legs.

"Your daughter. . . ." prompted Bianca.

"Yes. Two other kids. A boy, twenty." Zondra glanced at Vanmore. "Say twenty-two of your years. He's like Komordo. Then there's a girl, sixteen, like me." She gestured after the departing figure. "Ula's the middle one. Something went wrong in her prenatal modifications, and she wasn't fully viable. You know how it is sometimes. We've kept her head intact on an autojector, and the nerve channels are linked to relays to work her servoid." She turned again to Vanmore. "Her servoid is the prosthetic body she met you with. Later, we'll give her one that really looks like a woman—but that's going to need more maturity than she has just yet."

"Where is she?" asked Bianca. "Her head, I mean."

Zondra gestured towards the city. "Home. She's not completely immobile, you know. Rolls around on wheels. Beats us all at every electronic game we know. She doesn't like to have her servoid and transmitter too far apart. Interference."

Vanmore felt a mounting sense of horror. Horror at what these people could consider normal. While he was trying to rationalise it, Zondra gave a sudden shout.

"Food! I forgot. You must be starving."

"It's all right," said Bianca. "Max broke into a building to get me something."

Zondra spun around, her eyes shining. "Ah! He's one of us!" Suddenly she stepped forward and flung her right arm about Vanmore, crushing him against her. She was taller than him, but by bending her knees she was able to bring her lips against his. They felt different from any lips he had kissed. Warm, moist, muscular, intensely vital. While her right arm held him like a vise, her slim, quick-moving left hand caressed him in several places with a butterfly lightness. Then, as suddenly as she had seized him, she released him, stepping back with a deep, relaxed laugh.

Bianca moved close to Zondra and said something quickly that sounded to Vanmore like "He has a quasi," and the tall woman stepped back with a slight shrug, still looking at him with an inviting smile. He breathed deeply. Her embrace had driven almost all the air out of his lungs.

"Quasi?" he queried, looking at Bianca.

"Quasi-permanent woman."

"But she's a billion kilometres away—isn't she?" asked Zondra, still smiling.

"Tell her," said Bianca, looking earnestly at Vanmore.

"Eh?"

"Tell her about the *Mohenjo Daro*. You can trust Zondra. We've known each other since school."

It occurred to Vanmore there was an abysmal gap in the association covering the time Bianca had been away. He looked up and down the concourse. "Not here," he protested.

There was a moment's silence, then—"Let's go up to our place," said Zondra, and led the way across the building to an exit door bearing the number 89, corresponding with the gate through which he and Bianca had entered. He felt that they formed an odd-looking group, but the other groups of people visible on the concourse were just as varied—giants and gnomes, android figures and things he was uncertain whether to regard as persons or machines.

"I've just realised what's strange to me," he said. "Most of you people have very large heads."

Zondra glanced at Bianca. "I suppose we have, by primitive standards," she said.

It was Ula who supplied him with the explanation. "A couple of generations ago, our ancestors found some way of helping the growing human brain extend itself a bit further, almost doubling its size. Something like that is supposed to have happened from an unknown cause back in Palaeolithic times."

Outside was a vast parking space for airkars and airvans, compactly streamlined and different in styling from Earth craft, most very brightly coloured. Zondra led the way to a flame-red machine, and placed her open hand against a palmplate. All the doors immediately opened. She and Bianca took the front seats while Vanmore and Ula were assigned those at the back. As he was about to get in, Vanmore hesitated, standing with an unbelieving expression as he looked at another group of people emerging from a nearby aircraft.

"What's the matter?" asked Bianca.

Vanmore followed Ula into their machine. "That fellow over there has four arms," he said. "Like some Hindu god!"

Ula gave an unexpected ripple of laughter. "Max has just seen his first tetra, Zon. I think it upset him."

Zondra moved her head slightly to catch Vanmore's reflection in her rearview mirror. "That's what we call a tetrabrach. You'll see a lot of things here that are new to you, Max." She operated some control that closed the doors. "Remember, we don't worship stability the way your people do. We can't afford to. We're too new to our environments."

"To live equals to grow," murmured Vanmore.

"What was that?"

"Just something I heard somewhere. To live equals to grow."

"Sounds a good principle to keep in mind."

From outside, the airkar had appeared red. From within, its hull was faintly greenish and translucent. As it rose—without any physical sensation of movement, again—Vanmore had the sensation of sitting on a trapeze in empty air. Unconsciously, his hands gripped the edge of his seat.

Zondra, sitting in the left front seat, seemed to control the movements of the craft entirely with her right hand on a short, complex lever that she could move up, down, or to either side, twist, push, or pull. Her left hand rested on a console with minor controls. She flew quite low, as did a number of other small machines—evidently a system of traffic separation that kept them out of the way of large aircraft near the port.

Vanmore was still thinking about the tetrabrach, or whatever they had called him. "Listen," he said at length. "How could a person have four arms? Where do they get the other two? I mean, every human embryo starts out with only four limbs, doesn't it?"

It was Bianca who answered him this time. "Tetrabrachs have been around here a long time, Max. You'll find two of the arms are modified legs."

"But he had legs as well."

"You'll find they'd be mostly metal and plastic. Electric muscles, little atomic batteries to power them."

"Like these," said Zondra. Taking her hand from the lever for a second, she slapped it against one of her thigh-high boots. "On Chiron, I used to get around like Bianca. When I decided to live here, I needed more height and a longer stride."

"Why *did* you decide to stop here?" asked Bianca.

"Because this is where it's all happening, dear. All of it."

They followed the sweeping curve of the beach back towards

the main part of the city. Behind the beach was a strip of
foreshore park, and beyond that a broad boulevard. Then the
towering buildings began, spaced well apart, but rising higher
as they moved further away from the airport. Zondra began
climbing. To their left, the bay spread out, but even when their
machine had reached a height of three hundred metres or so,
the structures on the right soared as high above them as ever.
The boulevard was laid out in a series of straight sections a
kilometre or more in length, with curves sweeping gently into
the next straight. Zondra pointed ahead.

"There's our place—on the next curve."

It was a complex of buildings, its hexagonal central tower
surrounded by six shorter towers linked to it by bridges. High
up, the word ALTAIR showed white against purple.

"Why Altair?" asked Vanmore.

"Altair Starlines put up the building. We just lease some of
it," said Zondra. She flew in to a landing flange on level
75—it was marked in huge figures—and moved the airkar
smoothly in to a parking bay where a number of others were
standing. Looking up, Vanmore saw the name ZONDRA &
KOMORDO—BIO-ENGINEERING in black-shaded white letters
across a fluorescent blue band on the wall.

The doors opened, and Zondra stepped out of the machine
and strode across the flange towards a recessed doorway in the
silvery metal wall of the building. She put her hand against a
palm-plate.

"Looks as if Lars is working in his lab," she said. "Come
on in."

She took them in to a long room with bright, shadowless
lighting and benches loaded with complex apparatus. Lars
Komordo appeared to be seated at a control panel halfway
down the room, and he looked around as they entered. He was
a huge man, with a massive, leonine head, sandy fair hair, and
a jutting jaw.

"Lars," called Zondra. "This is Bianca Baru, and Max
Vanmore."

Komordo flicked off some switches, stood up—he must
have been two and a half metres in height—and strode around
the end of a table. Vanmore had the feeling he was in a
nightmare.

For Lars Komordo was a tetrabrach. He had four arms, and
they swung in a strange, complex rhythm as he strode down

the room. He wore a sleeveless tunic of a material that looked like red leather, and below it his long legs were of dark metal, functional, powerful, with no attempt to counterfeit living legs.

His voice was a thunderous basso. "Nice to meet you, Bianca, Max." He extended his upper pair of arms and shook hands with them simultaneously. "Sorry I couldn't be at the airport. Come through here and sit down."

He seemed to radiate superhuman energy. He strode towards a side door which slid open at his approach, and led them into a strangely furnished room with large, transparent doors opening into a sunlit area filled with plants, most of them weirdly exotic to Vanmore's eyes.

"Cafeno, anyone?" asked Zondra, moving over to an almost hidden autokitchen.

"Thanks," said Bianca, and Vanmore nodded. With a whirling movement of bare, muscular arms, Komordo swung two differently shaped chairs forward for Bianca and Vanmore. It was only when Vanmore sat down that he realised that he was tired, even though he had been sitting in aircraft seats for a considerable time.

Komordo stood in front of them, and suddenly his metal legs began to shorten. They tapered throughout their length, and Vanmore saw that both the thighs and the distal segments were telescoping smoothly. They stopped when they were only half a metre long, bringing Komordo's head level with Vanmore's. With his height reduced from two and a half metres to about a metre and a half, Komordo still did not appear small. His massive body looked wider than it was high, his head more than ever like a lion's.

"What part of Earth are you from?" he asked Vanmore.

"Australia."

"Ah, the isolated continent in the South. Interesting. That's not part of the Northern Alliance, is it?"

"No."

"I always thought Earth's next wave of initiative would come from outside the Northern bloc."

"The ship I was on really came from Nu Karnatika."

"Just as well, seeing what happened to the Australian ship, wasn't it?"

So they knew about the two ships! Vanmore felt a mounting tremor of panic. At this point, Ula moved across with a tray containing cups of cafeno, apparently a local drink that smelt like coffee. They each took one, but Bianca stood up with hers straight away.

"I want to see pictures of Zondra's other children," she said, and padded across the room.

"Through here," said Zondra, and led her out of another doorway.

"What *did* happen to the Australian ship?" asked Vanmore guardedly.

"I heard an explosion destroyed it."

"And the other ship?" He kept his voice level, but his heart pounded so violently that it seemed to him Komordo must have heard it.

"I don't know. It may be in orbit. Naturally, I'm vague, because it didn't concern me directly. But I could find out for you."

"I'd appreciate that," said Vanmore.

"You could do that for us, Ula," said Komordo. "The big screen."

"Right. I'll do a rapid scan of the last day's news."

After saying that, Ula seemed to do absolutely nothing, and Komordo ignored her as if she were no longer there. He turned and looked up at a large video screen on one wall.

Vanmore took the opportunity of studying him more closely. It was the first time he had found the chance to see just how a human body had been modified to produce a form like Komordo's. The head and the upper pair of arms and the shoulders seemed bigger than life size, but normal. The hips seemed to have been brought backward and upward so that the legs became arms reaching out below the other pair. The upper hands were perfectly proportioned though gigantic. The second pair had each two fingers and a thumb. Apparently the nerve channels for the other digits were used to control something else, probably the telescopic legs.

Suddenly the screen lit up with what must have been a replay of a television newscast, speeded up. An announcer said just a few words on a subject, then the picture switched to a different topic. A succession of disconnected pictures flicked past, until a spaceship appeared against a background of stars.

"Hold," said Komordo. "Run back to the beginning of that, and roll."

It was a newscast about the approach of two spacecraft

from the direction of the Solar System. The Alcenar people had known about them for a considerable time. There were brief pictures of both ships, then some relatively poor-quality shots taken *inside* the *Endeavour II*, and finally a view of the explosion. No explanation was given. Then an unrelated news item came on. At a sign from Komordo, the screen became blank.

"Well, that's all we know," said Komordo. "If you want more information, I can probably get it over at the observatory. Most of our observing equipment is in orbit, but the co-ordinating headquarters are here in Astralon." He looked across at Ula. "Find out when Horst will be at the observatory."

"Right," she said, and again remained absolutely immobile. After perhaps a quarter of a minute, she said, "Horst will be there in about forty minutes."

"Good," said Komordo. Then, looking at Ula, he said, "You might as well meet us."

Ula gestured with one of the narrow hands. "Zon and Bianca will be back in a minute. I'll roll in then. Meanwhile—more cafeno?"

"Thanks. Two."

As Ula walked across to the autokitchen, Komordo turned back to Vanmore. "One thing I don't understand about these ships from Earth. Why from two different countries?"

"Probably a prestige race."

Ula had walked back with two cafenos held in her slender metal fingers. She handed one to each of them, then stood beside Komordo.

"Lars likes meddling in the politics of other worlds," she said. "It's one of his hobbies."

"And why not?" Komordo put his hand around the blue plastic torso and drew it against him. "Comparing one system with another's a sure way to a better understanding of all of them." He looked at Vanmore. "I don't know how well you know history, Max?"

"Not as much as I'd like. We seem to have lost a lot of it."

"So I believe. Sometimes I think *we've* retained more of it than most parts of Earth. Anyway, more than two thousand years ago there was a Greek philosopher called Aristotle."

"I think I've heard of him. A shipping magnate?"

"I don't think so. But he examined the political systems of

more than a hundred and fifty different states—there were a lot of small city-states in his time—and he worked out a theory of cycles in government.''

"I've heard a garbled version of this. I'd like to get the full story.''

"I'll get it for you later, Max. Meanwhile—what do you think happened to the *Endeavour*?''

"Internal explosion, I'd say. I saw it from maybe eight kilometres away—''

"You *what*?'' Komordo's voice was a clap of thunder.

"I was on my way from one ship to the other in a shuttle.''

"You actually witnessed the explosion?''

"Yes. Our shuttle flew through the fireball.''

Komordo made some half-suppressed exclamation that Vanmore didn't understand. His large face was set like granite, and his eyes seemed to blaze into Vanmore's, a deep vertical furrow forming between his heavy brows. Suddenly he stood up, the telescopic sections of his legs lengthening silently. He turned and strode across to the visiphone booth, tapping keys.

"Horst there yet?'' he asked as the screen lit up. "I see . . . call me—as soon as he comes! This number.'' And he pressed another key.

Vanmore looked around for Ula, but she had gone. Komordo strode back across the room and stood, towering above him, four-armed, like a primitive god of destruction.

17

FOR A LONG time, Komordo stood looking down at Vanmore. Then he shortened the metal legs and descended slowly until their eyes were on a level. Down here, in a way, he seemed just as menacing, with his four powerful arms in restless movement, and his massive trunk like a rounded boulder in the red leatheroid wraparound tunic.

"Max," he said, "what brought your people to Alcenar?"

"Trade, as far as I know. And exchange of ideas."

"With enough explosive material to blow one of your ships to fragments?"

"Fuel, perhaps—" began Vanmore, but Komordo chopped his words off with a shout so loud that Vanmore felt the vibrations in his diaphragm, like the physically felt sound of nearby gunfire.

"Fuel, rubbish! We analysed the gases. That was an explosion of bombs!"

He had leaned forward, and the lower pair of hands gripped Vanmore's legs just below the knees, while the upper hands took him by the forearms. He was held absolutely immobile. When Komordo next spoke, his voice had a frightening softness.

"Our ancestors first came to the Alpha Centauri system in the last century. None of the planetary environments here suited us exactly, nor have those of the other nearby systems we reached. We've had to adapt our techniques of living, and make changes in ourselves as well as in our surroundings. We've come a very long way, very quickly, when you compare our progress with Earth history. You admit that?''

"Yes.''

"And you know why? For one reason, because we don't waste our energies in internal conflict. In war, or in argument over lifestyles. Someone doesn't agree with our way of life? Right—there's always room to move on. Sure, we have something like warfare going on, but the enemy is the environment, not sections of our own population.''

"So?''

"So, when an Earth ship comes to us loaded with bombs— well, put yourself in our situation. What would you think?''

"I wouldn't blast it out of existence without listening to what it had to say.''

Komordo's eyes seemed to darken, and he breathed in deeply. The four hands tightened on Vanmore's forearms and legs, and for a moment he wondered whether he was going to be torn apart. Then a buzzer sounded in the visiphone booth. Komordo released him, rose to his full height, and strode across the room. Light came from the screen.

"Ah, Horst,'' said Komordo. "I have a man here who witnessed the explosion of the Earth ship. . . . That's right. . . . He was in a shuttle a few kilometres away. . . . Says he was on his way to it from the other ship. . . . Right!''

He turned and walked back towards Vanmore, who stood up as he approached. At that moment, Zondra re-entered the room. She had changed into a blue net poncho that left her right arm and shoulder bare, and elsewhere showed the colour of her skin beneath it, reaching down to the shining black boots.

"Ready to eat?'' she asked.

"Go ahead without us, Zon. I'm taking Max over to see Horst.'' Komordo moved closer to Zondra, and there was a rapid exchange of conversation too swift and too quiet for Vanmore to be able to catch it. He felt fear, without knowing exactly what it was he feared.

Komordo moved closer to him and put his hand on his shoulder. "I think we might be able to put you in direct TV contact with your people in the remaining ship,'' he said. "Come this way.''

He led the way out through the garden of exotic plants and

around to the place where the airkars were parked. He did not go to the red one Zondra had used, but a silver machine next to it. He palmed the doors open, then looked back as if waiting for someone else to join them.

In a few seconds, something glided silently round the corner. It looked like a barrel-shaped drum of stainless steel, moving with its base a few centimetres above the pavement. Its domed upper portion—its "head"—carried a television camera lens shielded by metal mesh like a fencing mask, and from the sides of it protruded metal arms ending in three-fingered claws. Komordo motioned Vanmore into one of the back seats of the flier, then he climbed into the left front seat behind the controls.

The metal drum glided to the side of the machine opposite to where Vanmore was sitting. The slight hum coming from within it deepened, and it rose in the air until level with the seat. Then one of the short arms extended telescopically into the car and gripped the back of a seat, contracting to draw the drum inside. It settled on to the seat alongside Vanmore, the humming sound within it ceasing. Then Komordo operated the control that closed all the doors of the machine.

Like the red craft, this one had a hull which appeared transparent from within, and as it climbed steeply Vanmore again had the feeling of being on a trapeze.

Komordo flew like a stunt pilot—Vanmore didn't know whether he was trying to impress, or if he always flew that way. The towers of metal and tinted zannite, the broad elevated avenues, and the luxuriant, informal parks of the city swept below in a chaotic whirl of vivid colour. Keeping just below the velocity of sound, they flew out of the city and onward across multicoloured, contoured fields irrigated by canals, with the soaring escarpment of the ringwall forming a hazy, unbelievable backdrop to the scene ahead of them.

Looking upward, Vanmore could see metallic structures like monstrous aerials at the summit of cliffs perhaps ten or twelve kilometres high.

"Are we going up there?" he asked, pointing upward, but Komordo, glancing at him in his rear-vision mirror, laughed.

"Those are only relays. Practically no atmosphere up there. The ground base of the observatory is just ahead."

They were approaching a group of apricot-coloured buildings with a few large, parabolic dishes that seemed to be fo-

cused up at a steep angle to the equipment on the high ridge.
Komordo swept the aircraft around one of the buildings and
landed in a parking area alongside a number of other fliers.

He opened the doors and led the way into a foyer shielded
from dust by one of the force-films. Vanmore walked behind
him, with the drumlike thing gliding along on his right, its
base a few centimetres above the floor. They stopped in front
of a vision screen, where the hologram of a receptionist with
azure hair looked out at them.

"Identify for voice prints, please," she said.

"Lars Komordo, visiting Horst Yoritomo."

"Pass. Next?"

To Vanmore's surprise, a voice came from the speaker grille
of the cylindrical drum beside him. "Servoid of Ula Zondra-
Komordo, visiting Horst Yoritomo." It was Ula's voice—at
least, the same voice he had heard from the blue servoid.

"Pass. Next?"

Komordo stepped forward. "I'll be responsible for this
man. You'll have no record of him—he's from offplanet."

The woman in the hologram seemed to hesitate. "If either
you or the servoid are with him all the time he's on the
premises," she began, but at that moment Vanmore felt his
right wrist gripped by encircling metal fingers.

"Perhaps if I take his hand like this," suggested Ula's clear
voice, "he would find it impossible to break my grip."

"Very well," said the receptionist. "Pass."

Her image vanished, and a wide door slid open.

Komordo strode through. Evidently he knew his way about
the place. Ula—Vanmore had to think of the servoid as
Ula—glided forward, and he walked alongside her.

"This is ridiculous," he said irritably.

"But necessary, Max," answered Ula's voice. The lens
turned towards him. Her voice grille, as on the other body,
had been designed with the same upward curve, giving it the
identical, maddening caricature of a smile.

A wide, green walled passageway extended ahead of them,
but halfway along it a door slid open and a strange-looking
man with intense black eyes stepped out.

"Come in, Lars," he said. "Is this the man you spoke of?"

"Max Vanmore, from Earth. And my daughter, Ula."

"Ah, yes. We've met before, but a different package, I
think?" The room was an office with a number of vision

screens on one wall, and a tinted window giving a view of the escarpment. Horst sat behind a broad desk which appeared to be surfaced with ruby. He waved to seats opposite. Ula manoeuvred Vanmore until he was standing in front of a chair, then her hand, gripping his wrist, revolved with slow, irresistible force, so that he was compelled to sit down. She remained beside him. Komordo simply shortened his telescopic legs so that his height matched the others'.

With very little preliminary talk, Horst arrived at the matter that concerned him.

"Did you know the *Endeavour* was carrying bombs?" he asked Vanmore.

"I knew they had something highly explosive on board—I saw it explode."

Horst nodded. "Actually, it was a very potent, sophisticated type of bomb. We were able to determine that by spectroscopic analysis of the fireball."

"I flew right through that fireball in a shuttle. Was there any danger from radiation?"

"I'd say probably not." Horst came back to his original line. "Did you know beforehand that bombs were on board?"

"Kranzen—the captain of the *Endeavour*—was overcareful, I think. Prepared for any emergencies. But bombs? That seems—primitive."

"I know. But we saw them," said Horst.

"Saw them? How?"

"Perhaps I should explain. When the *Endeavour* was first sighted, I was one of the team monitoring its approach to our system. We gave it the customary signals to open communication with an incoming ship, but received no reply. You see, we have ships coming in to our system almost daily from the other systems we are opening up—Van der Kamp's planets around Barnard's Star, Bessel, orbiting 61 Cygni, the Altair planetoids—the list is growing every year.

"Well, receiving no reply from this ship, we sent out a probe and beamed close-range signals, but still no response.

"We assumed, then, that the automatic guidance mechanisms had brought the ship to its target area, but that something had gone wrong with the hibernation system. In other words, that the personnel were all trapped in hibernation. Would that seem to you a logical reason for boarding it?"

Vanmore nodded.

"Well, we boarded with a micro-surveillance unit. We have recordings of a number of conversations on the ship indicating that different people knew very little about the project other than their own particular niche. In fact, that was their downfall."

"What d'you mean?"

"We got to know Kranzen, Barton, and several of the other men quite well. An all-male crew, I think. Perhaps that led to tensions—but I digress. We have tapes of a discussion between Kranzen and Barton about projected use of their bombs."

"Is that really true?"

"We could play you the tapes. Some fixation on 'showing the flag,' as Kranzen put it."

"So you decided to blow them up?"

"No need. They did it themselves."

"*What?* How?"

"Our record chops off short of the actual end, but what happened seems to be this. They saw our surveillance unit, started shooting at it, followed it into their weapon silos. Then, we think someone who didn't know what the bombs were fired at our unit and hit a detonator." He flung his hands expressively upward and outward.

Vanmore sat silent for a time. "It looks as if I owe you an apology for what I thought," he said.

Horst leaned forward across his desk, a lock of lank, black hair falling across his forehead. "Tell me, what were you doing in the shuttle?"

"I was on the way to try to reason with Kranzen. We knew, on the other ship, he had bombs aboard. We were afraid he'd do something stupid and precipitate a war."

"Who was on the shuttle?"

"A young fellow called Das, the pilot—he was killed in the crash—Bianca Baru, because she was the only person on our ship who knew this system, and me, because I was the only one who knew Kranzen well enough to try to reason with him."

Horst looked at him for a long time without speaking. Finally he shifted his gaze to Komordo.

"It all checks," he said. "I've got a tape from Rajendra Naryan, on the *Mohenjo Daro*. They've had no contact since, yet their stories tally."

Vanmore sat upright, forgetting for a second the steel grip

on his wrist. "You've actually spoken to Rajendra?"

"Yes. We can reach him any time. You want to contact him?"

"If possible, yes."

Horst and Komordo stood up. "Ula," said Komordo, and made a gesture with his hand. Ula at once released Vanmore's wrist.

"Incidentally," said Horst, "it's fortunate you didn't reach the *Endeavour*. Kranzen was going to kill you."

"*What?*"

"I have tapes relayed from our micro-surveillance unit. At one stage, Kranzen said to Barton, 'This is finishing neatly. The last of the Vanmores. Their whole organisation's been a stumbling block to The Project.' " Horst shrugged. "Whatever they meant by that."

A few minutes later, in another part of the observatory buildings, they were standing before a large two-dimensional television screen, below which an operator moved some dials. A picture came and went, then stabilised. Vanmore found himself looking at a view of the control room of the *Mohenjo Daro*.

Rajendra Naryan himself stepped into the picture.

"Max! What happened to you?" His eyes lit up. "We thought you'd been blown up with the *Endeavour*."

"A lot's happened, Raj, some of it bad. Das is dead. The shuttle crashlanded in cloud. Is Rona there?"

Rajendra said something aside, and a few seconds later Rona appeared alongside him.

"Max! We thought you were dead! Thank God you're all right. But where are you?"

"Astralon."

"We're going down there tomorrow—they're sending a trade shuttle up for us. What are the people like down there?"

"Oh—they vary."

"Just like us?"

"Er—some of them are. Be terrific to touch you again, honey."

Rajendra moved into the field again. "We'll be with you tomorrow, Max."

"Good. When you land. And—Raj!"

"Yes?"

"There *are* roads of sapphire. I've walked on one. Star sapphires! And I ought to know—I make them."

"Good," said Rajendra, but his face said considerably more.

As they were leaving the observatory complex, Komordo said casually, "What was the interest in roads of sapphire?"

Vanmore, tired but relaxed, was sitting in the front seat alongside him. He pointed down to a blue, glistening road leading from the observatory back towards the city. "Sapphire, with us, is a precious stone. Here, you can afford to pave roads with it."

"So?"

"Well, that's one of the things that brought us here. If you have a matter converter that can produce sapphires cheaply enough to pave roads with them, we'd like to learn the technique. After all, we're far enough apart for there to be no competition."

"Matter converter? Where does that come in to it?"

"You have them, haven't you?"

"Yes. They operate at a couple of our universities, for research. Transmuters, they call them. They're not used much. Takes a tremendous amount of power to change a very small amount of one element into another. They use them in exploring the trans-Uranic elements, but they work in micrograms."

Vanmore felt a tightness in his solar plexus. "Then you don't use them industrially?"

"Of course not."

"You mean—you have no way of turning large quantities of one element into another?"

Komordo laughed. "If we were that short of a particular element, it'd be cheaper for us to bring it from some other planet."

Vanmore looked down through the transparent floor. "That road down there is paved with corundum, isn't it? Sapphire?"

Komordo glanced down. "That's right."

"Well, where do you get sapphire in quantities like that?"

"I'll show you." After a glance in his mirror, Komordo swung the machine around in a long curve, and began heading towards the ringwall. The areas of cultivated land were thinning out, here, into parched-looking native scrub.

"How much do you know about your own Moon?" asked

Komordo. "About the olivene they found on it?"

"Olivene?"

"Yes. I understand it's a semi-precious stone on Earth, but
on the Moon they found whole mountain ranges of it. That
was just one example of things like that. The Moon has no
granite, the Earth plenty, and so on."

He was flying lower, now, over a blue road on which large
trucks were travelling at intervals.

"All this land is the floor of an impact crater, where an
asteroid slammed into the planet a couple of hundred
kilometres back that way.

"Remember, the surface of Alcenar was formed under a
different sequence of temperatures from your planet. Just as
you have diamonds formed hundreds of kilometres below the
surface and brought up here and there by volcanic action, here
we have immense strata of corundum—aluminium oxide with
titanium—driven up along the ringwalls by the impact of the
asteroid. It's exposed strata that were once twelve or fifteen
thousand metres below. And here—" Komordo swung the
machine down close to a line of sparkling cliffs. "Here's one
of our sapphire quarries. There are probably hundreds."

He brought the flier down. Through a veil of sunlit dust,
Vanmore could see trucks being loaded by vast excavating
machines. Komordo opened the doors, and they stepped out
on to the dusty, shimmering ground. Vanmore stopped and
picked up a half-metre mass of fused sapphire crystals.

He had a strange feeling of emptiness, a sense of anticlimax.
He thought of the mighty race between Kranzen and Rajendra
Naryan for the prize of a technology that could pave its streets
with sapphire. And it had never occurred to anyone that on
this planet you could pick the damned stuff up for nothing.

At least Kranzen and his team would never find out now
about the void at the end of their rainbow.

"Coming?" asked Komordo.

"Right," said Vanmore dully. He threw the mass of
sapphire away, and walked slowly back to the aircraft.

18

NEXT MORNING, AN hour after the rising of the primary sun, Vanmore was standing in the terminal building of the Starport awaiting the landing of the shuttle that would bring the first group of people down from the *Mohenjo Daro*.

He found it hard to realise that he had been on the surface of this planet only a little over sixty hours, so much had happened in that short span of time to shake the very foundations of his lifestyle.

He wondered what Rona and the others would think of his new companions. Zondra wore a hooded cape of thick yet completely transparent plastic, showing the whole of her body above her thigh-high black boots. Her breasts were emphasised by a blue-tinted shading on their lower curves, and a touch of magenta makeup around the nipples. Komordo, striding restlessly about on his dark metal legs, wore a hooded red leatheroid coat with close fitting sleeves enclosing his four powerful arms. He looked over to Ula.

"Any time of arrival yet?" he asked.

"About nine minutes," she answered promptly. She had fitted a blue, hooded plastic cape over the servoid body she had used when Vanmore had first met her. All he could see of it was the round lens, the smiling grille, and the lower extremities of the stilt legs.

"How does she know that?" he asked Zondra, who was standing near him.

"She's watching a news telecast back in her room," she said, smiling as she noticed his bewilderment. "She uses one eye to monitor the camera in her servoid, and the other one is free all the time to look at TV screens, computer printouts, or whatever she needs for reference."

Ula had joined them while she was speaking. "I think it's the only way to live," she said.

"Where's Bianca?" asked Vanmore suddenly.

Zondra gestured. "She went to pick up a timetable of voyages between here and Chiron. If she goes there, she'll be back soon—I can tell you that. I couldn't stand it now." She looked at Vanmore with a sudden expression of candour, her eyes half a head above his. "You know, most of our ceilings there were only 150 centimetres high, because none of us stood a metre and a half tall!"

They were on the upper floor of the terminal building, and from the observation deck they could see out over the starport. It looked like an endless plain of smoothed rock with a hard, vitrified surface, beginning at the edge of the bay beside the main airport, and stretching so far inland that mirages glimmered on its surface like phantom pools of water.

"There!" shouted Komordo, pointing upward. The shuttle was coming down at a sharp angle, so swiftly that Vanmore felt apprehensive.

It levelled off over the sea and swept in at high speed across the flat ground, nose up to give its stubby wings a high angle of attack. It was red and yellow. It landed a long way off across the field, and a hovercraft-type vehicle went out to meet it. Ula's telescopic lens enabled her to see the people coming off the shuttle, but to the others it was barely possible to see any movement. At last, the hovercraft came skimming back to the terminal.

Vanmore didn't absorb much of the official welcome once he caught sight of Rona. She came down the ramp from the hovercraft in a lilac suit, bareheaded, immediately behind Rajendra Naryan. Raj stood regally a short distance from the end of the ramp, every centimetre of him a maharajah. He looked down for a few seconds at the blue rolled-sapphire pavement at his feet, then less confidently at the little group of people moving out from the terminal building.

Vanmore shouted Rona's name, and she saw him and began to run towards him—a little heavily, he thought, perhaps because she was not allowing for Alcenar's fifteen per cent higher gravity than the force to which she was accustomed. He went down a swift-moving escalator to ground level and rushed to meet her, feeling the threat of cramp in the backs of his own legs. Then he had his arms around her. He squeezed her against him as they kissed.

"You look wonderful!" he said.

"So do you. I thought—I might never—"

Suddenly they were holding each other tightly, and he felt her trembling. He stroked her until the tremors gradually subsided. Then her old, mischievous expression returned as she tilted her head back.

"What sort of competition do I have here?"

He grinned. "Take a look," he said, and swung her around.

She looked at the group of people near the terminal building. "My God! They're not true!"

"They are. Come and meet some of them."

Rajendra was talking with an official welcoming party, one of them a small, gnome-like man with an enormous head, seated in a metal chair suspended in the air, another a tall tetrabrach female in a ground-length grey dress, with her four arms sheathed in full-length fluorescent yellow gloves.

Vanmore led Rona across to his own group. Bianca had now joined them, and Rona gave a cry of recognition. Bianca introduced her to the others.

"This is Rona Gale, Max's woman, from Earth," she said. "My friend Zondra—"

Rona drew her breath slightly as the huge bulk of Zondra towered in front of her. Her eyes took in the transparent cape, the makeup of the firm breasts, the dense triangle of golden hair above the long boots—then Zondra's right arm slid out of a slit in the cape and swept Rona against her, lifting her easily off her feet and swinging her around.

"This is my partner, Lars Komordo," she said.

Vanmore was astonished to see Komordo's face suffused with an electric charm.

"Beautiful!" he said, and his legs contracted until he had his eyes slightly below the level of Rona's. "I must apologise for our gravity here."

"It *is* heavy for me," she admitted, smiling.

"Here—until you get used to it—" Suddenly his four arms were around her, cradling her against his massive body while his legs lifted him to his full height.

"Whee!" said Rona, looking down at Vanmore. "Do they do this to all the women who arrive here?" Her face was crimson.

"Only the attractive ones," came a cool voice and she looked down at the upturned lens of Ula.

"Perhaps she'd better get used to your gravity by walking in it," said Vanmore.

"Plenty of time for that," said Komordo easily. "Let's go over and meet your friend." He strode across to where Rajendra Naryan was still talking with the gnome and the tetrabrach woman. Raj and the woman were about the same height, and the gnome had raised his floating chair so far above the ground that their heads were on a level. Strangely, when Komordo joined the trio, the woman's height increased smoothly until it almost equalled his two and a half metres—apparently she had the same kind of extending legs as he did.

The gnome-like man stayed with his head level with Rajendra's. His enormous skull was covered with fine brown hair, and his eyes were large and dark. The lower part of his face was small, and the trunk of his body was almost globular, about the same size as the head. A pair of skinny hands seemed to grow directly from the shoulders, their fingers sprawling across complex keyboards at the sides of the supporting chair. If he had legs, they were hidden. His voice was shrill and clear.

"Still collecting interesting ladies, Lars," he said.

"This is Rona," said Komordo, as if he had known her for years, "and this is her man, Max." Holding Rona in a sitting position against his body with three of his arms, he used the other to make the introductions. "Two members of the welcoming committee for new arrivals—Yaki and Mara."

The big woman flung her four yellow-gloved arms wide in an exuberant gesture. "We like to help people feel at home when they arrive here," she said.

Vanmore could hardly think of any two people less likely to make an Earthborn person feel at home.

"Put me down, Lars," said Rona quietly. "I feel like a baby, held like this."

"Of course," he said, and set her down on her feet. She moved across beside Vanmore and rested her hand on his arm.

At once, Yaki brought his chair down to a level where his face was in line with Rona's, and he darted silently forward until he floated directly in front of her, less than an arm's length away.

"You're very attractive, Rona," he said, and gave a high-pitched laugh. "I can say things like that, because I consist mostly of a head. We need women like you on Alcenar."

"I don't intend to stay permanently," she said.

"Don't decide as quickly as that," said the piping voice, and the head and chair swivelled in the air to catch the attention of the big woman. "Do something to make the girl think twice, Mara."

"This is the advancing edge of human development, Rona," said Mara, flinging her arms wide. "Look at what we have, first. Then decide."

Lars Komordo stepped between them. "She's tired. I suggest she and Max come back to our place. Have something to eat, sleep for a while. Right?"

"Good idea," said Vanmore.

"Thanks," said Rona.

"I'll see you later, Raj," added Vanmore.

"Excellent, Max. I'll be with these people."

The woman linked one yellow-gloved arm through Rajendra's, and put another across his shoulders. She was now matching his height exactly. The gnome glided to the other side of him, and the three of them moved away.

"Come," said Komordo, extending his four red-clad arms.

"I'll walk, thanks," said Rona, and she quickly slipped an arm through Vanmore's.

"We have a vehicle outside," said Komordo, and strode towards one of the film-shielded exits. Zondra and Bianca, talking animatedly together, began to follow him, and suddenly Zondra squatted beside her friend and they each flung a massive right arm around the other. Then Zondra simply straightened her slim, electrically powered legs. Though the combined weight of their bodies might have equalled that of four average Earth people, the long, black-covered legs carried them along without apparent effort. Ula walked demurely beside them.

Rona brought her lips close to Vanmore's ear. "What *is* that thing in the blue cape?" she whispered.

"It's what they call a servoid here. The girl who uses it is Zondra and Komordo's daughter, but she runs it by radio."

"God, aren't there any normal people about here?"

"I used to think I was. Now—I'm not so sure."

Out in the airkar park the breeze coming across the bay was still cold, but the slowly rising sun was giving the promise of later heat. Rona shivered suddenly, folding her arms across the front of her body. A little ahead of them, Ula turned and stood waiting for Rona and Vanmore to catch up.

"Are you cold?" Rona looked at the round lens and the red-outlined grille, as if uncertain where to direct an answer. She nodded.

"This should fit you." Ula's thin, three-fingered metal hands unfastened the blue cape she was wearing, and she strode briskly forward and put it around Rona, pulling the hood up. "I don't need it—I only use it for decoration." She gave a sudden laugh. "Colours clash horribly, but they'll think it's Earth styling."

Komordo's vehicle was different from the one in which he had flown Vanmore out to the observatory—in fact, when he had first seen this machine earlier in the morning, Vanmore had thought immediately of pictures of the old twentieth century flying saucers. Almost circular, finned, silver, yet transparent from the inside outward, it had a round seating arrangement so that all the occupants—it could have held about eight—sat facing inward. The rear section of the seat was raised slightly behind a control console, so that the person flying the craft could look out over the heads of the others, but still be part of the group.

Vanmore wondered about distractibility, then came to the conclusion that people like these could handle it.

At the door of the machine, Zondra turned to Rona and Vanmore. "We'll go straight to our place for a meal. Best way of making an adjustment to our way of life, we think. I suppose home life is the same anywhere, isn't it?"

"People are always people," said Rona, although Vanmore could detect a flicker of doubt in her voice.

"Right," said Komordo. "Let's go."

He turned and stepped in to the machine. He did not bend to go through the doorway. He simply retracted his telescopic legs and stepped straight in on the floor of the machine. Where a moment before he had towered to a height of two and a half metres, now he became a squat, monstrous figure waddling to the control console and sitting behind it. Ula, too, retracted her stilt legs in the same way, and now, looking into the aircraft, Vanmore saw that the circular seat was practically at floor level.

They helped Rona in next, and he followed. Sitting on the seat, backs to the transparent outer wall, they found their legs extended uncomfortably across the floor almost to the opposite side. It was warm inside the round cabin, and Komordo had already thrown off the leatheroid coat, stowing it somewhere behind the control seat. Without it he was practically naked—a hairy, almost spherical body with four immense, muscular arms and a black, leather-like garment about his hips, linking his trunk with the metal legs.

Bianca simply stood, now as tall as anyone in the cabin. Zondra slipped off the transparent cape and climbed in to the machine, sitting beside the door, her legs extended across the floor. She reached inside the flared tops of her black boots and snapped some kind of control, then slid the boots and legs off, revealing a pair of strange, white-gloved hands with blunt fingers evidently surgically modified from toes. She flexed them, as she folded the legs and put them beside her. They were connected at the top to form a single unit, and she touched something inside to lock them in a bent position. As she put them on the seat, Vanmore could see inside the tops of them, into carefully shaped recesses with hollowed control keys which could be operated by the toes.

Just then, Komordo lifted the aircraft almost vertically, and Rona clung to Vanmore as the ground dropped away beneath the transparent floor.

"It's all right," he reassured her. "This kind of thing happens all the time, here."

They swept back around the curve of the bay towards the gleaming towers, Zondra pointing out various landmarks below: yards where parts of spacecraft were built, prior to being flown into orbit for final assembly. Distant structures across the plain, where metals were mined and other, more sophisticated materials produced.

"This area sounds self-sufficient," said Vanmore.

Zondra made a movement of her brows that was an equivalent of nodding. "It is, really. Iron, titanium, aluminium, tungsten—we don't have radioactives mined near here, but we can bring them in.''

Bianca, who had been standing next to Zondra, reached out and touched the gloved toes. "Those are useful, Zon. Who did them?"

Zondra stripped off the white gloves, revealing the strange, finger-like toes jutting from her groins. "Our own microsurgeon. Young fellow called Jay. You'll meet him today—he's one of our extended family."

This time, as they approached the Altair Building, they did not fly in on the seventy-fifth level, but much higher, above the two hundredth floor of the central tower, which Vanmore estimated must have been more than eight hundred metres above the ground. On the side away from the bay, the hexagonal tower was cleft by a vertical indentation with landing stages for aircraft at every second floor, set within like shelves. Apparently the idea was to shield aircraft from the fierce winds that sometimes blew at this height.

Komordo flew the saucer-like craft in to one of the stages, which opened out in the heart of the building into a much larger area than Vanmore expected. While still seated at the controls, Komordo operated something that made a door slide open in the inner wall of the building, and he drove the machine neatly in to a room bathed in white light from a luminous ceiling. He touched other controls, and the outer door closed, while the door of the aircraft slid open.

He stepped out, lengthening the telescopic legs and striding into a softly lit passageway that curved out of sight. Ula followed him, but Zondra sat near the door of the machine as if waiting for something.

"Go ahead," she said. "I'm using my skimmer."

Without knowing what she meant, Rona, Bianca, and Vanmore emerged from the machine, and as they went towards the passageway something glided past them. It looked like an oval, padded board floating a few centimetres above the floor. It stopped at the door of the aircraft, and Zondra swung her heavy body out to sit on the device, her toes resting on control keys. She pulled up a flexible purple cover with a zip that held it firmly about her hips, then, picking up the folded legs and tucking them under her arm, she glided past the trio up the passageway.

At one point along the passage, she opened a sliding door and stowed the legs away among a number of other pairs, some obviously of different lengths.

She spun round to face the others. "Let's eat! I'm starving."

"So am I," answered Bianca. Zondra whirled round and glided on. Her body and the skimmer seemed to form a single, perfectly co-ordinated unit.

The passage ended in a huge, bright yellow room with floor-to-ceiling windows along two sides that met at a 120-degree angle—obviously it was in one of the corners of the hexagon.

Komordo was standing in front of a visual display terminal, while in the far corner of the room a girl with pink hair stood in an autokitchen. She looked like a young version of Zondra, but as yet without her poise. She wore legs like the ones Zondra had worn, but they were much shorter, giving her a stocky look, and as she turned she seemed slightly clumsy in the way she used them. Zondra glided up to her and put her arm around her, swinging her around to face the newcomers.

"My younger daughter, Gisela," she said. "A teacher of mine, Bianca Baru, and two people from Earth—Rona Gale, Max Vanmore."

The girl greeted them, but Vanmore noticed that she looked sharply at Rona's head, then at his. He was suddenly conscious of the fact that these people all had braincases at least twice the size of his or Rona's.

"Are you going to stay here?" Gisela asked.

"For a while," said Rona. "Not permanently."

The girl looked her up and down. "No. Our gravity would knock your body about before long." Then she turned her attention back to the autokitchen.

The meal was different from anything the visitors had ever experienced. Some of the food was synthetic, but there were also strange vegetables and curiously flavoured sauces. They sat around a long oval table slightly low to the floor for Vanmore's taste, Zondra and Komordo at opposite ends of it, Vanmore and Rona facing the huge windows, and Gisela and Bianca with their backs to the view. Ula stood a little away from the table, but shortened her legs so that her lens was on a level with the faces of the others.

"This food is marvellous," said Rona, looking across at Gisela.

"Naturally," said the girl. "I programmed it." Her expression was sullen.

"You'll have a heavy day ahead of you," said Komordo suddenly, looking at Rona and Vanmore. "After you've eaten, I suggest you sleep, say until hour fourteen. By the way, you'll need watches for our thirty-eight-hour day. Ula or Gisela can take you to select some later in the day."

Gisela's cloudy mood changed abruptly. "There's a good watchmaker down at the shopping centre on the hundredth level," she said. "I'll take you both down to her."

They went on eating, Vanmore aware of some kind of tension in the family that he couldn't quite place.

A bell chimed somewhere in the apartment, and Zondra touched something on her skimmer. A few seconds later, two people walked in to the room, and Zondra glided to meet them, turning to introduce them.

"These are two of the people from Earth—Rona Gale and Max Vanmore. This is our microsurgeon, Jay, and Jay's Woman."

They walked forward in perfect step, like a pair of simultaneous dancers, until they were standing quite close to Rona and Vanmore. Jay had an enormous head and a lugubrious face with a hard, down-turned mouth, and a sharp nose with half-lensed glasses perched low down, so that he looked over the top of them. His compact body was like a hunchback's, with a short cape of thick green plastic that hid his arms, and his long legs gave him the overall appearance of an adjutant-bird.

The woman beside him seemed at first the most normal person they had seen since arriving on the planet—a strongly built woman with a fresh face and short brown hair almost hidden under a close-fitting cap that made her head look absurdly small.

"Interesting to meet persons from Earth," said Jay in a high-pitched, precise voice, and then, just as if he had not heard Zondra introduce them, he said, "I'm Jay, and this is my woman." He said it with an air of ownership, as a man might say "This is my car."

Vanmore gave a slight bow, and Rona said, "Nice to meet

you, Jay." She turned to the woman. "And your name is—"

The woman gave a broad, rather empty smile. "I'm Jay's Woman. That's name enough. We're always together."

Rona said nothing. She had obviously given up. Jay and his woman sat at the other side of the long table, next to Gisela, who put some plates of food across in front of them. The woman picked up a forklike implement from the table and began feeding both herself and Jay, mouthful for mouthful. He did not bring his hands out from under the cape, but simply ate what the woman put in his mouth, chewing as if his thoughts were on other and possibly more sublime things. Vanmore caught Bianca's eyes, but after a fleeting glance at the pair of newcomers she gave a slight shrug, her expression blank.

"You two had better have your sleep, now," said Zondra, moving around the table to Rona and Vanmore. "You're used to only 87 per cent of our gravity. I'll show you where your room is. Come."

She glided ahead of them on her skimmer, leaning slightly inward as she went around corners. Their room, like the other, had floor-to-ceiling windows, and Rona gave a delighted cry as she went across to stand looking down between the scattered skyscrapers to the bay.

"It's like our penthouse room at Amadeus," she said.

"It rings some other bell with me," said Vanmore thoughtfully. "I know. That other penthouse on top of the hotel in Apia—back where it all started."

Rona looked across at him. "You mean—when you got the telegram that told you about the assassinations?"

He nodded. "That was the beginning of everything, wasn't it? But for that, we'd still be in Queensland producing star sapphires."

"Well," Zondra's deep voice cut into his thoughts. "If the room evokes memories, I hope most of them are pleasant." She glided quickly about, showing them how to make cafeno in a tiny autokitchen set in an alcove, and where to hang their clothing.

At the door, she spun around, and as if on impulse she moved over to Rona and put her arms around her, hugging her against her massive body. "Glad you came, dear." She held her for a few seconds, then was suddenly at the door again. "Get the weight off those legs," she said, looking at Vanmore now as well as at Rona. "There's a control—there—that can tilt the bottom end of the bed up. You might like to experiment with it."

"Thanks," said Rona. After Zondra had gone, she smiled at Vanmore. "She's rather sweet when you get used to her, isn't she?"

Vanmore shrugged. "Maternal, I'd say. She probably thinks of us as a couple of kids."

He lay down on the wide bed alongside Rona. She rolled towards him and put her arm across his chest, nuzzling his cheek.

"Good to lie down," she said. "You don't really notice that gravity much, but—what was I going to say?"

He parted his lips and blew some strands of her hair away from his mouth, and then, suddenly, she was asleep. He lay looking up at the softly luminous ceiling for a while. Reaching over to the controls beside the beds, he darkened the windows until the outlines of the buildings outside showed black against a dark violet sky. He played around with another dial that dimmed the even glow of the ceiling, and he found a slide control that made the glow of the ceiling yellow or violet, or any shade on the gradation between. He wondered how it was done, but decided there was plenty of time to find out things like that. He caressed Rona's arm, listening to her regular breathing.

How long he slept in the darkened room, he did not know.

But he awoke with the chill touch of metal on his forehead.

19

THE ROOM WAS still in darkness, except for the faint violet
glow filtering through the windows. Some kind of figure was
leaning over him. He reached out his hand for the ceiling light
control and turned it full on.

Rona screamed, and Ula, who had been bending over Vanmore, straightened up.

"I'm sorry. I was trying to waken Max without disturbing
you. Max, there's a call for you."

"A call?" He yawned and sat up. "But nobody knows I'm
here."

"It's Rajendra Naryan."

He stood up, stretching. "What time is it?"

"Nearly seventeen. We thought it best to let both of you
sleep." Ula gestured to a hologram alcove in the corner of the
bedroom. "I can switch the call here."

"Thanks."

As she went out, Rona rolled over on her elbow. "How long
was she here?"

"I don't know." He glanced at his wristwatch, then
dropped his hand irritably. "Two thirty. Means nothing.
Shiptime. Seventeen, she said. That means nothing, too." He
turned the dial that lightened the windows, and the white
sunlight streamed in from close to the meridian. At that moment, Rajendra's image appeared on the hologram. He looked
fatigued, his eyes dark-shadowed.

214

"I trust you've rested, Max. These people seem to move very fast. They've arranged a meeting for me with a man called Dorlan down at their Trade Centre. He's something to do with a team that monitors imports—they called him their vegetation expert. He's had a group examining samples of the seeds we brought with us. I think their findings determine the value of the seeds we've brought. That won't mean much to us in local currency, but it governs what we can afford to take back with us. Could you come along with me, Max?"

"How do I get there?"

"Oh, we'll pick you up—we know where you are. That's one of the disconcerting things about these people—they seem to know everything, or they're able to find it out in a flash, which adds up to the same thing."

"All right, Raj. I'll come with you. When?'

"About ten minutes?"

Vanmore whistled. "They move fast, as you say—no mistake about that. Ten minutes, then."

Rajendra gave his customary namaste, and the image flicked out.

"The Trade Centre," said Rona. "That's the building Zondra pointed out on the way in from the starport, isn't it?"

"I think so. You get some more sleep, honey."

"I'll try. Don't know whether I can, now. I won't know what's likely to wander in."

He grinned. "Never know your luck. See you." He kissed her, and went out. In the living room he encountered Zondra and Komordo.

"What should I wear down at the Trade Centre?" he asked Zondra.

"Almost anything." She looked at him critically. "Pity you can't cover those legs up—they look as if you've just walked out of a jungle. Still, they know that, don't they?"

"Where I come from isn't exactly a jungle," said Vanmore.

Komordo gave a short laugh. "You'll find the Trade Centre's a tougher jungle than any you've known," he said, and he and Zondra laughed together.

A few minutes later a bell chimed, and Zondra touched the door release on her skimmer. A squat, broad woman in a plain grey tunic waddled into the room on bowed legs. Her head, which would have been of normal size by Earth standards, looked small in comparison with those of the other people in the room, its smallness emphasised by a close-fitting little hat. She looked about her.

"Which is Max Vanmore?" she asked.

"I am."

She looked up at him. "I'm Yaki's Woman. I'm to take you to the Trade Centre." She turned and waddled to the door, stopping for him to follow.

Unexpectedly, Jay and his woman appeared. He stalked up to Vanmore, his downturned mouth straightening in an attempt to smile. "Good luck," he said, "and don't let them rush you. They'll try to get you to give decisions without taking your time to think. Remember that—just take your time."

"Thanks," said Vanmore.

"Come," said Yaki's Woman, and with a wave to the others Vanmore followed her out to a small airkar. The doors of it opened as they approached. Vanmore climbed in, and the woman got in beside him. She did not take the controls. In fact, there was nobody at the controls. The door closed, and the machine simply took off with no visible agency flying it. It swung down in a smooth curve from the tower and joined a stream of other small aircraft travelling in the general direction of the Trade Centre.

"Who's flying this thing?" asked Vanmore, and the woman looked at him in surprise.

"I don't know. But they'd be quite efficient," she said, and then she looked straight ahead as if there was nothing further to say.

When the digital clock on the bedroom wall indicated 17:50, Rona got up and went in to the adjoining shower recess. Somehow her baggage and Vanmore's from the shuttle had been brought in to her room, and she spent a little time after her shower hanging up her garments. She put on an iridescent blue wrap-around dress, and went out along the passage to the living room, where Zondra was working on some papers at a table, and Ula was looking out of the window.

"By the way, Ula," said Rona. "I forgot to thank you for lending me your cape. It was cold out there this morning."

The dark lens flashed reflected light as it moved to survey her. "You should get some clothes, Rona. Good ones. You have a beautiful, classical body shape."

"Thanks," said Rona.

Zondra looked across at the servoid. "Why don't you come out and meet her face to face, Ula?"

Rona glanced at Zondra, then back at the robot figure. "Why not?"

The figure turned and walked to a door, which it left open after passing through. Zondra glided across to Rona and lowered her voice. "I'm trying to get her to meet people more directly. When a person deals with others through a servoid all the time, they're apt to become introverted."

A minute later, Ula came back through the same door, wheeling what looked like a perambulator with a body made of pink fibreglass. It formed an enclosed ovoid shell, and from the top of it protruded a human head. It was a large head, with plump cheeks and a sullen mouth, and blonde hair pulled up in an oldfashioned ponytail. The right eye was covered by a pink plastic cup with fine insulated wires running down beside the neck, and a smaller cup covered the right ear. The one visible eye looked somehow young and old at the same time. It was grey, darkly shadowed beneath, with an expression of unshakable boredom.

The lips moved, but the voice seemed to come from a grille in the front of the pink shell. "Well, Rona, here's the organic part of my little team."

Rona managed a smile. "Hi, Ula. I feel as if I've met you already."

The grey eye rolled sideways. "Am I interrupting anything, Zon?"

"Not just now, dear."

"Can I borrow your guest for a while?"

"If you return her in good order."

"I promise that." The servoid body reached over and swung the perambulator so that the head was directly in front of Rona. Looking up at her, the eye seemed to light up. "Come along to my room, Rona. I'd like to show you my things."

Rona glanced at Zondra, then nodded. The servoid turned the perambulator around and wheeled it out through the doorway, one of its metal hands making an adjustment to the blonde ponytail. It led the way along a passageway with a moving mural on one wall, and turned in to a round room without external windows, its walls all of a soft pink.

Rona looked about her. Around the walls were pictures, most of them pictures of women, mostly young girls, and many of them nude. They varied to an astounding degree in type, in race, and in physique.

Exactly in the centre of the room was a barrel-shaped column of pink plastic, a little over a metre high. The servoid wheeled the perambulator alongside the column, then lifted the head upward. It was mounted on a pink cylinder half a metre long, with its lower surface bristling with countless small metal prongs and three larger locating pins.

Carefully, the servoid fitted the cylinder in to the top of the barrel-shaped column, pushing it down until something clicked solidly within. Then it stepped back.

The head and the domed top of the cylinder rotated silently, and various things happened about the room. Lights flicked on and off, as if being tested, and some TV screens and display terminals lit up briefly. A large, drumlike cylinder with a camera lens and metal arms slid out from a recess in the wall, moved its arms, and returned. A small, doll-like figure with a lens and metal claws, no more than ten centimetres high, strutted out from some place of concealment, then went back. Then the head swung around to look at Rona again.

"Sit down, Rona. Would you like something to drink?"

Rona shook her head. The servoid body walked across to a section of wall that slid open at its approach, revealing a number of differently coloured garments hanging within. It took out a golden cloak and fitted it around the barrel, fastening it by magnetic catches. When it stepped away, the figure in the centre of the room looked simply like a short, blonde, one-eyed woman in a gold, barrel-shaped cloak, her head tilted arrogantly back.

"Easier to talk with, now?" she queried. Her amplified voice came from an external speaker. Rona nodded, and the grey eye sparkled as Ula smiled.

"You know, Rona, you're the first Earth girl I've actually met. Not through the camera of a servoid body, I mean, but here in front of my own eye. Would you mind taking off your dress?"

"What did you say?"

"Your dress, darling. Nothing can happen to you. I'm simply a head on an autojector—a head on a barrel, as some of my people rudely call me. But I can be quite a useful friend.

"Now, Rona, please—your dress . . . ?"

The Trade Centre was an impressive complex of buildings.
Because of its proximity to the airport it was low and
spreading, with long colonnades of white and orange stone
laid so that the colours formed transverse bands. The airkar
landed neatly in an inner courtyard—one of many—and the
doors opened.

Yaki's Woman stepped out and motioned Vanmore to
follow her. She led the way along one of the colonnades and
through an archway into a cloister bordering a small, luxuriant garden.

"Easy to get lost around here," he said.

"Not when you learn the overall pattern of the buildings,"
she said. At a certain point she stopped and pressed a button
alongside a door. A voice squawked from a speaker, and she
said "Yaki's Woman," whereupon the door slid open, revealing a suite of offices.

The woman led the way into a large office lined with shelves
of oldfashioned-looking files, together with a number of the
ubiquitous cathode ray tubes. Seated on the far side was Rajendra Naryan. As soon as he saw Vanmore he stood up.

Yaki, who had been sitting opposite Rajendra in his floating
chair, turned around and immediately rose in the air until his
massive head was on a level with Rajendra's again.

Rajendra looked worried. "Sit down, Max," he said.
"Yaki's been explaining the procedures here. I think you'd
better hear them."

However, just as Yaki was beginning to speak, a voice came
from a loud speaker on the wall.

"Professor Dorlan will see you now."

A door slid open to give access to an inner office lined with
vision screens. Dorlan was a considerable shock to both Vanmore and Rajendra. What they met was a servoid, over two
metres tall, with a broad, ovoid body of what looked like
stainless steel, balancing easily on thin, functional legs like
metal stilts. The domed "head" carried a hooded camera lens
like Ula's, but set in the front of the metal body was a square
television screen, from which the face of the man who operated the servoid looked out at them.

"My name is Dorlan," he said, his lips on the screen forming the words, while the sound came from a rectangular grille

beneath the lens. The head, as far as they could see through the screen, seemed to be immobile against foam padding, its right eye covered by a black plastic cup by which it was evidently able to see through the camera lens. The other eye was blue and observant-looking. The servoid gestured with one of its metal hands.

"Sit down. This shouldn't take us very long."

Vanmore didn't like the sound of that. When they were all seated, Dorlan rested his hands on the desk in front of him. The right hand was human-scale, with five fingers. The other, three-fingered, was a powerful, functional vise.

"My team is still examining the samples of the seeds you have brought," he said. "Some will have to remain in plant quarantine for a considerable time—say ninety or a hundred days. But with many, it's not worth our while to run tests at all."

"Why not?" asked Rajendra.

"Because we grow the same species ourselves—but ours have already been adapted carefully to local conditions. Wheat, rye, oats, Australian eucalypts, Indian tamarinds— our early settlers brought seeds of all those. Coconut palms, pines, firs—almost everything you have brought."

"I didn't know that," said Rajendra in a flat voice.

"Obviously not. The trouble is in the lack of communication for such a long period between Earth and Alcenar. As a result, you don't have very much of value to trade. What did you want in return for your seeds?"

"Technical information, mostly," said Rajendra. "For one thing, the anti-inertia device you use on your aircraft and other vehicles."

"The antiner? That might pose a problem. First, it needs a very sophisticated technology to make it work safely. Second—I doubt if my people would release it to yours."

"Why?"

"The technology behind it can be used to produce some really terrifying weapons. I won't plant so much as the germ of an idea of any of them, but such things have been used. I think my people would feel that yours, as yet, lack the necessary stability—"

"*Stability?*" Vanmore exploded into the conversation. "Good God, stability is what our civilisation is all about! If we were any more stable, we'd be a museum display!"

The metal figure on the other side of the desk did not move, and the face on its screen kept a perfectly controlled expression. "Apparently, we mean different things by stability. What I'm talking about is emotional stability. Perhaps a better word to have used would be maturity."

"Are you accusing us of being immature?" demanded Vanmore.

"I'm not accusing you," said Dorlan. "I'm merely pointing it out."

When Rona left Ula's room, she had a sudden desire to be alone. She went out into the observation gallery with its transparent outer wall, and stood looking down over the city. After a while she became aware of someone standing beside her, and turned to find that it was Jay's Woman.

"Hello," she said.

The woman smiled. "They get a bit overpowering for a halfhead, don't they?"

Rona frowned. "What d'you mean by halfhead?"

Jay's Woman smiled more broadly, pointed to her own head, then to Rona's. "We're halfheads, sis. I think we should stick together."

Rona was suddenly furious. "We both have perfectly normal heads."

The woman laughed. "Maybe normal where you come from, sis—but we're halfheads around here."

"Where did you come from?"

"I don't remember. I think I've been erased. I only remember since I've belonged to Jay." Very briefly, her expression was troubled. "I suppose I came from a primitive settlement. The family must have got me for Jay."

"But why?"

"He's been specialised for microsurgery. His arms have tiny bones like a bird's, and thin, double-jointed fingers. He can't use them for general work—he wears them in a sling inside that protective cape. I have to do everything for him. Except his operations, of course."

"How old was he when they decided to make him a microsurgeon?"

"Probably before he was born. They can predict abilities fairly well, when a foetus is unusual in any way."

"God!" said Rona. "I think the whole place is mad."

"There's one advantage, of course. He's always been assured of a career. We go all over the planet."

"But what sort of a life is that? What about love?"

"Oh, I go through that from time to time. Jay doesn't mind. He's very understanding. Very mature."

Suddenly, she held up her finger, and seemed to be listening to something.

"What's the matter?" asked Rona.

The woman turned her head and pointed to something like a small hearing aid in her left ear. "Excuse me," she said, "Jay wants me." And without one more word she turned and hurried out. Rona looked after her for a moment, then went to her room.

An hour or so later, Vanmore returned. He kissed Rona, then sprawled on the bed.

"You look flattened," she said.

"I am. Road roller victim."

"What happened?"

"They're tough. Fellow we had to contact said he'd got over ninety per cent of the species Raj was trying to introduce. Trouble is, they could be lying. No way we can be sure."

"But if they didn't want the seeds, they'd be bound to return them, wouldn't they?"

"They make the rules, here. Anyway, they've had them for testing. They could keep some. I don't know, though—he showed us pictures of coconut palms, pines, gums, saltbush, you name it. Seems their early settlers brought seeds of everything they could think of. Raised them in sealed buildings, controlled environments, until they could adapt them for outside areas." He made a gesture of disgust. "It was bad enough about the sapphires. Now we look like we're going home almost emptyhanded."

"You mean they're giving you nothing at all?"

"Not exactly. They've offered us some improved equipment for the ship, and they're filling our tanks with a more advanced fuel that they've developed. But as to anything that changes our civilisation—forget it!"

"How about these things that float in the air?"

"They're a cheap byproduct of a very involved and very expensive line of technical development that they won't give to us. The stuck-up bastards say we're not ready for it!"

He was sitting up on the edge of the bed, now. Rona knelt on the bed behind him and began massaging his neck and back.

"How about coming to bed, Max. These people seem to sleep whenever they can fit it in."

He looked morosely at the windows. "Perhaps that's what's wrong with them." He yawned. "You haven't been through their full day, yet. This time of the year, you get nineteen or twenty hours of sunshine like this, then about the same time of red sunlight. They call it the redtime."

"What do they do here during the redtime?"

"I spent it down in the Wetlands. Nobody down there. All that happens is that things hunt. Eat each other." He shivered.

Rona began to undress. Sprawling back, his eyes half-closed, Vanmore watched her happily. Then, abruptly, he sat up.

"What the hell's that?"

"What?"

"That gold stuff around your navel."

"Oh, that?" She gave a wry smile. "You know, that Ula woman's weird—if you can call her a woman. She's a voyeur to end all voyeurs."

"How do you mean?"

"After you'd left for the Trade Centre, she took me along to her room to show me her things. After a while she asked me to undress—said she wanted to have a look at an Earth girl all over. Then she showed me pictures of other girls she'd had there, some with designs painted all over their bodies. She asked me to copy one of the designs on myself, here and there—this is just one part I forgot to clean off. Eerie, don't you think?"

"You didn't have to go along with it, did you?"

"Well, no—I suppose I'm soft-hearted. It seemed to me she wouldn't get much fun. There's just her head and neck, with thousands of little electric relays that pick up nerve impulses in her neck, and amplify them so she can operate all sorts of things. She can even add or subtract hormones in the flow of blood pumped through her brain, so she can be anything from a mystic to a tigress."

Vanmore thought of the visit to the observatory during the long morning, with Ula's unbreakable steel grip on his wrist.

"I wouldn't worry about her, honey. I think she gets all the fun she can handle. Now, let's forget all these damned people for a while."

He put his arms around her, and they lay for a time looking out of the tall windows. A few other high towers stood out against the sky, silver with dark green windows, copper with deep blue, green metal with amber windows. Her lips were warm and vibrant against his, her body responsive. After a few moments, he reached over for the dial that darkened the windows, turning the sky a deep purple and everything else a silhouette of black.

During the next few days, the complexity of everyday life in Astralon overwhelmed them like an avalanche. It was close to the time they called mid-year, from Day 122 to Day 130, when the planet was between the two suns and there was no real night. The pulsing life of the metropolis surged on throughout the whole thirty-eight-hour day, and while most people took a couple of siestas their hours of sleep were a matter of individual choice. The flow of activity of the city did not pause.

During the redtime, the overall light was supplemented by floodlighting on buildings, and by the skylights. The skylights, a line of brilliant stars northward of the zenith, were actually a chain of orbiting solar mirrors above the equator.

Vanmore and Rajendra spent over a hundred hours at the Trade Centre during the next ten long days. Throughout the same period, Rona saw more of the city and its surroundings than they did, mainly in the company of Gisela, who began to accept her as a friend, and the servoid of Ula, whom she now looked at in quite a changed light.

"These people are very different from the way I had them summed up at first," she said to Vanmore one day. "I'd imagined them all brain and cold logic."

"I know. Raj and I have been running in to the same thing down at the Trade Centre. Sure, their intelligence has made a gigantic leap upward on the evolutionary scale, but along with it there's been an explosive increase in adrenal, thyroid, pituitary, and other hormones. I think they vary, psychologically, far more than people back home."

"You mean they can get further away from normal, and still function effectively?"

"Something like that. I suppose it's a trend that's been going on a long time. Tolerance to diversity."

Rona nodded. "I see what you mean. Among savages, no one can afford to be much different from the others. We can tolerate more variation in behaviour, ideas, styles of life—and these Alcenar people carry the same trend further." She laughed. "I went shopping today with Gisela and her brother, Kano—he's like a young version of Komordo—and his girlfriend, Glaya. She grew up on one of their asteroids, light gravity. Tall and thin, stalks along in an exoskeleton, all rods and harness. Yet she and Kano are crazy about each other."

"How did you get on with them?"

"Fine. I even get on well with Ula, now I know more about her."

"Exactly. They can live happily with variations that would drive Earth populations into separate armed camps."

Rona was silent for a while, then she gave a bubbling little laugh.

"What's funny?" he asked.

"I was just thinking. When we go back to Earth, if all else fails, you could become a charismatic leader preaching tolerance."

"I can't see it," he said, shaking his head.

"Never mind. Neither can I," she said, and they both laughed.

By the time the date set for the *Mohenjo Daro*'s return voyage had drawn near, it had been stocked with an impressive array of advanced machine tools and other products. Perhaps the item Vanmore valued most highly was a microtaped copy of the ninety-volume Centauran Encyclopedia, which covered a staggering range of information taking in not only the Alpha Centauri system, but Earth and a number of bizarre worlds where groups spreading out from Alcenar had opened up unbelievable horizons.

While he was working on an inventory of equipment one redtime, Lars Komordo came to him. Tired, Vanmore rose from his seat and stretched his arms, looking out at the dark towers against the flaming sky.

"You're going back to a very primitive planet, Max," said Komordo.

"I wouldn't call Earth primitive, Lars. Not most of it, anyway."

Komordo made a curious gesture with his hand. "Matter of definition, perhaps. But I can give you something that might make life easier."

"What is it?"

Komordo produced a thing about the size of a medium automatic pistol, with a large butt and two short, parallel barrels about ten centimetres apart. Between the barrels was a short, thick telescopic sight. Vanmore looked at it in some horror.

"We use these in the Wetlands," said Komordo. "Predators can come at you with very little warning, there—from the bushes, out of the air, even out of the rivers." He held the weapon out and pointed.

"It fires two streams of charged particles, contained in vortex beams and powered by an atomic battery. Not nuclear. Atomic. Safe, and it lasts for centuries."

"But I don't want to kill anything," protested Vanmore.

"You don't need to. Both streams must strike the target, and with the slide control there, in the green, the shock will merely startle an animal. Around here in an animal the body weight of a man, the charge will stun it. To kill, you'd push the slide up into the purple section."

"But, Lars, I don't need a thing like that back home."

"It will be sixteen of your years later than when you left. How do you know?"

With a shrug, Vanmore took the weapon from him.

20

FROM ORBIT, THE Earth looked the same as when they had last seen it sixteen years earlier.

"It looks mild, somehow, doesn't it?" said Rona, as she and Vanmore looked down at the blue and white globe. Rajendra was in the radio room, trying to make contact with his people in Nu Karnatika. "After Alcenar, I mean—it hasn't got those terrible, jagged mountains sticking out above the atmosphere."

"Mild from up here," said Vanmore thoughtfully.

Rajendra came back from the radio room without speaking, and glared morosely down at the planet.

"Everything all right at home?" asked Vanmore.

"No. It's not all right." Rajendra turned to face him, his eyebrows tensed into a deep V. "There have been changes. Nu Karnatika is under the control of an oligarchy of technical experts."

"But what happened to the aristocracy that was developing?"

Rajendra shrugged. "Nothing dramatic. Compensation, things like that. They tell me the Palace is now a combined museum and restaurant."

"What?"

Rajendra managed a mirthless smile. "I'm told they have a statue of me outside the restaurant. In any case, they're sending a shuttle up in about nine hours."

"I'd better try to contact Vanmore Titanium."

"Go ahead. Hope you have better fortune than I."

Vanmore went to the radio room. The operator established a link with the Australian network, and Vanmore sat in front of the screen and tapped out the area code for Amadeus and the number for Vanmore Titanium. A girl's face appeared on the screen.

"I'm sorry. The number you have called is not listed. Will you please check Directory?"

He punched out the call sign for the Australian Directory, followed by the area code number, and rolled the series of names up the screen. There was nothing in the Vs showing Vanmore Titanium, and nothing under Titanium at all.

"Perhaps you've been nationalised," said Rajendra.

Vanmore tried his own relatively small sapphire business in Queensland, but there was no trace of that. At some time in the intervening sixteen years it had vanished.

While he was still sitting at the screen, one of the radar men came in and went to Rajendra Naryan.

"Something coming up to us," he said.

"But our shuttle's not due for nearly nine hours."

"This is grey. No markings."

The grey shuttle had a purposeful appearance, the shark-like outline of its hull broken by what looked like weapon pods. It matched orbit with the *Mohenjo Daro*, moving close alongside, and suddenly the luminous marking "AI9" appeared on its side.

"We used to have an intelligence department called AI7," said Vanmore. "Perhaps this is an offshoot." He grimaced. "I hope not—I've clashed with them before."

"It was sixteen years ago, Max," said Rona. "These people wouldn't know you."

"But their computers remember."

At that moment a signal came through from the grey ship. "AI9 here. We're coming aboard." It was not in the form of a request. It was a statement.

The shuttle docked, and three men came in through the airlock. All were in grey, close-fitting spacesuits with very small, short-life backpacks, and as they came inside the ship two of them removed their helmets. The third man remained near the door of the airlock, a laser gun in his hands.

The leader looked about the cabin, then centred his attention on Rajendra.

"Rajendra Naryan?"

"Yes?"

"AI9. We've come to take possession of our share of the sapphires, or the machine which produces sapphires."

"Sapphires? What are you talking about?"

"There's no point in wasting our time." The leader took a laser pistol from its scabbard.

"But the sapphires are all on the other ship," said Rajendra coolly. "The *Endeavour II*. It's following our course."

The leader seemed to hesitate. He took a small radio from his belt and spoke into it in a low voice. He put it away and looked at Rajendra. "It's unbelievable that you would put all your eggs in one basket, to use an old saying. We'll just take our share from the first consignment."

Vanmore stepped forward. "I might be able to clear this up," he said. "You'll need a special key to get to the sapphires. It's been programmed to respond only to me."

"Where is it?"

"In my baggage. I can get it in a minute."

"Go with him," snapped the leader to the man beside him.

Vanmore led the way, with the guard walking behind him with a drawn laser pistol. "It's an ingenious type of key," said Vanmore over his shoulder. "There are two prongs on it, and a slide that has to be set to exactly the right point on a scale. The butt has been palm-printed for my hand alone."

He opened the bag containing the weapon Komordo had given him. While apparently still rummaging through the things in the bag, he switched on the atomic battery and saw the tiny green light. He thumbed the slide control to just below the purple section at the top of the scale.

"Now," he said, "I put the prongs in these—just a moment, could you move aside?"

As the guard was stepping aside, Vanmore swung the two thin shafts of light across his throat. His face became a distorted mask as his body convulsed and tumbled sideways. Vanmore took the laser pistol and thrust it into his belt, then stooped to look at the guard. His eyes were closed, and a faint pulse fluttered in his wrist.

Vanmore went into the bathroom and took a small towel, which he draped over the weapon, holding it with both hands as if it were something heavy and bulky. He went back to the cabin, and just as he reached the door he looked irritably over his shoulder and said, "All right—there's no need to keep prodding me in the back with that thing."

The leader and the other guard seemed to relax, as if their colleague had matters in hand. Vanmore, as he moved through the doorway, directed the twin beams at the guard near the airlock. He went down like a felled tree. The leader looked at the sprawling figure, and before he could bring his attention back Vanmore tossed aside the now smoking towel and raked the beams across the leader, chest high. He switched off the battery and stood looking down at the two grey-clad figures, lying like overthrown statues.

"It's not the way I meant it to be," he said aloud.

"Are they dead?" asked Rona in a shaking voice.

"Stunned, I think." He walked over and picked up their weapons, handing the pistol to Rajendra.

"What did you hit them with?" asked Rajendra.

Vanmore held up the weapon. "Thing Komordo gave me. I didn't want to take it. Looks as if he knew more about our way of life than we did."

"What happens now?" asked Rona.

"I don't know yet," admitted Vanmore. "One thing's sure—they're not going to stop trying. They've got the idea the ship's full of sapphires, and they're not going to be put aside by a slick answer."

"Who are they?" asked Rajendra.

"I think they're a bunch of Australian Intelligence that's gone bad. Or maybe a shipload of sapphires was too big a temptation for them to keep playing it straight. Listen, I think we may have a way out."

"What's that?"

"The suits these fellows were wearing hide their identity with the visors down—look at the one by the door. They're somewhere about our size—the leader and the one back there. Suppose we got into their suits, put Rona in her own suit, and marched her in to their shuttle. Now, once inside—well, this thing of Komordo's doesn't look like a weapon at first glance, and it's too quick for the fellow on the receiving end to have a second glance. Is it worth a try?"

Rajendra shrugged. "If we wait here, we're sitting geese."

"Exactly. Rona—get into your own suit. We'll take these."

It was easier than they expected. They wound a nylon rope around Rona's wrists as if they were tied together, although by a single tug on the rope she could free herself. Rajendra, closest in build to the leader of the AI9 trio, walked close behind her with his hand on her shoulder, a drawn laser pistol behind her. Vanmore, carrying a bundle which hid Komordo's weapon, walked at the rear. They went through the airlock into the shuttle, and into the long cabin.

It was only when Vanmore was sure he had all the remainder of the shuttle's crew in sight—three of them—that he shouted "Drop!" On the pre-arranged signal, Rajendra dragged Rona down, and Vanmore swung the twin beams in a frenzied series of arcs that took in the three standing men. They went down like grass under a scythe.

While Rajendra and Rona checked the stunned figures for weapons or radios, Vanmore searched the remainder of the shuttle. There was no one else aboard.

They dragged the three men back through the locks into the *Mohenjo Daro*, where Rajendra left it to his crew to tie them up. Then they took their personal baggage into the shuttle, Vanmore including his microtaped copy of the Centauran Encyclopedia. They closed the airlocks and uncoupled, Rajendra at the controls because he had the widest piloting experience.

"If I go to Nu Karnatika, we'll be picked up as we arrive," he said.

"The same may be true of Island Lagoon," mused Vanmore. "Could you land this thing on an ordinary airstrip?"

"I think so."

"Let's try Amadeus. Unlike Island Lagoon, the strip's in the middle of a town. We could lose ourselves in minutes."

"Good," said Rajendra. "Since we didn't succeed in getting the antiner out of them, fasten your seat belts."

It was about eleven o'clock at night when they came down over Central Australia. The moon was close to full, and it lit up the broad sweep of the lake. There were no lights in the vicinity of the airstrip, and few in the rest of Amadeus—none whatever in the dark tower of the Titanium Building.

Rajendra brought the shuttle down in a fast, extremely professional landing, using almost the full length of the strip even with reverse thrust.

Vanmore walked over to the dark terminal buildings. There were a couple of electric ground cars at rental meters, and he took out some money he had taken from one of the stunned guards and secured one of the machines, driving it back to the shuttle and picking up Rajendra, Rona, and their baggage.

He drove down to the lakeside and looked around the curved foreshore drive. Out on the point, he could see a light in the last house—Quade Gannon's house.

Did Gannon still live there? Sixteen years was a long time—he was beginning to realise that. He drove around to the green brick house on the point. The trees shielded it densely, now, so that from the road he could hardly see it. There were three vehicles under the carport that he did not recognise, but this hardly surprised him. He didn't even know the models —they must have appeared during the time he was away.

He drove the rented car into the driveway, then got out and knocked on the front door. After a few seconds a light came on above him, and the door was opened by an elderly, square-faced man with white hair. In spite of the added years, Vanmore recognised him at once. Evan Hart, the shop steward of the Amalgamated Titanium Workers' Union. At first, he didn't even recognise Vanmore.

"Yes?" he said.

"How are you, Evan? We never did have that meeting I promised you sixteen years ago."

"Good God! Max Vanmore, isn't it? Come in." He turned and shouted into the interior of the house, "Quade! It's Max Vanmore."

Gannon looked heavier and greyer than when Vanmore had known him, and he was wearing glasses. "Max! I thought I'd never see you again. You remember Evan, don't you?"

"Course he remembered me," said Hart. He looked at Gannon, then back to Vanmore. "Suppose you didn't expect to find us two together, eh?"

"I hadn't thought about it."

"Used to be adversaries, weren't we, in the old days." Gannon looked across at Hart. "Some time after you left, the Titanium Company became Titanium Co-operative. Worker participation. Evan and I were both on the board."

"What happened?"

"Long story. Lot of clashing between different factions. Place only worked about half the time." Gannon gave a resigned shrug. "At last, a big, growing Brazilian crowd took it over, found it uneconomic in comparison with some of their plants in other countries, closed it down."

"They still mine titanium in Australia," Hart put in. "But they process it in Brazil. Of course, Brazil's got a direct outlet to the Pacific, now—you wouldn't know about that."

"Lot of things I don't know, yet. I'm just back. I don't even know what happened to my own plant in Queensland."

"The sapphire plant?" Gannon laughed. "You can thank young Ferris and his story for that. Bottom fell out of the sapphire market. Folded."

"Anyway," said Hart. "Quade's job and mine finished up when the Co-op went. We're both too old to bother about shifting. No more need to be enemies. We're neighbours, we both play chess, so—" He spread out his hands. "Want something to drink?"

"In a moment. Say, I have Rona and a friend outside—"

"Bring 'em in," said Gannon promptly. "I'll get Meiko. Of course, you haven't met Meiko yet."

When Vanmore took Rona and Rajendra Naryan into the house, Gannon had been joined by a dark woman with eyes that reminded Vanmore of Horst Yoritomo's.

"Rona!" said Gannon as soon as he saw her. "You don't look an hour older than when you went away!"

Meiko stood looking at her with her head slightly on one side. "What marvellous clothes. Where did you get them?"

"Oh, this is what they were wearing on Alcenar when I was there," said Rona. Actually, she was wearing a blue net cloak and matching boots. An Alcenar woman would have worn nothing else, but Rona had added a flesh-coloured body stocking—"cheating," as she had said to Vanmore.

"If you need a partner as a fashion designer, I'm here," said Meiko. "I suppose if you steal an idea from four light years away it counts as designing."

Gannon had moved close to Vanmore. "What happened to Bianca?" he asked quietly.

"Fine, when I last saw her. She's among friends."

"Good. Good!" Gannon suddenly turned his attention to Rajendra. "I remember you, now. At the funeral."

The conversation shifted to their impressions of Alcenar.

Vanmore found he was talking about the more easily be-
lievable things, like the skylights and the cloudbreakers. He
did not touch subjects like sapphire quarries, or bio-
engineering as the Astralon people had developed it. He was
editing his descriptions. Somehow, in the back of his mind, an
idea began to form. . . .

"How would you say the Alcenar people differ from us?"
asked Evan Hart.

"More varied than us," said Rajendra, "and more tolerant
of variation. What would you say, Max?"

"Less bound by traditional methods, perhaps. More open
to new ideas, for sure."

"How about their social setup?" asked Hart.

"Looser than ours. Something of the Polynesian extended
family, yet less restrictive." Vanmore gestured. "Certainly, I
didn't see anything like those AI9 people."

Gannon gave an exclamation of disgust. "AI9! You don't
want to worry about that. It's a spent force. Corrupt. No real
teeth in it."

"But a team of them raided our ship," protested Rajendra.
"They thought it was full of sapphires. Actually, we have a
few, but they were looking for a shipload."

"What happened?"

"We overpowered them—thanks mainly to Max's quick
thinking. My crew have them securely held."

"Probably a renegade team that had hijacked one of their
own craft. Otherwise, they wouldn't have been so easy to
overcome."

"That did worry me," admitted Vanmore. "It went too
smoothly for us."

"Sounds as if the whole place is running down," said Rona.

"It is," agreed Gannon, and poured himself another drink.
"We could have had the leading country on Earth—*and we
blew it!*" He swallowed and sat looking glumly at his half-
empty glass. "I suppose the whole Earth is going the same
way. Everyone feels that life has become too complicated for
him to have any control over it. Perhaps it's as well Alcenar
and Earth are four light years apart. They've moved so far
ahead of us that our people would feel out-classed, if there
were closer contact. They'd stop trying. Like a primitive race

under the impact of a highly organised civilisation."

"Remember Aristotle, Max?" said Rajendra. He turned to include Gannon and Hart in the conversation. "There was a theory of cycles in government invented long ago, right here on Earth—and we had to go to Alcenar to find out all about it."

"Yes," said Vanmore. "I remember, all right. It looks as if, while we've been away, the country and the whole planet have slipped down sixteen years further along the way to break-down."

"Until the next charismatic leader comes along and stirs them up again," mused Rona.

The half-formed idea that had been thrashing in the background of Vanmore's mind suddenly integrated.

"Until—what did you say?"

"Until the next charismatic leader—" They looked at each other. Vanmore looked at Rajendra.

"Are you thinking what I'm thinking?"

"I hope not, Max."

"When you have a breakdown or deadlock, you have millions of confused people waiting for The Answer. Why don't *we* give it to them? You in Nu Karnatika, me in Australia?"

"But what 'Great Truth' can we give them? Do we know any?"

Vanmore paced up and down the room. "Raj, take a look at some of the 'Great Truths' that have moved millions of people in the past! The ideas behind the Crusades. The jihads of Islam. And what about the supremacy of the Aryan race? There wasn't really any such race—it was a language group-ing. Some of the ideas weren't even true, yet they shook the world!"

Evan Hart shook his head. "I hope I wake up and find I'm dreaming all this," he said. "I feel as if I'm present at the hatching of one of those ideological monsters that's a ra-tionalist's nightmare."

"I don't think so, Evan," said Gannon slowly. "I think he has something."

Vanmore suddenly felt as if he had been fired by some of the enthusiasm that surged in Lars Komordo. "It's a matter of giving people a target to shoot for. Most of them feel our civilisation's over the hill. We could show them there's still a way up!''

"The best of luck to you," said Rajendra.

There was a long pause. Then Gannon said, "I still have a key to the penthouse on the Titanium Building, Max. Want it for the night?" He turned to Rajendra. "I have a spare room here. You're welcome to put in the night, if you like, before Max starts shaking the world."

Out in the car, Rona said, "That frightens me, a bit."

He put his arm around her and held her against him. After a while he stroked the front of her neck with the back of his forefinger, from the chin downward. She murmured with pleasure for a few seconds, then suddenly stiffened.

"You learned that trick from Bianca!"

He looked at her in surprise. "How did you know?"

She looked quickly away, and he caressed her rhythmically until the tension slowly went out of her.

"Remember what the historian Toynbee wrote about withdrawal and return?" he asked, and she shook her head. "No matter. I was thinking of that holiday of ours that was interrupted in Apia—back when it all started. It'd be a nice, relaxing place to do some thinking. Planning. . . ."